THE HAUNTING AT SEBRING HOTEL

J.S DONOVAN

❀ Created with Vellum

MIRROR, MIRROR

$\mathcal{I}$n the misty woods and under the star-speckled sky, the 1923 Art Deco hotel stood. Leafy vines crawled up its brick walls. Hidden from the naked eye, faded Masonic symbols and strange icon were etched into the brick awning and other parts of the exterior. A foggy glass pyramid capped the peak of the four-story structure. From a top-down view, one could see mismatched stones forming two overlapping circles in the woods. The obelisk-like hotel was erected at the center of the circles' overlap. The initiated would know this architectural formation as the phallus of Osiris. To the rest of the sleeping world, it was a strange design choice by the hotel's mysterious creator.

In Suite 204, Alma Milford quietly rose from her bed. She yawned deeply. A strand of brown hair stuck to the corner of her mouth. She swiveled out of bed and accidentally stepped on her lover's shoe.

"Ow," she mumbled, faint pings of pain throbbing in her bare foot. She looked over her shoulder. The man had his back to her. Covers cocooned his body. Alma pursed her lips. She used rationality to drown her shame. *It's a dog eat dog world. We all lie to get ahead. You're just like everyone else.* The amoral philosophy left her feeling empty and bitter. She walked to the window and parted the curtains.

The rising sun bled its vibrant colors across the indigo sky. The Atlantic Ocean twinkled far beyond the surrounding woods. Just like in the postcard, a long line of maple trees flanked the only road to Club Blue. She didn't know why the hotel had such an odd name. It seemed like horrible marketing on the owner's behalf. Alas, Club Blue's secrecy was its greatest selling point. Without an invitation, it was near impossible to find the place.

After showering, Alma sat in front of the large desk mirror. She put on Chanel lipstick and popped her lips. The crimson shade nicely contrasted her glossy green dress.

The man rose from her bed and grabbed his crumpled clothes off the floor. Alma's attention stayed fixed on her reflection. The man behind her might as well have been out-of-focus. Partly dressed, he kissed the side of her neck. "See you tonight."

Alma smiled insincerely and watched the man's reflection leave. She continued putting on her make-up, hoping that her beauty would hide the rot in her heart. She reached her hand into the decorative flowerpot on the desk and removed the micro camera.

At midday, she arrived at one of Sebring's fancy restaurants. There was a large divide between the rich and poor in the coastal northeastern town. The wealthy folks from the surrounding city used Sebring as a refuge from the stresses of the outer world. The lifelong residents were mostly crab fishers and workers in the lumberyard trapped in the town by low income.

Holding her little purse close to her side, Alma stood in the restaurant's entrance. The dim lights shined over quiet tables. A fireplace glowed at the center of the small lounge.

She spotted the man in the three-piece suit. He waved her over.

Alma joined him.

"How was he?" Carl asked, a wicked smirk on his face.

Alma smirked back. A sickening feeling pitted in her stomach. She opened her purse and removed the camera's SD card.

"No time for small talk? Then again, what can I expect? I'm not one of your clients," Carl teased.

She put the SD card on the tabletop and held it below two fingers. "Make the transfer."

"Tsk tsk." Carl clicked his tongue. "Not until I see it."

"We've worked together enough to know I'm good for my word," Alma replied.

"And I've been around long enough to never pay for something that wasn't vetted first," Carl replied. He gestured to the card.

Sighing, Alma slid it to him.

He pulled out his phone and SD card reader. He pushed the card inside and fast-forwarded through the video. Carl chuckled. "His wife's not gonna be happy when she sees this one."

Alma glanced around the restaurant, paranoid people were watching her. No one was, of course. Carl disconnected the SD card reader and slid it and his phone into his blazer's inner pocket. Before he could take his hand out, Alma said, "The transfer."

"Right," Carl said as if almost forgetting.

He removed his cellphone, dialed a number, and told the person on the other end his bank router number. After a moment of waiting, he said, "Thirty thousand... yes... thank you." He hung up. "Any other women in your position would get less than a tenth of that."

They're not as good as me. Alma checked her banking app on the phone.

Carl said, "It'll take a few minutes."

Alma asked, "So who wants the video?"

"You know I can't tell you that," Carl replied.

"Higgins Capital?" Alma asked.

"Not saying," Carl lied.

Alma hated the nature of her business. She'd screwed a lot of big-name people, literally and figuratively. Some wanted to kill her while others sacrificed everything they owned to be with her. She made sure never to see any of them again. Things were easier when her business was back home in Mexico. There were plenty of places for the elite to indulge themselves without anyone noticing. To them, Alma was just another pretty chica. In the States, she had to be more careful. She'd been in the northeast for a few years. Her handlers had created a nice profile for her. Currently, she was a wealthy socialite who was happy to discuss business with anyone.

After two long minutes, the money appeared in her account. An invisible weight lifted off her shoulders.

The waiter arrived. He placed the 18oz prime rib and loaded baked potato in front of Carl. The waiter turned to Alma. "And for you, ma'am?"

"Not hungry," Alma replied. She scooted out of the booth.

Mouth full, Carl asked, "Where are you going?"

Alma ignored his question. "Until next time, Carl."

"I look forward to it," Carl replied, watching her leave. He stabbed his fork into a chunk of steak and took a bite. Watery blood trickled down his chin.

Alma returned to her room. She started to pack her suitcase when a thought came to mind. There was a private party in the ballroom tonight. A lot of movers and shakers would be there. She'd get a chance to scope out her competition and maybe collect some dirt on Higgins Capital's CEO. She needed leverage in case he tried to burn her. Thirty Gs was a drop in the bucket to these people, but they were still fickle when it came to spending money.

Alma unpacked her bags. *One more night,* she promised herself. *Be gone before sunrise.*

She glanced at her reflection in the mirror. It felt like someone was watching her from the other side. Alma set aside the paranoid feeling. She meditated until dinner.

Wearing her vibrant green dress, she outshined the crowd. She flirted with the fat cats, said things that made them blush, and eventually took one back to her room. The man from last night was too drunk to notice. After getting the secret video she needed, she sent away Higgins' CEO. The man was ignorant of his board's plan to blackmail his rival. That made him an even better target for Alma if his people tried to betray her.

After a few hours of rest, Alma grabbed her packed bags and headed out of the room. The second after she left, a part of the suite's wall popped open, revealing a hidden door. A figure stepped out of the darkness. His gloved hand squeezed the knife's hilt. He followed Alma.

HOTEL DEVILLE

*A*nna Hall kept one hand on the steering wheel and drove farther away from her old life. She wore mustard-colored pants, a cardigan, a gold and white vertical striped shirt, and low black heels. Her hair matched her auburn eyes, and years of polite smiles left laugh lines on her pretty face. At forty-two years old, she never thought she'd get a fresh start, but here she was. Blue skies were above her head and the open road lay before her. Maine never looked more beautiful. She kept her attention on the road. Her spacious Kia Sorento cruised.

Fourteen years old and youngest of Anna's two boys, Asher sat in the back seat and played on his tablet. His skinny thumbs rapidly tapped the screen. His rectangular glasses captured harsh explosions and assault rifle muzzle flash. He wore a green polo, straight-legged jeans, and sneakers. His style hadn't changed since sixth grade. He took a break from his game to use his asthma inhaler. He returned to his game without ever looking up. James's death hit him hard. To be without a father at his age would leave a long-lasting effect. Anna heard his softs sobs through the walls at night but didn't know how to comfort him. Anna's oldest son was much more closed off.

Having the front seat leaned back as far as it could go, seventeen-year-old Justin Hall watched the world blur by in the window. Methodical bass and obscene hip-hop leaked from his large headphones. He paid Anna no mind. The boy was tall and athletic. He wore a thin hoodie and a t-shirt with a woman's lips and tongue sticking out, much like an adult version of the Rolling Stones icon. Justin's hair was short and messy. He had a well-defined jawline, handsome dark eyes, and an uncaring expression. He has more walls up than Fort Knox. At any given time, she didn't know if he was going to lash out or tell her he loved her.

Anna's heart ached. She wondered if her boys' issues were a product of her parenting or the media-centric society around them. From day one, most Gen Z'ers had access to unlimited porn, smut, and trash that came with the internet. Anna fought vigilantly to keep their eyes and ears safe, but it was an uphill battle she failed daily. Asher was on the web more than his older brother. The asthmatic boy could go days glued to his computer screen, scrolling through endless social media feeds, playing the latest gory video game, or streaming Netflix's darkest shows. His reclusive tendencies skyrocketed when he hit puberty last year. His many allergies might've gotten slightly better, but his social anxiety crept into most parts of his life. It doesn't help that his older brother called him gay all the time. Asher wasn't, but older brothers will do what brothers do.

Unlike Asher, Justin would do everything he could to escape the house. Anna was supportive of that, but he never told her where he'd go and would come home smelling like pot. Anna confronted him a few times, but Justin backtalked. Though James could put the boy in line, his methods shook Anna. She glanced over to her eldest son, pondering if she spent enough time nurturing him. He was her firstborn, and unexpected at that. Once Asher came into the picture, frequent trips to the hospital consumed most of Anna and James's time. Justin learned to fend for himself.

"Hey," Anna said.

Justin's music blocked her out.

"Justin," Anna said firmly.

Seeing that her methods were failing, she started dancing to faint music leaking from his headphones. Asher noticed pretty quickly. Still playing his game, he bobbed his head to the steady thump of the bass. A good five seconds passed before Justin glanced over to her and then back to the window. He did a double-take and removed one headphone. His annoyance was palpable. "What?"

Anna said, "I'm not allowed to say I love you?"

Justin moved the speaker over his ear again and turned up the music.

Asher shrugged.

Anna chuckled.

They drove by the wooden welcome sign for Sebring, Maine. A lighthouse was painted on the front. Population: 2344.

Anna glanced at the rearview. "We're almost there."

Classic New England homes and farmlands lined their trek. Autumn touched one leaf out of every hundred trees. Fall season seemed to hit here before anywhere else. Anna's SUV rumbled as she drove over the downtown's cobblestone roads. There were mom-and-pop restaurants, antique shops, a century-old butcher shop, and old brick buildings with blocky designs.

They followed the road alongside the coast. The Atlantic Ocean hammered the rocky shores. The chilling waves smashed against the jagged stone. There was no sandy beach, and the 52 degrees Fahrenheit water dissuaded swimmers. A picturesque lighthouse stood on its own island two hundred yards from the short pier. As sunset drew closer, the lighthouse turned on and cast its rotating beam of light. The old cylindrical building connected to a small home. An elderly fisherman entered carrying a bucket of crabs.

The road took Anna away from the ocean and through the woods. She turned down a single-lane street. Fat maple trees flanked both sides, forming a portal of sorts toward the grandiose four-story motel at the end. Anna's excitement stirred as the building came into view. It was made of red brick and white stone. Vines climbed the walls and stopped just below the second floor. Stone pillars supported the grand awning fit for an ancient Roman temple. A glass pyramid shape capped the building but was barely visible from the road. The building looked like it belonged in New York City and deserved another twenty floors. But no. The strange structure was hidden away in the small coastal town of Sebring, virtually unknown to the world. Etched in stone in the beautiful awning were the words "Club Blue." Two hexagrams made from two interlocking but oppositely oriented triangles were carved on either side of the words.

Asher glanced up from his game. His eyes went wide in awe. "Whoa."

"Pretty cool, huh?" Anna replied.

Two human-sized statues of bearded mermen flanked either side of the glass front doors. One held a trident and the other sounded a conch horn.

Anna let the boys out and parked around the side. There were only six other vehicles at the extended-stay hotel. Anna entered the large lobby. Her heels clicked on the glossy tile floor. Beautiful wall lanterns and chandeliers illuminated the vast and tall room. The receptionist counter sat midway through the room and on the right wall. The entrance to an upscale, dimly lit but currently empty bar was opposite of the counter. Soft piano music drifted out of the bar and into the lobby. Open doors to the ballroom were at the back center of the room. On the same side as the counter but near the back of the room was the elevator and entrance to the stairway. The restrooms were nearby.

Anna and her sons lingered at the empty front desk. Peeved to see no one was working, Justin dinged the desk bell. The sound echoed off the walls. The place was grand, intricately detailed, and strangely empty.

Justin took off his headphones. "Are they always this late?"

"They know I'm coming," Anna reassured him. Following the advice of a realtor friend, she had stopped by once before and fell absolutely in love with the place.

Wearing a slim suit and having slicked-back grey hair and a thin mustache, the concierge arrived at the desk. The man was tall, gentleman-like, but also timid. His eyes were bloodshot. He wore a weary smile at the sight of Anna. As a night manager herself, it was not something you wanted to see. He said, "Good evening, Ms. Hall. I'm pleased you arrived safely from your journey."

"I have. The countryside is beautiful this time of year." She put an arm around Asher. "This is my youngest, Asher. And that's Justin."

Asher smiled awkwardly.

Justin seemed uncaring.

The corner of the concierge's mouth twitched. "I'm sure you'd like the grand tour."

"That would be wonderful," Anna said.

The concierge sifted through his key ring and found a key that was old and small. He walked to the bar. "Club Blue has maintained its same level of excellence since its inception in 1923. Staying true to Marco Blanc's vision, we've avoided electronic locks and a modern redesign in favor of something more classical. Here is the lounge, a favorite among our patrons."

Soft piano music played in the dimly lit room. The wooden wall panels and bar shared the same lavish tint. Justin lagged behind. His non-expressive gaze gravitated to the glass cabinet behind the counter. Hundreds of types of liquors, wines, and spirits stood on the smooth shelves.

"As you can see, we have no bartender," the concierge said. "Every drink is made to order by yours truly."

"You wear many hats," Anna complimented.

"Just like Mr. Blanc. He set the example of excellence for all who have followed. When you're ready, I'll show you the billiard room."

Asher mumbled to Justin. "He sure does like to use the word excellence."

"Shut up, homo," Justin mumbled back and walked ahead of him.

Asher followed after. "Takes one to know one."

Justin set his jaw in annoyance.

Asher chuckled.

Anna looked over her shoulder and glared at them both. She mouthed, "Enough."

Asher pointed his finger at Justin. Anna was aware of her youngest's antics. He'd scream the loudest when something went wrong, but he conveniently left out the part where he goaded Justin.

Double doors at the back of the bar opened to the billiards room. Anna could imagine Depression-era businessmen and ladies gathering in the hazy room. The space was tidy and clean, with seven billiard tables and a rack of cues and triangles.

The concierge said, "Patrons have access to the pool room as long as the bar is open."

Asher and Justin traded smirks. Their competitive spirits sparked.

The concierge took them to the massive kitchen next. It was fit for a hotel two times the size.

"Wow." Anna's voice carried through the room. "You can feed a small country from in here."

The concierge replied, "Yes, Mr. Blanc would host some of the finest chefs from around the world and wanted to provide them adequate space. Also, large banquets were commonly held in the ballroom."

"You don't have them anymore?" Anna asked.

The concierge's smile wavered. "Not many, I'm afraid."

He took them to the meat locker and used a key on his ring to open the lock. They looked into the rectangular room as if peering down a corridor. Two lines of meat hooks dangled from the ceiling. A large counter and sink were flush against the right wall. Anna felt a cold chill.

"Though we no longer serve food at Club Blue, the inspection report cleared with flying colors and the freezer is usable. Just for you, of course. This entire area is only accessible by the staff," explained the concierge.

He took them out of the kitchen and into the ballroom. Circular tables with white chairs formed a U around the dance floor. An imperial staircase led up to a wrap-around mezzanine balcony on the second floor. The steps were made of green stone. An interesting array of geometric patterns were etched into the wall's upper trim. Hand-painted art occupied the hexagonal frames inlaid on the ceiling. The paintings depicted angels, clouds, blue skies, and ladders. A massive chandelier hung at the center. The light at the center of the chandelier was the shape of a giant beehive, three feet tall and two feet wide.

Just like the first time she saw it, Anna was in awe. The ballroom alone was worth the purchase. She pulled at

Asher's sleeve. "This place was popping in the '20s. Dancing, champagne, and live music. While the rest of the nation was experiencing Prohibition, here the police chiefs, business moguls, and wealthy heiresses partied until sunrise."

The concierge smiled nostalgically. "Indeed."

To Anna, it was the coolest thing in the world. The boys were still thinking about the billiard room.

The concierge led the three of them through an unmarked passage and into a two-lane bowling alley.

"Sweet," Asher said.

The concierge explained that the bowling lanes were updated in the late 1980s with "cosmic lights and sounds," though the concierge tried to keep it close as he could to the original design.

On the opposite side of the ballroom was a similar corridor leading to the gym. It had mirrored walls, free weights, and treadmills below mounted TVs.

They returned to the lobby. The elevator only had buttons for the basement and first three floors. They went to the second floor. Suites 201-215 were standard. Suite 216, 217, 218 were the owner's suites. The concierge showed them a standard room and then his own. His suite had a king-sized bed, an elegantly-furnished living room, a mini-kitchen, and a large window that overlooked the woods below. Some of the rooms had different designs and layouts. The concierge described Marco as an artist. He wasn't content with making just another motel. He wanted *the* motel. Every time you stayed, you'd get a different experience, but a welcoming one. He took them to the third floor. It consisted only of suites. There were thirty-three usable suites through the hotel.

"Forty-four," the concierge clarified. "If you count the fourth floor."

Justin took off his headphones. "What's up there? Why isn't there a button for it in the elevator?"

"It's been closed off since the fire in 1962," the concierge explained. "I'm sure you'd like to see it, though."

He took them up the stairwell and to the locked door. He drew out an older key not on the ring, twisted it in the lock, and pulled the door open with a *creeeeaaak*. With no artificial lights, the corridor was a black tunnel. Scorch marks tarnished the floors and broken walls. The hallway groaned as the wind struck the hotel.

Asher took a step forward. Anna grabbed his shoulder and pulled him back. "It's not safe."

Having a pensive expression, the concierge observed the darkness. "The fire damage was contained to the fourth floor only. None of the electric or plumbing damage affected the lower floors."

Justin said, "It's a waste not to rebuild it."

"It wasn't my place to do that," the concierge replied.

He shut the door, locked it, and returned downstairs. Anna followed.

Justin and Asher traded looks. Something was up with this guy.

They saw the basement next. Massive industrial washers and dryers occupied the laundry room. Steam stumbled out of the boiler room nearby. The rest of the basement was open storage.

Lastly, the concierge led them down a small hallway behind the front counter. They entered into the spacious office. It had a fine wooden mantel, a bookshelf holding old books, a lounge chair, a globe, and other knickknacks on the desk. "This was Mr. Blanc's personal workspace. I've worked for many years to maintain his aesthetic, and even more time managing the hotel from here."

Anna said, "I say we get down to business. You still asking the same price?"

The concierge took a seat at his desk. "It's lowered."

Anna stayed standing. "To what?"

"Six."

Anna hid her surprise. The hotel was eight million previously, fully furnished. That was already a steal. Anna played along. "I see. Is it because of the damaged fourth floor?"

The concierge pinched the bridge of his nose. He sighed and turned his bloodshot eyes to Anna. "I've been here for a long time, Ms. Hall. I'm tired. I want to rest."

The price was tempting. She'd reviewed the inspection reports during her last visit. Everything was up to code. All but the fourth floor. She'd have to rebuild that part from the ground up. Having the extra living quarters could turn a nice profit.

Like the concierge, she'd aim to maintain the integrity of the original design, but would need a fresh spin to market it. Currently, there were no advertisements to promote the hotel or any effort on the concierge's side to sell the four-acre property. Anna had heard about it from a realtor eight months ago. The concierge expressly told her only to promote it by word of mouth. That was a huge red flag. A property like this was worth fifteen million at least. Why was he selling so low? How stupid would she be to turn down that price?

"Mom, you're not serious about this, are you?" Asher asked.

Anna told the concierge. "One moment."

Anna and her boys stepped out of the office.

Asher asked, "I thought you said we were just checking out the place?"

"We are, but this deal is too good to pass up."

"What's so bad about our home?" Asher complained.

Justin said, "We're moving, idiot. Get over it."

"But Brandon, Dillan, and I were going to start high school together," Asher complained.

Justin replied, "Forget them. They're all faggots anyway."

Asher lowered his head and mumbled, "Shut up."

Anna said softly, "Yeah, we'd have to find you two a new school. That's okay. Change is good."

"Where are we going to live? Are we getting a new house? Are we going to have to buy that too?" Asher asked.

"Nope. We'll be staying here," Anna replied.

Justin scoffed and shook his head.

Asher looked disgusted. "Have you seen this place? It's terrifying. There's probably some frigging pedo hideout or something."

Anna couldn't hide her shock. "Pedo-what?"

"Yeah!" Asher doubled down. "Where are all the people, huh? If it was a normal hotel, there would be people walking around. Families. I've not heard anyone since we got here."

"Mr. Ferguson showed me the financial records on my last visit. The place had a rough couple of years," Anna admitted. "But that doesn't mean things can't turn around. It just needs a little love. Besides, each of you will get your own suite."

Asher stopped complaining and his eyes lit up. "You're lying."

"Cross my heart," Anna replied. "You'll able to play your game and stay up late without me bothering you."

Justin said, "There's a catch."

"Kind of," Anna replied. "You'll have to help out."

"What do you mean *help out*?" Asher asked.

"Cleaning, greeting guests. It's all part of your new adult lifestyle. You guys are growing young men. You can handle it."

Asher didn't like the sound of work.

Anna said, "If you do a good enough job, I might even pay you."

Asher pondered that. "It's better than fast food."

"What are your thoughts, Justin?" Anna asked,

"I don't get a say," the seventeen-year-old replied.

"That's not true. We're all in this together," Anna said.

"You've already made up your mind," Justin said. "I knew you did the moment you arrived."

Anna couldn't say he was wrong. "Look, guys, I won't buy it if you'll be miserable, but do I want it? Yeah. I'm not planning on managing a Motel 6 for the rest of my life, and with James... well, it's just us now." She opened her arms in a showmanship gesture. "Look at this place. We can build something here. A family."

"We already are a family," Asher said.

Justin set his jaw, his expression turning bitter.

"A better family," Anna elaborated. "So... are we going to do it or what?"

"Whatever," Justin replied and put on his headphones.

Asher's mouth scrunched to the side. His brow wrinkled as he thought deeply. "My own suite..."

"All yours," Anna replied.

Having formed a consensus, they returned to the office.

The concierge asked, "Have you decided?"

"We have," said Anna confidently.

The concierge pulled out the proper paperwork.

The next few weeks breezed by. Anna had already resigned from her position as the manager of the Motel 6. She put her old house on the market and left her realtor in charge of selling it. Another friend auctioned off most of her furniture and James's Jeep. Anna burned through James's life insurance and savings quickly, took out a few loans she hoped to repay with the sale of her old house, and left everything else to chance. She was optimistic though. She loved

Club Blue. She'd cherish it like one of her children. One day, it would surpass its former glory. Once the boys' school transcripts were sent to their new high school, York, Pennsylvania was no longer apart of Anna's life.

Not everything was perfect. The day she moved into Club Blue, the working staff staged a walkout. They didn't explain why. As they went out of the door, she offered them raises but they ignored her. The concierge didn't help, either. He rarely returned her calls, and when he did, he sided with the leaving employees. The extended-stay patrons saw the change of management as the time to pack their bags. Anna was left with a thirty-three-room facility. She had no housekeepers, handymen, electricians, and marketers. Nobody but her two sons. They weren't happy to shoulder the extra weight. Anna was downright pissed off.

She moved into the concierge's suite, replacing the large bed with her own. Despite her profession, she hated sleeping on other mattresses. She brought in her wardrobe and personal dining table that belonged to her mother. Her parents were alive but distant. Retired, both of them left America to travel the world. She rarely spoke to them. She brought her recliner, desk chair, and favorite lamp, too. Asher and Justin weren't allowed to bring any furniture. Their rooms had everything they needed.

After getting their own set of keys, they all settled into their own rooms.

At night, Club Blue was silent.

The lobby door was locked. Dry air lingered in the vast room.

Frank Sinatra's voice was distorted as it spilled out of the lavish bar.

Dim orange light shined in the neglected bowling alley. Like clockwork, all the neon and flashing lights activated in a sudden noisy burst.

Deep in the dark kitchen, metal hooks dangled in the meat locker. Rust spotted the barbed tip hooks. They were fit for cow ribs.

The floors creaked in the vacant halls.

The door to the fourth floor was locked tight.

Anna tossed and turned in her sleep. She awoke, forgetting her nightmare immediately. Cold sweat doused her body. She panted. Eyes heavy, she stared at herself in the tall wall mirror. All she could see was her own silhouette. She swung her legs off the side of the bed, wiped the sleep from her eyes, and stood. Her soles touched the cold hardwood floor. She pulled open the window curtains. The forest surrounding her little castle was still covered in darkness. As thin as a hair, the sunlight breached the horizon. She threw on some clothes, a jacket, and put her hair in a bun. Slipping on her running shoes, she exited her room and tiptoed down the hallway. It was out of habit. She followed the stairs to the emergency exit. The northeastern air nipped at her. Though she was capable of walking, she decided to drive to the seafront.

She parked at the visitor lot and followed the trail to the rocky coast. The sliver of light had grown larger. She took a seat at the edge of the water. Soft waves slapped the rocky wall, but none reached Anna. A cool breeze brushed against her face. She thought about James. His kind smile. His often-humorous seriousness. The way they laughed early in their marriage.

Anna's eyes watered.

He was gone. Killed in her bathtub.

3

BURN NOTICE

*A*sher pushed a laundry cart through the hall. Its dummy wheel spun rapidly. Using the keyring Anna provided for him, he unlocked suites, pulled off bed sheets and pillowcases, and added them to the growing pile. In certain suites, photographs of old white men hung on the walls. They wore tailored suits and had on large aprons that looked like envelopes. Heavy medallions hung around their necks. Badges decorated their breasts. A symbol that had the letter G inside a measuring compass and squire edge was hidden in the photographs and deftly etched in the wooden furniture. He had seen the symbol before on the internet. It was of Freemasonry. He didn't know too much about them, but he was privy to the Illuminati conspiracy theories that circulated around his old school.

In the ballroom, looking down from the wooden band around the upper part of the room, was a large eye surrounded by a pointy sun. Asher felt something was *off* about this place. It was like he was constantly being watched.

It didn't take long until the mountain of sheets piled over

the rim of the hamper. The job was boring, but Justin had it worst. He had to clean bathrooms.

Asher pushed the cart into the elevator and pressed the "B" button. The elevator smoothly descended.

Ding!

The door slid open. Asher pushed the cart across the basement's concrete floor. Like the seedy underbelly of the beautiful city, the basement of Club Blue was drab, grey, and had a spiderweb infestation. The fluorescent lighting tubes cast a white hue throughout the corridor. A few tubes flickered. Others hummed. The light they projected agitated Asher's eyes. Damp, mildew-tasting air hovered like an invisible cloud. Being alone got his heart pumping. He kept his hand close to his inhaler and scanned his surroundings. He pushed the cart a little faster.

He arrived at the industrial washing machine. It was large enough to take all the sheets in at once. Since the sheets and pillowcases were all white, Asher didn't have to bother separating them. He tossed them inside, poured in the detergent, and started the load.

Suddenly, he heard a woman breathing in his ear.

Asher twisted back.

The basement was empty.

The lighting cast harsh shadows in the hall and dark boiler room.

Asher swallowed a glob of spit. "H-hello?"

Hearing no reply, Asher left the cart and sprinted to the elevator. He wasn't taking any chances. He quickly pressed the "1" button. The doors closed two seconds later. It felt like an eternity. He didn't know if the whisper was in his head. Probably. He was an imaginative guy.

He arrived in the lobby. Not seeing his mother or Justin, he headed to the bar, wanting to practice his billiards skills for a few minutes.

Justin stood behind the bar's counter and was reaching for a whiskey bottle on the top shelf.

Asher adjusted his glasses. "You shouldn't be doing that."

Justin grabbed a glass, put it on the counter, and poured a splash inside. Looking Asher in the eyes, he gulped it down.

Asher said, "Whatever, bro."

Justin poured another glass and deftly slid it across the countertop. It stopped an inch from Asher. "Drink."

Asher chuckled nervously.

"Come on," Justin said. "Drink."

Asher's smile fell away. He stared at the glass. His palms started sweating.

A hand reached out beside him and grabbed the glass.

Asher skittishly jumped aside, seeing his mother. He didn't hear her enter.

She wore a white t-shirt, sweats, and tennis shoes. Her hair was in a loose bun. "You two should be working."

Asher was too terrified to speak. She was going to ground him for at least a year. Even Justin seemed nervous.

Anna said, "School is starting soon. I don't want you to getting behind on your hotel responsibilities." She downed the glass in a single gulp. Wincing, she put it back on the counter. "I have to finish the rest of the paperwork. I want every room perfect, just like I showed you. Spit shine the floors if you have to. The hotel opens tomorrow."

She headed for the door.

Asher and Justin traded looks. Did they just get away with it?

In the doorway, Anna looked over her shoulder. "You get one drink. Period."

She exited the room.

Asher pulled out his inhaler, shook it, and blew a jet into his mouth. The cool air calmed him.

Justin poured another glass. "You in?"

Asher shook his head.

"Suit yourself." Justin downed it like a shot.

He put the bottle back on the shelf and sealed the glass cabinet. He grabbed his custodial cart and pushed it out of the room.

Asher got bored waiting on the wash to finish and decided to explore. He walked through the ballroom and craned back his neck. The portraits of angels, clouds, and ladders captured his interest. His imagination ran wild. What if this place was hiding a large sum of gold? It seemed implausible, but he read about something like it in a book before.

He hurried back to this room, opened his backpack, and grabbed his lock-picking tools. His father had taught him how to pick locks years ago.

Asher went upstairs and reached the door to the fourth floor. As he expected, none of the keys on the ring worked. He used the lock-picking tools instead. It took a lot longer than he expected. He was about ready to give up when he heard that final satisfying click.

He entered the charred hallway and pulled the neck of his shirt over his mouth to protect him from dust. He turned on the flashlight on his phone. The light shined over broken walls and the burned floor. He traveled carefully and peered into a few of the rooms. The metal bedframes rusted on the ground. Chucks of woods and sharp nails were haphazardly strewn across the floor.

He found a broken mirror in one room. Behind it was a skinny corridor that ran the length of the wall. *Secret passage*, he thought. He peeked his head into the hidden corridor. Jagged wood and broken furniture packed the inner walls, as if someone had intentionally clogged the way.

He continued his expedition down the normal hallway. Double doors at the center of the hallway opened into a lounge. The leather on the furniture had burned away. Broken glass littered the minibar. Decrepit seats and circular beds were placed throughout the lounge. *Strange.* He returned to the hall and continued farther away from the elevator.

Unburnt and painted red, the door to the final room looked new.

Asher cautiously approached it.

He turned the knob.

Locked.

He checked the keys on the ring. One matched the room's number - Suite 440.

It worked.

"What the heck?" Asher mumbled. He turned the doorknob and let the door open on its own.

A nicely-furnished suite presented itself before Asher. Nothing was burnt. The bed was unmade, as if someone had recently slept in it.

Asher walked inside. "Hello?"

He flipped the light switch. No power. There were electric lanterns scattered throughout the room. Asher turned one on. It glowed. He found men's clothes in the dresser and an expensive watch on the lampstand. He went to the bathroom and tried the sink. Clean water poured out of the faucet. It must've been connected with the rest of the plumbing. He lifted the toothbrush. His eyes widened. The bristles were damp.

He faced the closed shower curtain in the mirror's reflection.

Asher gently put the brush back and bolted out of the suite.

The shower curtain parted. Someone stepped out and watched the boy race down the hallway.

4

SCRUTINY

*A*nna waited outside of the hotel while the cops entered. One of the officers was a tall, dark-skinned man and the other was a short and wide white male. Both were middle-aged and checked Anna out the moment they saw her. She smiled politely. Her boys stood beside her. Asher looked especially nervous. Anna didn't believe his tall tale until she saw the room for herself. She called the cops soon after. From what she knew, the stairs were the only way to the fourth floor. She wondered if the previous concierge knew anything about the uninvited guest.

A long twenty-five minutes drifted by until the officers returned, chatting quietly.

"Well?" Anna asked nervously.

"We didn't find anyone," the short cop said.

Anna said, "Can't you run a DNA test or something?"

The officers traded looks and laughed.

"What's so funny?" Anna asked.

The dark-skinned cop said, "This isn't a homicide case."

"Or even a robbery for that matter," the short cop added.

"We open tomorrow. What if the squatter comes back?" Anna asked.

The dark-skinned cop said, "I suggest you change your locks."

The short cop stepped closer to Anna. "You want us to go the extra mile, you got to go the extra mile with us."

He looked her up and down.

Anna had no words.

Justin stepped between the cop and his mother. He stared the cop down.

The short cop taunted, "Come on. Hit me."

"Justin," Anna said firmly. "Back off."

Fuming, Justin stayed put. The vein in his neck bulged.

The black cop said to his partner. "Let's just go, man."

"No no no, I want to see what this kid is made of," the short cop replied.

Justin balled his fists but kept them at his sides.

"I'm for real, man. We don't got time for this," the black cop said to his partner.

His short cop stood inches from Justin. "Mind your temper, boy."

Justin glared. He held his ground.

The short cop smirked. He walked forward, bumping shoulders against Justin on the way to the police cruiser.

The black cop followed, saying to Anna, "Get new locks... and some security cameras while you're at it. Call us if you have another problem."

They drove away.

Anna mumbled, "A-holes."

Justin set his jaw.

Asher asked, "They aren't going to do anything?"

Justin replied, "For a nerd, you aren't very smart."

"Justin, that's enough," Anna said.

Justin's expression turned bitter and he returned inside.

Anna said to Asher. "Let's take a walk." They toured the hotel. As they passed through the corridor, Anna asked, "Why did you go upstairs alone?"

Asher shrugged. "I was bored, I guess."

Anna said, "Next time, ask me, okay? I don't want anyone going up there alone."

Asher lowered his head. "Yes, Mom."

"Now, tell me what else you found while you explored."

Asher's mood took a one-eighty turn. He smiled. "This way."

He showed Anna the various Freemason symbols hidden within the wood trimming and in paintings hanging on various walls. Anna wasn't too surprised. The place got the name Club Blue from somewhere. If the owners were Masons, why should she care? True, the hotel had a vague history, but Anna was more concerned about her uninvited guest. She left Justin in charge while she and Asher went to the hardware store. They bought new locks for the fourth floor. At Anna's command, Justin took all the furniture from the unburnt room and tossed it into the dumpster.

In the meantime, Anna tried contacting the concierge. His number had been disconnected. Annoyed, she sent an email, inquiring about someone living upstairs. She made it sound urgent.

Over the next week, a number of guests arrived. The first was a dapper-dressed old man. He had combed-over hair, a temperate demeanor, and a kind smile. His name was Andrew Warren and he acted like a gentleman from a bygone era. He claimed to have stayed in Club Blue many years ago and happily signed an extended-stay agreement. The next guest was a trucker who stayed only for a night. He wore a cap, a stained shirt, and Wrangler jeans. He'd come from the south to deliver food to various supermarkets.

"Not many people come up this way, you know," he said

as he got his key. "You would've done better to have a hotel closer to the city."

"But it wouldn't be this charming now, would it?" Anna joked.

The trucker said, "Yeah, but you'd actually make money."

Anna kept her smile, choosing to forget the offensive statement.

The honeymooners arrived after the trucker left. The beautiful buxom woman wrapped herself around the tall, handsome man as they planned out their weeklong stay.

"You're beautiful," the vixen said.

"Aw, thank you," Anna replied.

The vixen looked Anna up and down. Getting the room key, her husband swept her off her feet and carried her to the elevator. She giggled the whole way as her man whispered sweet nothings to her.

Anna put all the guests on the second floor. It was easier to clean and keep track of who was where.

She checked the fourth floor daily, making sure no one had taken residence in the unburnt room. It was empty.

She sent more emails to the concierge. He didn't reply.

The boys were well-behaved and played billiards frequently.

While Anna was working at the desk one rainy evening, a middle-aged man wearing a windbreaker, jeans, and running shoes entered into the lobby. Water dripped from the corners of the jacket and splattered on the checkered floor. He had brown hair parted at the side, a strong chin, and deep brown eyes. He approached the counter, leaving droplets of water in his wake.

He noticed Anna and mustered a smile. "Isn't this a surprise."

"Have we met?" Anna asked politely.

"Eight months ago," the man said, "York Police Department."

Anna's heart skipped a beat.

The man said, "I was there when Detective Casey was interviewing you. It was in regards to your husband."

Anna eyed the man. She kept her composure. "I think you might be mistaken."

"Anna Hall," the man said, calling out her lie.

Anna's kind smile faltered. "Are you a cop?"

"FBI agent. I deal in homicides mostly. There was some strange circumstance about your husband's drowning. Passed out drunk in the bathtub. What are the chances of that?"

Anna's heart raced. "This is my husband you're talking about."

"Whoa. Calm down. I'm just making an observation," the man replied. "I was hoping to rent a suite."

Anna wanted to turn him away, but she set her feelings aside. "Can I see your ID?"

He pulled out his wallet and drew out his driver's license. "Cameron Ryder. It's good to meet you, Anna."

The man was strange. There was a small threat behind his grin.

Anna put him on the third floor, as far away from her suite as possible. "Suite 315. There's a cable channel list on the nightstand. How long do you plan on staying?"

Cameron replied, "I don't know yet. Probably a few weeks."

"Can you be more specific?" Anna asked.

"Put me down for two weeks. I'll let you know if I plan to stay longer," Cameron said.

"Alright, Mr. Ryder," Anna said. "One of my boys will help you with your luggage."

"I got it. Thanks," Cameron said. "Enjoy your night, Anna."

He walked out into the rain and returned holding a single suitcase. He nodded at Anna as he went to the elevator. The moment the elevator door closed behind him, Anna felt like she could breathe again. *He thinks you killed your husband. Who wouldn't? You were the one who put him on that life insurance policy. You were the one who purchased this hotel with his fortune.* Anna nibbled on her fingernail.

Lightning flashed outside.

The power in the lobby flickered out.

Thunder crackled.

Her laptop screen became the only source of light.

A moment later, the lights turned back on. She added faulty electric to the list of things that needed to be fixed.

She searched Cameron's name on the internet. He had a weak web presence. All of his social media accounts were private. She found a picture of him with a few other men. After researching them, she discovered they were FBI agents. Cameron was the real deal. Why the hell was he here?

5

TERROR

*A*nna drove to Sebring High School. It only had six hundred students, and most of them had spent their whole life in this little town. The line of cars neared the flag pole. The morning sun was still low in the sky, and the clouds were a steely gray. Justin was in the front seat. His headphones blasted dirty music into his ears. His backpack slouched between his legs. He eyed the students exiting the bus in front of him. Asher was half-asleep in the backseat.

Anna reached the drop-off area. "Have fun."

Justin grabbed his backpack and left the SUV quickly. He slung the strap over his shoulder and started for the school's double doors.

Anna noticed Asher hadn't moved. "Is everything okay?"

"Yeah, I'm… I'm fine," the fourteen-year-old said, enviously watching the other children joyously greeting each other after a short summer break.

Anna leaned between the two front seats. "In a few weeks, none of this will be weird anymore."

Head down, Asher opened the Kia Sorento's sliding door.

"Oh!" Anna exclaimed. "You have your inhaler?"

Embarrassed, Asher's face turned blood red. "Yes, Mom."
He closed the door.

Anna rolled down the window. "Stay safe! I love you!"

The boy was already halfway to the door.

She wished she could hold him in her arms and tell him everything would be okay. He wouldn't believe her. He hated school.

A few cute girls eyed Justin. He smirked at them and kept walking.

Like a ghost, Asher was completely ignored by everyone he passed.

The driver behind Anna pressed their car horn.

"All right!" Anna shouted and started accelerating. The school shrank in the rearview. The start of the new school year worried Anna. She remembered how nervous she used to be at their age. Nevertheless, she quickly became head of the yearbook committee and made a lot of friends. In contrast, Justin was an expert at burning bridges and Asher could be crippling shy at times. Around Anna, he was a chatterbox, but he was as silent as a church mouse among his peers. Anna wanted him to sign up for after-school clubs, but Asher rejected that idea. Even the anime club didn't appeal to him. Clubs didn't interest Justin either, but Anna didn't know half the stuff Justin liked.

She returned to the hotel and spent most of the morning conducting interviews. She needed a hotel cleaner and a good handyman. It was a daunting task, but she found a few good candidates. Most of them were shocked to have found the job listing. According to them, Club Blue hadn't hired new employees for decades. Anna told them that a lot was going to change around here. She found most of her interviewees to be young and inexperienced. She needed someone she didn't have to train. Eventually, she found an elderly woman who'd been in the hotel cleaning business all her life. Her name was Lilith.

Anna hired a plumber named Harry to be her handyman. He was a chunky man and kind of smelly, but his resume and references said that he was the best for the job. Best of all, he was a jack of all trades. Once Anna started to make some more money, she planned to hire a marketing specialist. She'd be her own PR person until then.

Anna returned to school in the afternoon. Exhausted, Justin and Asher tossed their backpacks in the SUV and dragged themselves inside.

"How was it?" Anna asked as they put on their seat belts.

"Fine," Justin said.

"Sucks," Asher replied at the same time.

"Did you meet any nice kids?" Anna asked.

Justin put on his headphones.

Asher silently looked out the window.

Anna decided not to push them into a conversation.

The hotel was mostly quiet for the rest of the day. The honeymooners spent their day out and about. The finely-dressed old gentleman took a walk outside and read a book on the bench out back. He sprinkled bird feed on the stone pathway and waited. One crow arrived and then another. Before he knew it, a murder of crows was waddling around his feet, *caw*-ing and eating seeds. The old man grinned softly.

That night, Anna ordered Chinese takeout. She and the boys ate in the large ballroom. Soft instrumental music echoed off the walls. They were the only people in the massive room. The dim lights reflected off the checked tile floor. Asher dug into his Kung Pao chicken. Both his elbows rested on the table. Justin ate pork and broccoli. Anna twirled noodles around her chopsticks. Like most family meals, the three of them ate in silence. Anna wanted to break the status quo.

"Do you guys want to play cards?" She asked.

Asher perked up. Justin kept eating.

Asher moved his plate away. "I'll play, but I'll probably have to destroy you two."

Anna raised a brow. "Oh really?"

"Yep. I'm undefeated in gin rummy," Asher bragged.

Anna popped the clasp on her purse. "I'll guess we'll see."

The ballroom door opened.

The three of them turned that way. Holding a pizza, Agent Cameron entered. He walked halfway through the room, grabbed a nearby chair, and pulled it up to Anna's table.

Anna glared at him. *What the hell are you doing?*

"Howdy," Cameron popped open the lid to his pizza. Steam rose from the cheesy meat lovers pie.

"Um," Anna cleared her throat. "Mr. Ryder. How are you enjoying your stay?"

"Can't complain," he replied and lifted the slice to his mouth. He took a bite and winced. He spat it out. "Hot."

Justin leaned back his chair and crossed his arms. He glared at the agent.

Cameron dabbed the corner of his mouth with a napkin. He turned to Asher, who was looking at Anna with a confused face.

Cameron asked, "What's up, man? Have you played the latest Call of Duty?"

Asher said, "That's lame."

Cameron raised his brows. "Really?"

"Everyone is on Fortnite now," Asher explained.

"We'll see about that. Xbox or PlayStation?" Cameron asked.

"Xbox. Do you play?"

"Heck yeah," Cameron said. "You think I'm living under a rock or something?"

Asher laughed. "You get the latest expansion?"

"*Save the World?* Oh, yeah. I've been killing the game on that map."

"Awesome," Asher said, getting excited.

Anna interrupted, "Cameron. Why don't you introduce yourself?"

Cameron said, "I'm Cameron. I'm an FBI agent. A few months ago, I worked in York, Pennsylvania. That's where you all are from, right?"

Asher nodded, a large smile on his face.

Justin hadn't taken his eyes off the agent since he sat down. He wasn't buying Cameron's charm. Anna stayed hospitable and calm. She didn't want to make a scene. *He's a guest. Treat him like a guest.*

Asher asked, "Do you stop killers?"

"Only sometimes," Cameron replied. "A lot of the time, my job is interviewing people and reviewing crime reports."

"What gun do you use?" Asher asked.

"In game or real life?" The agent asked.

Asher said, "Real life."

"I'm rocking a Taser currently. It's nonlethal... mostly." Cameron reached into his unzipped jacket. Anna's glare stopped him.

Cameron said to Asher, "I'll show you some other time."

Awkward silence swallowed the conversation.

Justin took his first bite since the man got here.

Anna hated having him so close to her children. She stayed polite. "What did you do today, Cameron?"

He finished chewing and lowered his slice. "I took a walk on the beach and decided to test the water. It's cold." He chuckled.

Anna chuckled, too, but it was all an act.

Justin stood from his seat.

"Oh? Are you finished?" Anna asked.

"Yeah," Justin said.

"Why don't you stay seated with us?" Anna asked, begging him with her eyes. "I'm sure you'd want to hear some of Cameron's stories."

Justin didn't catch her hint. He said, "I'm good," and left the room.

Asher took the leftovers from Justin's plate and scraped them onto his own. He started eating.

Anna turned her attention back to Cameron. "Where are you stationed?"

"Philly originally," Cameron said, "But they've moved me around a lot. I prefer the northeast."

"Do you have a family?" Anna asked.

"Not really," Cameron admitted. "I didn't have the best dad. That kind of turned me off on the whole idea of kids."

Anna said, "They can be quite a handful. Teenagers especially."

"I'm right here," Asher said.

"Oh, sorry. I didn't see you," Anna joked.

Cameron said, "They seem like a good bunch."

"We've been through the thick and thin of it together. I don't know how I would've gotten this far without them," Anna said.

Cameron smiled to himself.

Anna glanced around the ballroom. She spoke in a hushed tone. "So what's your big mission, Agent?"

"You know I can't tell you that."

"That's no fun," Anna flirted, hoping to get information out of him. "I won't tell a soul."

"Cross your heart?" Cameron asked.

Anna used her index finger to cross her heart. Cameron

spoke in a quiet tone and leaned over the table. "They'll still fire me if I tell you."

He leaned back into his seat.

"You're no fun," Anna said.

"A common pitfall among professionals," Cameron said.

"Are you sure you don't want to share?"

Cameron's dark brown eyes locked on her own. "Maybe I'm here for you."

Anna faked a laugh. She made it pretty convincing. "You're funny after all."

Cameron smiled slyly.

Asher finished his plate.

Anna said, "You have any homework?"

"Not yet," Asher said.

Anna closed up the rice container. "We should still get you to bed anyway. I don't want you exhausted on your second day of school."

Cameron helped seal the to-go containers.

Anna said, "You don't have to do that."

"It's my pleasure," Cameron said.

She had Asher carry the leftovers. Walking out of the room, she thanked Cameron for his company. Cameron remained seated and finished his pizza slice.

After making sure both of the boys were in their rooms, she returned to the front desk. Cameron walked in a few moments later, smelling like cigarette smoke. "Staying up?"

"Someone has to," Anna said

"Insomniac," the agent replied, a wry smile on his smug face.

Anna smiled back at him. "Enjoy your night, Cameron."

Her smile faded the moment the agent left.

Two days later, Harry called Anna into one of the rooms. The bearded handyman had a beer belly, a sagging tool belt, and an ugly mug. He directed Anna to the open coat closet. "There," he said, breathing loudly through his open mouth.

"What am I looking at?" Anna asked, a little peeved that he pulled her away from the desk.

"On the wall," Harry pointed. Anna moved past him. She noticed the perfect circle burrowed into the wall. It was about the width of a pencil. She got a peek through. She could see the bed in the room beside it.

Breathing loudly, Harry said, "Someone's been naughty."

"Seal this up." Anna stood. "If you find any more, seal them up too."

The last thing Anna needed was a lawsuit.

HER NAME WAS MCKENZIE MICHAELS, and she was a bomb-shell. Seventeen years old, blonde, and Justin's type of crazy. She wore a tight button-up shirt, a cardigan, and a short skirt. She had a few drinks in her from the party. Just like Justin. In the passenger seat of the Kia Sorento, she stretched and crossed her legs on the dashboard. "You really steal this from your mom?"

Justin smirked. "She'll never know it was missing."

He drove on the maple-tree enclosed road and arrived at Club Blue.

McKenzie ogled the large hotel. "You live here?"

"Yeah. It's boring as hell." Justin said, parking on the side of the building. "Come on. I'll show you upstairs."

McKenzie bit her lip. She followed him to the side entrance. Justin used the master key to unlock it.

McKenzie said, "You know people died here, right?"

Justin hushed her and shut the door. He glanced up the stairway. "Third floor."

McKenzie led. "That fire in the '60s killed, like, eight people."

Justin kept an eye out for his mother. They reached the third floor.

McKenzie stopped at the threshold. "Imagine being trapped in a place like this when that happened. Fire everywhere. No hope of escaping."

Justin closed the door behind her. "There's only one guy staying on this floor. You can have any room but the last one."

McKenzie jogged ahead. She wobbled. Justin caught up to her and she fell into Justin's arms.

Justin held her. "You okay?"

McKenzie giggled.

Justin asked, "How drunk are you?"

"Me? This is how I always act," McKenzie said, unintentionally loud.

Justin hushed her and helped her balance.

McKenzie giggled even more.

Justin unlocked Suite 304.

McKenzie entered first. Justin checked the hall one last time before entering.

"I like the place," McKenzie said, flipping on the light switch.

Justin grabbed her upper arms and shoved her against the wall.

"Hey!" she exclaimed, but her shout was cut off by his kiss.

She was rigid at first but then rubbed her hands up the back of Justin's neck and into his hair. She grabbed a handful and tugged, pulling Justin's face away from her. He sucked air through his teeth, feeling hairs pulling at his scalp.

Lustful passion burned in McKenzie's luminous blue eyes. She kissed his neck and bit him, drawing a little blood.

Heart pounding, Justin grabbed the neck of her shirt with both hands and pulled, ripping off the two top buttons.

McKenzie stopped kissing him and cursed. "This shirt cost seventy dollars!" She slapped Justin across the face. "Jerk."

Feeling the hot pain on his cheek made Justin more passionate. He pushed McKenzie harder against the wall. She pushed back. Justin stumbled back a few steps and fell on the bed. McKenzie crawled on top of him and disrobed. "You owe me a shirt."

"Have your dad pay for it," Justin said.

McKenzie gawked at him. "Douchebag."

Justin grabbed her and rolled her over so he was on top.

Suddenly, the world blurred, and Justin was staring at his naked reflection in the bathroom mirror. "What the..."

He touched the large, bloody hickey on his neck. His back burned. Grimacing, he turned his back a little bit, seeing the long claw marks down his back.

He mumbled a curse.

His head throbbed. He didn't remember anything that happened after they got in bed.

The bathroom door was closed. He grabbed a hand towel and dampened it under the sink. He wiped himself down and took a dump. His mind was scattered, trying to figure out what triggered the blackout.

A bloodcurdling scream erupted from the bedroom.

Finished wiping, Justin jolted from the toilet seat and burst into the bedroom.

Half-clothed, McKenzie was curled up in the opposite corner of the room. She pulled her knees close to her chest and screamed bloody murder.

"McKenzie, stop!" Justin rushed over to her.

She hid her face in her hands.

Justin grabbed her wrists and pulled them away. "Stop."

She sobbed uncontrollably.

"What happened? Tell me!"

Her face was ugly with tears and snot. Justin glanced around the room. It was just the two of them. He turned back to her. "Talk to me."

She trembled, wailing loudly.

Justin shook her. It made her crying worse.

Unsure what to do, Justin hugged her. McKenzie's horrified, bloodshot eyes looked over Justin's shoulders.

"Shh," Justin said calmly.

McKenzie's sobs quieted into a whimper.

"It's okay. You're okay," Justin said. He was terrified because she was terrified.

Justin held her until he felt like it was all right to let go. He grabbed her skirt, shirt, and cardigan from the floor. He shoved it into a bundle. "Put these on. We need to go."

McKenzie kept staring past him.

Justin looked over his shoulder. "What? What are you looking at?"

McKenzie's face flushed white. Mascara tears trickled down her cheeks. She was petrified.

Justin guessed it was the tall wall mirror mounted into the wall.

"Get dressed," he said urgently. "I don't know if anyone heard us."

McKenzie didn't move.

"Hurry, darn it!" Justin said.

Seeing she was unresponsive, he put on her cardigan for her, slipping her arms through the sleeves and fitting it backward to hide her small breasts. He lifted her to her feet and slipped her skirt on her. He shoved her shirt in her hands. She squeezed it tightly.

Justin put on his jeans. "If this is some sort of joke, say it now before I get really pissed."

McKenzie held her shirt close to her. She trembled.

Justin slipped on his shirt. Putting one hand around her,

41

Justin ushered her to the door. He opened it a crack and peeked into the hallway. Not seeing anyone, he quickly rushed her to the stairs. She wouldn't move from the hallway.

"What the hell is wrong with you?" Justin said in a harsh whisper.

Grumbling, he swooped McKenzie off her feet and held her with one hand under her knees and the other under her upper back. Feeling the strain in his lean, toned muscles, he carried her downstairs, used his back to push open the side entrance, and got her to the SUV. He sat her in the front seat and shut the door.

Stress levels skyrocketing, he got into the Sorento and slammed the front door. He turned the key and floored the accelerator. He drove down the tree-lined road, getting farther from the hotel. He glanced over at McKenzie. She stared forward, hugging her shirt. Her teeth chattered.

"You have to tell me what's going on," Justin said.

The girl was silent. She barely blinked.

"Hello? Can you hear me?" Justin asked, annoyed and terrified.

McKenzie didn't move the whole way back to her house.

Justin parked outside of the driveway of the nice suburban home and turned to her. "You call me, okay?"

McKenzie opened the passenger door. It was the first sign of life he'd seen. She dragged her feet to the house's front door. Justin stayed in the vehicle. The house lights turned on. Her father opened the door.

"McKenzie, what did I say about going out at night— Wait? What happened?"

The father saw Justin's vehicle. He shouted. "Hey! What did you do to her? What did you do?!"

Justin floored the gas.

The tires screeched. The Sorento bolted down the road,

leaving behind two black wheel marks on the asphalt. The father shouted curses at him. Justin kept his eyes ahead.

"Crazy chick," he mumbled to himself, pulse raging.

The memory of her scream echoed in his ears. He'd never heard anyone like that before. It was one of absolute terror. The kind you couldn't fake.

ACCUSATION

*A*nna awoke suddenly, drenched in cold sweat from another nightmare she didn't remember. The digital clock read 5:32 am. Feeling miserable, Anna forced herself out of bed, hurried to the bathroom, and vomited in the toilet.

Tasting bile, she pulled off a piece of toilet paper and wiped her mouth before flushing it down. Money troubles, the boys starting school, and the FBI agent lurking around left her feeling queasy. She knew she wasn't actually sick because of how many times she'd stress-vomited in the past thirty years of her life.

Helluva way to start the day. She rubbed her tears away and stood up. She looked at her reflection and pinched her stomach. She was nearing one hundred and forty pounds. It was not a bad weight at all, but the idea that she had put on five pounds made her feel sick again.

She grabbed her woman's business suit out of the closet. She stopped herself from closing the closet door and checked for any peepholes. Not finding any, she got dressed. After she fixed her hair and put on make-up, she headed to the front desk. She organized her pen collection, booted up her laptop, and made sure everything was in tip-top shape. Old ledgers rested in a locked drawer beneath the counter. The last concierge wrote everything by hand. Anna was jealous of that type of patience. It was so much easier to catalog using her hotel software.

Anna stood behind the counter for a long hour. The wall clock's ticking echoed off the walls. It was Saturday morning. Things were slow. She poured a glass of coffee from the nearby machine and made sure the candy bowl was full of mints. Seeing it was, Anna had nothing to do but wait. She decided to email the concierge again. She was convinced he was ignoring her.

The front doors opened. A middle-aged married couple entered. The man wore a heavy jacket and had a clean-shaven, round face. His wife was short, thin, and had streaks of grey in her hair.

Hands folded over her lap, Anna greeted them. "Welcome to Club Blue. How might I serve you?"

The man spoke with a hostile tone. "Is that your blue SUV parked outside?"

"Uh," Anna replied, taken completely off-guard.

"The Kia," the man belted.

"Yes. Why? Has something happened to it?"

"You got a son? Tell me where he is," the man demanded.

"I don't understand—"

"Where is he?" The man shouted.

Anna said, "Sir, I'm going to have to ask you to calm down."

"Calm? Calm! Your son attacked my girl last night!"

The wife stood behind her husband, her head lowered and nervously twiddling her thumbs.

Anna said, "There must be a mistake. My son is here all night, every night."

The man said, "He lied to you."

"I don't appreciate your tone," Anna said. "Tell me what's going on before I call the police."

The man panted. Sweat dotted his red face. "My little girl and your son went to a party. When it was over, he dropped off my girl at 2 am, drunk, half-dressed and… and…" The man got so worked up, he could hardly speak. "He did something to her. She won't look at me. We had to force her to leave her room."

His wife rubbed his back, calming him but only slightly.

Anna asked, "Are you sure it was Justin?"

"He was in your car," the man replied. "I saw him myself."

"Wait here," Anna said. "I'll be right back."

She sped-walked to the elevator. She pushed the button a few times, anxious for it to open. When it did, she quickly ascended to the second floor. Her mind spun in circles. She refused to believe any accusation until she talked to her son.

She hammered her fist on Justin's door. "Hey, it's me. Open up."

She waited.

Frustrated, she pulled out her key ring, found the right key, and put it into the lock.

The door suddenly opened.

Wearing boxers and t-shirt, Justin loomed over her. His tangled brown hair looked like a rat's nest. Dark circles brushed under his bloodshot gaze. "What?"

A nearby door opened.

Dressed for a morning run, one of the guests stepped out.

Anna pushed past Justin, knocking into his shoulder. "Shut that."

Justin closed the door and turned back. He crossed his arms and waited for Anna to speak.

She noticed the purple hickey on his neck, seeing that her fears were well-realized. "You had a girl here last night?"

"No," Justin said.

"Don't you lie to me," Anna barked.

"I'm not."

"Justin, I swear—" Anna stopped herself before going off on him. "That girl's parents are downstairs right now. They say you and their girl…" The thought nauseated Anna.

"What?" Justin asked.

"Did you?" Anna asked, letting him fill in the blanks.

"What are you talking about?"

"Don't play dumb," Anna snapped. "You have a hickey on your neck."

Justin touched it and cursed.

Anna rubbed her forehead. "Listen, we're going to go downstairs, and you're going to tell them the truth--"

"We banged. So what?" Justin interrupted.

"Politely. Apologetically," Anna coached. "Don't say anything you wouldn't say to a police officer."

"McKenzie just started flipping out for no reason," Justin said.

Anna didn't know what to say next. Looking at her baby boy caught up in this made her want to tear her hair out. Knowing that he was sexually active made her light-headed. Knowing that he might've forced himself on a woman made Anna almost faint. "Get some clothes on. Something nice. First impressions mean a lot."

She walked to the bathroom while her son got changed. Closing the door partway, Anna blinked the tears out of her watery eyes. She composed herself in the mirror. *Professional. Hospitable. Kind,* she thought to herself. She felt her chest tighten as if her heart were being crushed. She controlled her breathing. She promised herself not to vomit again.

"Hey," Justin said on the other side of the door. "I'm ready."

Anna stepped out.

The seventeen-year-old wore skinny jeans, nice skate shoes, a white V-neck tee, his sports jacket, and a scarf to hide the hickey. His unruly hair was brushed over to the side. He still looked like a skater punk.

"Is that the best you got?" Anna asked.

Justin frowned. "It is."

"It's fine," Anna said half-heartedly. "Come on."

They headed down the elevator. Despite Justin's flat expression, his eyes couldn't conceal his distress. They arrived in the lobby.

The middle-aged couple stood by the front desk.

The father stormed toward Justin. "You little bastard!"

"Daniel!" His wife shouted.

The father stopped inches from Justin's face. "I ought to wring your neck."

"Daniel, please," his wife pleaded.

"Not now, Sherry!" he shouted, spittle flying from his teeth hitting Justin's face. He jabbed his finger into Justin's chest, knocking him back a half-step "You hurt my little girl."

Anna cautiously approached. "Everyone, take a breath."

Daniel said to Justin. "I'll make sure you rot in a cell for the rest of your life."

Justin tried to act like the words didn't affect him, but his silence was proof of his terror.

"Please, there's been a misunderstanding," Anna said. "Let's talk in my office."

Daniel shouted, "We'll talk right here!"

"Okay, okay, just—let Justin share his side of the story. There's no need to do anything stupid," Anna said.

Daniel looked ready to punch Justin's face in. Sherry calmed him down. "Please, Daniel. Not now."

"Alright, boy. Spit it out," Daniel said.

"Give him a little room," Sherry said.

Daniel took two steps back.

Justin glanced at his mom for guidance.

She nodded.

Justin said to Daniel, "McKenzie and I... we, we came here after drinking."

All eyes were on him. The chandelier reflected on his sweaty brow. "We made out and... after we finished, I went to the bathroom and McKenzie started screaming. She saw something and it must've scared her. That or, she's, uh, she's crazy. Does she take any medication?"

Daniel glared. "My little girl was perfectly fine before you came along. Man up and tell the truth, son."

"I am," Justin said.

"Liar," Daniel barked. "I'm going to make sure the police burn you."

Seeing this was going sideways, Anna asked, "What did McKenzie say?"

Daniel got quiet.

Sherry said, "She hasn't said anything."

"How did you find my car?" Anna asked.

"Daniel's best friend works in the police department. He ran the plates," Sherry explained. "We have a lot of friends in high places."

The threat wasn't lost on Anna. She asked, "Have you told the cops?"

Sherry replied, "Not yet."

Daniel kept his eyes on Justin. "We wanted to hear it from your boy first."

"I'm innocent, man," Justin exclaimed. "She's the crazy one."

"You lie one more time and I'll put you on the floor," Daniel threatened.

Justin opened his mouth to protest, but Anna cut him off. "Look, it's clear we don't have all the facts. These claims against my son, if they're false, will ruin his life. It will ruin my life. It will ruin his little brother's life. We shouldn't make any hasty decisions."

Sherry asked, "And if he raped her? My little girl. What about her life?"

Anna glanced at her son and then back to the woman. "If that's the case, he deserves to be tried through the proper legal channels."

Sherry said, "So what do you propose we do?"

Anna walked behind the front counter. She punched a code into the lockbox mounted under the desk and pulled out her checkbook. "We discuss our options. If McKenzie talks, we proceed to the next logical step. Until then—" Anna put a number on the check. "Let's handle this civilly."

Sherry read the number. She gestured for Daniel.

He walked over. "You think you can bribe me?"

"No, sir," Anna said. "But I want to compensate you for the grief my son caused you." She handed him a business card too. "Here's my number. Call me when McKenzie talks."

The couple exchanged glances. Silently agreeing that the money will hold them over, they took the check.

Daniel said, "If I see that little monster around my daughter—"

"That won't happen," Anna assured him.

"And if you try to leave town—"

"We're not going anywhere," Anna said.

Sherry sighed. "Let's go, Daniel. My migraine is coming back."

Shooting Justin a nasty glance, Daniel followed his wife out of the building.

Anna walked to the glass doors and watched them enter their sedan. Justin lingered behind her.

"How much?" Justin asked.

"I don't want to talk right now." Anna was so pissed she couldn't even look at him.

In a huff, she retreated into her office. She shut and locked the door behind her, now five thousand dollars poorer. It was more money she'd have to repay the bank. She rested her back against the door. She wondered if Justin really hurt that girl.

There was a knock.

"What?" Anna asked.

"I'm sorry." Justin's muffled voice carried through the door. "I didn't hurt that girl. I swear on my life."

Anna balled her fists. Anger and frustration raged through her.

"Hello?" Justin asked.

Anna unlocked and yanked open the door, startling her son. "Justin. I will say this once. No more parties. No more girls. No more stupid stuff. You will go to school, you will make As, and you'll come here and work. That's it."

Justin protested. "But she's the one who caused this! It's all a setup!"

"I don't care. If you don't clean up your act this year, I'll take you out of school and you'll be cleaning toilets for the rest of your life. Do I make myself clear?"

Justin set his jaw to the side. He boiled.

"Do I?" Anna repeated herself.

"Yeah," Justin said venomously and stormed off.

Anna returned to her office. She needed a breather. How could he have hurt that girl? Her little boy used to be so sweet. Nevertheless, she'd seen violent bursts in his father. He could be a very dangerous man. Was Justin becoming him?

7

COSMIC

*A*sher stepped out of the elevator and into the lobby. The glossy floors captured the chandelier lighting. Cool air lingered. The bar was closed. No music today. The front counter was unoccupied.

"Mom? Justin?" His voice carried through the large, empty room. "Hello?"

He adjusted his crooked glasses.

The late evening sky cast its golden glow through the glass front doors. Asher walked behind the counter, through the short hallway, and opened the door to his mother's office. She wasn't there.

He returned to the counter. He watched his feet as he walked. His mind was on his homework. Math was easy. It was English that worried him. Standing behind the counter, he glanced up and noticed the tall man and teenage girl standing in front of him.

Their sudden appearance startled him. He composed himself.

The man stood over six feet and wore a sports jacket that

had patches on the elbows. He had horn-rimmed glasses, gaunt cheeks, silvery grey eyes, and a long face. Likes veins of iron, streaks of grey ran through his dark wavy hair. The teenager was five foot eight. Straight, raven-black hair poured down her slender shoulders. Dressed in black, her cute collared day dress hugged her slim body. She wore black leggings and Converse shoes. Sleepless circles brushed under her coal-colored eyes. She didn't wear make-up, but her ivory skin was blemish-free. She eyed Asher but had a natural expression. Her father had a distant gaze.

Asher forced himself to smile. He looked about as awkward as he felt. "My, uh, mom is around here somewhere."

He glanced around the lobby, feeling alone. His social anxiety built up. He wanted to use his inhaler just to have something to do but stopped himself. He said, "I can check you in, though. How long do you plan to stay?"

"Three weeks. More probably," the man said. "I have to finish my book."

He scratched the back of his head aggressively.

"Oh, okay. Three weeks," Asher mumbled. He shook the mouse, waking up the computer. He tried to remember what his mom showed him about the registration software. It took longer to load than he expected. He nervously shifted his weight from one foot to another.

He asked for the man's ID.

The man opened his wallet and put it on the counter. "David Hunt," Asher mumbled as he typed in the name. He was from Minnesota. Asher opened the glass key case behind him and pulled out one for Suite 212, which he placed on the counter. "Cash or credit?"

The man pulled out a fat money roll and counted out a few hundred.

The teenage girl kept staring at Asher. He smiled awkwardly and nervously looked away. Asher put the money in the register. "You're all set. Enjoy your stay."

David Hunt and the teenage girl walked to the elevator. The girl glanced over her shoulder at Asher, giving him one final look before ascending.

Asher's breathing quickened. He felt an attack coming on. He quickly pulled out his inhaler and pushed the top, blowing the dry jet air into his mouth. Relaxed, he stayed at the counter until Anna returned twenty minutes later.

"Where were you?" Asher asked.

"Getting groceries. Help your brother." Anna walked behind the counter.

"I checked in some guests into Suite 212," Asher said. "They paid in cash."

"Awesome. Thanks," Anna replied, her mind obviously somewhere else.

Asher and Justin brought the groceries to Anna's suite. Hers was the biggest and had an oven and a large kitchen space. They packed the fridge full. Justin seemed to be in a bad mood. He didn't say anything to Asher the whole time.

After that was finished, Anna had Asher and Justin clean the hotel. The brothers washed windows, mopped the marble ballroom floor, and made beds. Offering to clean the bowling alley all by himself, Asher separated from his work partner and entered the bowling alley. He shut and locked the door behind him. He parked his cleaning supply cart and stretched. He pulled out his phone, sat in one of the plastic seats, and booted up a platformer video game. He'd had a craving to play the classics like Castlevania and Metroid Prime.

Slouching, he started fighting the game's boss. A sudden explosion of noise and color filled the bowling alley. Asher nearly fell out of his seat. Flashing lights suddenly blasted on and distorted Techno tunes played through the speakers. The neon lights on the walls glowed.

Asher glanced around. There was no one else around to trigger the lights.

The belt in the ball retriever rotated. A ball rolled out. He pocketed his phone and grabbed it. Asher aligned the shot and rolled it down the lane. The ball curved into the gutter. He waited for it to return and tried again.

"Dang, I suck," he mumbled.

Crash!

A loud noise sounded behind the pins.

"H-hello?" Asher asked.

Someone replied, but his or her voice was muffled.

"What?" Asher asked. "I can't hear you."

The person shouted, but Asher couldn't make out the words.

He contemplated getting help from someone else, but he didn't want to leave the stranger alone. What if they were hurt? He could always call his mom.

"I'm coming over!" Asher shouted. He walked down the strip between two lanes and reached the pins. There was a dark corridor behind them.

"Hello? Can you hear me?"

"In here," a female said.

Asher got on his hands and knees. He crawled past the pins, knocking one down. The pin retriever started to lower. He reached the other side before it could touch him. He stood to his feet and brushed himself off. He stood on a wooden floor and was surrounded by machinery. The teenage girl from earlier stood a few feet away.

"What are you doing here?" Asher asked.

"I was exploring," the girl replied.

"What made that noise?" Asher asked.

"What noise?"

Asher mimicked the crash.

"I didn't hear anything," the teenage girl said.

"You shouldn't be back here, you know," Asher said.

The girl smirked. "Are you going to throw me out?"

Asher didn't know what to say. If he said yes, she'd think he was lame. If he said no, she could run amok in his mother's hotel. "Just don't do it again, okay?"

The girl didn't seem phased by his remark. "What's your name?"

"A-Asher."

"I'm Raven. My dad is the A-hole who named me after a bird. You think I got a big nose?" She leaned closer to Asher.

He took a step back, keeping a comfortable distance. "No. It's fine."

"Fine?" Raven asked.

"Very—" Asher was going to say cute, and it was, too. Like a little button. He felt himself about to stutter and settled with, "Fine."

"You're nervous," Raven said.

"What are you talking about?" Asher rubbed the back of his neck.

"Nice save," Raven said, easily calling his bluff. Suddenly, she turned around and started for the thin door at the end of the stubby corridor.

"Where are you going?" Asher asked.

"To explore," Raven said. "Are you going to come or be a wimp?"

"I'm fourteen," Asher declared as if that was a reason for why he couldn't be a coward.

"And I'm fifteen. You don't see me crying about the rules," Raven replied. "Hurry up, I already found a lot of cool places around here."

Conflicted, Asher followed after her.

He heard a low rumble from the bowling alley.

Both of them twisted back, seeing a ball hit the pins and landing a strike.

Raven asked, "Are you with someone?"

"No. I even locked the door behind me."

Raven looked alarmed.

Wanting to seem brave, Asher got on his knees and looked through the pins. There was no one in the room. The door on the way in fell shut as if someone just ran out. "What the—"

"Who is it?"

"I don't know," Asher said.

"Let's keep moving," Raven said.

Asher followed close behind her. The only other person it could've been was Justin, but why? It didn't make any sense.

They pushed open the thin door and were inside a wide workman's closet. This was where the handyman stored his tools and repaired things on the workbench. Raven huddled over a bucket of tools.

Asher slowly approached. "You probably shouldn't be messing with that stuff."

Raven quickly twisted, holding a saw to her throat. Her chin was up and her head tilted to the side. Her eyes were wide and crazed. A wicked smile grew on her lips.

Asher screamed in a high-pitched voice.

Raven giggled and lowered the saw. "Scared ya, huh?"

Asher put a hand on his racing heart.

Raven said, "My dad uses me as the inspiration for a lot of his novels. One was about a fifteen-year-old serial killer just like me."

"That's cool," Asher said, unsure how to reply.

"F-ed up is a more apt description." Raven tossed the saw back in the bucket. "You like horror movies?"

Asher shrugged. "Depends."

"How about books?"

Asher said, "I don't read too often."

"You should," Raven said. "There's a lot of F-ed up stuff out there. I read this one book where this guy got his face ripped off. How crazy is that?"

The thought made Asher nauseous.

"Show me something cool around here," Raven said.

"There's a meat locker," Asher said.

"Oooh." Raven was intrigued.

Asher regretted mentioning it. "I don't have the key."

"Can you pick it," Raven asked.

"Yeah, but—"

"Yeah?! You know how to pick locks?" Raven asked.

"I have some experience," he said humbly.

Raven said, "That's wicked."

"Really?" Asher said, excited. He recovered quickly, "I mean, yeah, it's cool I guess."

Raven was giddy with excitement. "Show me."

They stepped into the ballroom. Raven craned her head up to the ceiling. "Jacob's Ladder?"

"Uh, what?" Asher asked.

"It's a bible story. Jacob was alone one night when he saw angels descending and ascending from heaven."

"Huh," Asher said.

"You think Jacob really saw it?" Raven said as they walked.

Asher shrugged. "I never really went to church."

"That doesn't answer my question," Raven said.

"I don't know. Maybe," Asher said. "I kind of believe in that stuff, but I've never seen it."

"What would you do if you did?" Raven asked.

Asher said, "I never really thought about it, I guess."

Raven stayed quiet.

They turned into one of the off-shooting hallways and entered the kitchen. Asher led Raven to the meat locker. He removed the lockpicking tools from his wallet. There was a master lock on the hatch. Raven watched him, making Asher nervous. He wasn't good around people, especially not girls. His palms were damp. He trembled slightly. After ten minutes, he got it.

"Sorry," he apologized.

Raven said, "We're in. That's what counts."

Two rows of hooks ran down the dark freezer. A metal counter with a faucet-less sink ran the length of one wall.

Raven flipped the light switch and allowed Asher to step in first. The chilling air shocked him. Raven closed the freezer door behind her.

"Hold up," Asher said.

"Relax. We'll be fine," Raven said.

Asher nervously buried his hands in his pockets. The meat locker wasn't very cold, but it was still working.

"Watch this," Raven jogged down the middle of the room and leaped. She grabbed onto one of the hooks.

"Careful!" Asher said.

Raven giggled. She swung to the next hook and the next. "It's like that ring thing you'd see at a gymnasium."

Asher's teeth chattered. He didn't know how many health codes Raven was violating, but it was probably a lot.

Raven noticed Asher's stern expression. "Light up, Asher. Live a little."

"I'm good," Asher stayed by the door, watching the girl swing. Breaking all these rules was starting to annoy him. Mom had enough issues to have to worry about Raven messing something up. Even worse, she could get hurt and all the blame would fall on Asher. He should've never brought her here. He opened his mouth to tell her to stop, but couldn't. He didn't want to think he was a coward. *What would Justin do?* he asked himself. It was a stupid question. His big brother would've been swinging with the girl.

Raven let go of the hook and landed on her feet. She put her hands up, like a gymnast completing a great feat.

"Are you ready to go?" Asher asked.

"Cold?" Raven asked.

"You're not?"

"This is nothing," Raven replied. "We get feet of snow in Minnesota."

Raven pushed against the locker door. It didn't budge. Her expression turned dreadful.

Asher's heart sank to his stomach.

"Just kidding," Raven said and pushed the door open.

Asher released his loaded breath. He followed her out. As he locked the door, Raven asked, "What's next?"

"I have an essay I have to write."

"Do it later," Raven said.

"It's one thousand words. I should really get started," Asher said.

"Whatever," Raven replied. "I guess I'll just have to explore by myself."

Her words plagued Asher with guilt, but he'd entertained her long enough. "I guess so."

Raven put a hand on her hip and glared.

Asher broke eye contact immediately. "I should probably... yeah."

"You live around here, right?" Raven asked.

Asher didn't want to disclose the information. Nevertheless, he had a feeling that she'd find out if he lied. "Yeah."

"Cool," Raven replied.

Asher walked to the ballroom. Raven went the same way. It was really awkward. He turned into the bowling lane hallway. He pressed his back against the wall and peered out, watched Raven hiking up the left side of the imperial staircase. She walked along the mezzanine balcony, looking bored. Asher returned to the bowling lane and grabbed the supply cart. He mopped the floor quickly. When he finished, he placed the wet floor sign there and pushed the cart to the supply closet. He went up the stairs and headed to his suite. It was strange having his own room, but it made him feel like a real adult.

He walked over to the desk. His backpack slouched on the floor nearby. Sighing, he pulled out his English and Algebra One textbook. Keeping his Word software open on his desktop monitor, Asher had a hard time starting. He couldn't stop thinking about Raven. Part of her annoyed the crap of Asher. The other part, he found highly intriguing. In his short few years of life, he'd never met a girl like her.

Thump!

Asher glanced up. The noise came from the other side of the wall.

Thump!

Asher grunted. He reviewed his writing prompt.

Thump!

"That's it." Asher got up. He went into the hallway and knocked on the door next to his own. Keeping his hands in his back pockets, he waited.

Justin came walking down the hall.

"Hey," Asher said, "Who stays in this suite?"

Justin replied, "No one." He unlocked the door to his room and vanished inside.

"That can't be right." Asher pulled out his master key and unlocked the door. "Room service. Coming in."

The lights were off. He lingered at the entrance. There was no one inside. He mumbled to himself. "You must be hearing things."

He shut and locked the door.

He returned to his studies, not hearing the thump again.

As he typed his essay, a half-inch latch silently moved behind a nearby painting, opening up a small peephole. It was completely hidden to the casual observer. Asher's studies stole his attention. He didn't know he was being watched.

8

THE GUEST

*D*ressed for the day, Anna searched the bathroom frantically for her favorite hair clip. It wasn't in her toiletry bag or drawer. Peeved, she settled for an old one. Like always, she entered the lobby early in the morning and started brewing coffee. Returning to the desk, she noticed her pens were gone too. She had four of them. She barely used them, but it was the fact that they were gone that angered her.

She took a few deep breaths, trying to not start the morning on a bad note. She adjusted the flowers in her vases and replenished the mint bowl. She couldn't bring herself to have the place any less than perfect. Club Blue was more than a hotel. It was her home.

Yawning, her boys exited the elevator.

Asher played a game on his phone.

Justin had his backpack slung on one shoulder. The top of his skateboard stuck out of the top.

Anna said, "Not happening."

Justin glared. "I'm not going to ride it to school."

"Did I not make myself clear before?" Anna asked rhetorically.

Grumbling, Justin removed the skateboard from his pack and handed it across the desk.

Anna put it under. "An Uber is waiting outside. Hurry up. I don't want you to be late."

"You're not taking us?" Asher asked.

"I'm too busy," Anna replied.

Asher seemed let down. The boys exited.

The housekeeper arrived a little while later. Lilith and Anna exchanged small talk. The elderly woman asked about the fourth floor.

"It's closed off until further notice," Anna said. "Just make sure the rest of the hotel looks pretty."

At 9 am, Anna's first guest of the day arrived. He was of average height and build. In his late thirties, he had spiked blond hair, chubby cheeks, oily skin, a stud in his ear, and wore a hoodie above his Hollister shirt. The man walked with a confident swagger to the counter. He rested one elbow on the countertop. "Hey, precious. You have any more available rooms?"

"Plenty," Anna replied. "What are you interested in? Queen. Twin?"

"Where's Ferguson?" the man interrupted.

"He no longer owns this establishment," Anna said.

"You're kidding, right?" the man asked.

"Not at all," Anna said. "I purchased Club Blue two months ago."

The man's disappointment was papabile.

Anna asked, "How long do you plan on staying?"

"A week," the man said.

"ID please?"

Anna's question offended the man. "Ferguson didn't do that."

"It's a new company policy. Safety reasons. I'm sure you understand," Anna said.

"That's ridiculous. Whose safety?"

"It's in case of an emergency," Anna replied. "Something gets stolen or broken, we want to be able to contact the owner... or the police for that matter."

The man said, "Ferguson valued privacy. That's what made Club Blue so great."

"ID or I can't help you," Anna replied.

"What if I paid in cash?" the man asked. "I'm sure you could use the money."

"I'm sorry," Anna said.

Grumbling, the man pulled out his wallet and showed his driver's license. Lance Colby. Thirty-eight years old. Kansas City. Anna typed his name into the online ledger. "We'll set you up in Suite 207."

"Okay, can I have access to the back door?" Lance asked.

Anna was confused. "Sure. As long as you have your key."

"Good. Good," Lance said, thinking. "At least it's not gone completely downhill."

After accepting the key, Lance walked to his black Mercedes sedan and parked it around the side of the building. He returned a moment later, rolling a large suitcase behind him.

At midday, Harry approached Anna. His tool belt sank his pants an inch. He wiggled as he pulled it up to his rotund waist. Loudly breathing through his open mouth, the handyman told Anna about a few creaky floorboards, a leaky sink, and a slew of little but annoying problems. Anna gave him permission to buy whatever he needed to fix the issues. She expected to build trust by giving him freedom. If Harry did a good job, she'd extend him more responsibility.

Harry seemed grateful. "One more thing," he said. "I was thinking of ways we can refurbish the fourth floor."

"It's a mess," Anna replied.

"Not entirely," Harry replied. "Some of the water lines still work. We just have to look at replacing the AC and the electric... and the walls."

"And the carpeting, bedding, etc.," Anna said.

Harry shrugged. "Whatever you want to do. At the very least, let me inspect it."

Anna did want to get the fourth floor repaired. Obviously, she didn't have the money for it at the moment, but it would be good to get an estimate. She closed the front desk, leaving a number to text her if anyone showed up. She followed Harry up the stairs and unlocked the door. Harry entered the damaged corridor first. He gave Anna a flashlight. "Hold this."

Anna took it and aimed the light down the hallway. The place looked like it was going to fall in any minute. Harry pulled up the notepad on his phone. He took notes and pictures. He touched holes in the wall and grumbled to himself. Anna followed him around. He used unfamiliar jargon referring to the different electric currents they needed. Anna nodded along. The air scratched her throat. She coughed.

Harry stepped into one of the bedrooms. A few loose ceiling beams hung overhead.

"Maybe we should wait on this, Harry," Anna said, feeling more and more uncomfortable the farther they got away from the exit.

"There's nothing to worry about," Harry said. He peered into the three-foot-wide gap between two bedroom walls. "It looks like a tunnel."

"Like a hidden passageway," Anna remarked.

"Uh-huh," Harry said, "You know I heard rumors about this place."

"Oh yeah?"

Harry gestured Anna to follow him back through the room. "The rich and famous would come up and engage in all sorts of—"

Snap!

A ceiling beam broke free.

"Watch out!" Anna shouted.

Harry let out half a scream before the beam hit his head. Dust puffed around him as his body hit the burnt carpet.

Anna stared in horror, the beam resting on Harry's head. Blood started trickling out.

"Harry?" Anna rolled the heavy 4x4 beam off.

The man wasn't moving.

"Wake up," Anna shook his shoulder.

Dread filled her. "Please, Harry. Wake up."

She pressed her fingers to his neck, trying to find a pulse. After a moment, she found it. He was alive. Anna pulled out her phone and dialed the police.

She stayed alongside Harry as she waited for the ambulance to arrive. The walls and ceiling creaked around her. Her flashlight and phone were the only sources of light. She felt like she was being watched. Tears welled in her eyes.

Ten long minutes later, she heard footsteps in the hallway. She cautiously left the room, seeing the paramedics approaching. "In here." She gestured for them to enter. "Be careful."

Unable to wake Harry, they put him on a stretcher and walked down a set of stairs before turning onto the third floor and descended the rest of the way via elevator. The paramedics claimed the man had major head swelling and probably a fractured skull.

Anna nervously chewed her nail as she watched Harry get carted off. Sirens screaming, the ambulance raced down the road. Anna returned to the office. Guilt tightened her chest.

If she had never allowed him up there, this would've never happened.

The boys returned home from school. Both of them were exhausted and miserable. Anna gave them their space. She needed them rested in order to take care of Harry's duties in the coming days. If Harry's condition was detrimental, she'd have to find another handyman to replace him.

That night, she got a call from Lilith, who was within the hotel.

"I-I fell," the older woman said.

Anna found her sprawled out on the floor of one of the suites' restrooms. She couldn't stand. The ambulance returned, after only being gone for eleven hours. They carted Lilith away. It was most likely a broken hip.

Distraught, Anna ordered takeout for the boys while she worked the desk. No new guests showed up. She decided to take a break and head to the bar. She walked behind the counter, unlocked the liquor cabinet, and poured herself a drink.

"Bar open?" Agent Cameron lingered in the doorway.

"Come on in," Anna said.

Cameron sat on the bench. "You got any spiked lemonade?"

Anna checked the cold storage and pulled out a glass bottle. "Four bucks."

"Put it on my tab," Cameron said. He used his shirt to pop off the lid. "I saw the ambulance early today. What happened?"

"More like what hasn't happened," Anna said. "I lost my only two employees in the last twenty-four hours."

"Crappy coincidence," Cameron remarked.

"The strange timing hadn't escaped me. When it rains it pours, I guess," Anna replied.

"How are the kids?" Cameron asked.

"Annoyed with school," Anna said. "It looks like it's going to be another one of *those* years. Their father's death hit them hard."

Cameron said, "I'm sorry. How are you holding up?"

Anna gave him a nasty look.

Cameron said, "Relax. I'm asking as a friend."

"Pretty dang bad, honestly," Anna said.

"You could've fooled me," Cameron said.

"James would've been flipping tables if he went through what I had to go through today."

"Your husband James?"

"Yeah."

"Tell me about him," Cameron said.

"When did you become my therapist?" Anna asked sarcastically.

"I'm just curious," Cameron said.

Anna eyed him suspiciously, "My husband was a flawed man, but we had a few good years. I wouldn't have wished his fate on anyone."

Cameron took a swig from his bottle. "You ever think about tying the knot again?"

Anna said, "Not anytime soon. What about you? Where's Mrs. Ryder?"

"She doesn't exist," Cameron said. "My lifestyle doesn't suit most women."

"In the line of danger too often?" Anna asked.

"I wish. I travel a lot. The agency has a lot of guys like me."

"Single and depressed?" Anna asked, a wry smile on her lips.

"That, and we're less distracted."

"Do you have any kids?" Anna sipped her drink.

"Nope," Cameron said, taking a swig. "I have the job

J.S DONOVAN

though. There's nothing more rewarding than capturing a killer."

"How many have you caught?" Anna asked.

Cameron said, "Six. A few rapists as well. Some of them are remorseful. Others are not. I liked to put the fear of God in both."

"That doesn't sound like you got very many," Anna said.

"Wow. Thanks," Cameron said sarcastically.

"What do you do all day?"

"Research. Interviews. I look over dates and crime scene files. Maybe something will hit and we can proceed with the case. Most of the time, it's desk work."

"Well, thanks for your service," Anna said.

Cameron toasted her.

The instrumental soundtrack occupied the silence.

Cameron said, "You're a remarkable woman, you know that?"

Anna replied, "Are you flirting with me, Agent? That's not very professional."

"Relax. I'm just saying that I admire your hard work. Being a single mother and full-time manager takes a certain type of grit. Not everyone has that," Cameron said.

Anna shrugged. "I do what I got to do to survive."

"There are easier ways of making a living," Cameron said.

Anna replied, "True, but I'm building something here. If it turns out well enough, it'll be here long after I'm gone."

"Ah," Cameron said, nodding. "A legacy."

"Just a nice hotel," Anna replied.

"My father would've liked you. He always talked about leaving his imprint on the world," Cameron said.

"What did do?"

"He was a cobbler. His business wasn't very successful, so he spent a lot of his time grooming me," Cameron replied.

"You going to take over the family business?"

"In a sense," Cameron replied. "Sometimes I feel like I'm becoming more and more like him."

"Dreaming of making shoes?" Anna teased.

"Bitter," Cameron said. "Towards the end, he wasn't a happy man. His passions didn't fulfill him the way they used to. It was sad watching him go. He left this world miserable and alone."

"I'm sorry to hear that," Anna said. To lighten the mood, she said, "You might want to start looking for a wife."

Cameron smirked. He finished his drink. "How about your parents?"

"Both of mine are using their retirement to travel the world," Anna said. "The memories they're making is the type of thing I want to leave my residents with here."

"That's romantic," Cameron said.

"I'm a sucker for that type of thing," Anna replied. She checked the wall clock. "I should get back to the desk."

"Mind if I stay a little longer?" Cameron asked.

"Not at all," Anna pulled out two more lemonades. "Enjoy."

"Generous," Cameron said, surprised by the gift.

Anna smiled at him and returned to the desk. She left the door open.

The next day Anna got the news that Harry was comatose. His wife wasn't happy and wanted Anna to pay worker's comp. Anna added that to her building debt. Lilith had a broken hip. She wouldn't be back for months. Seeing that her boys had to go to school, Anna took over Lilith's duties. She washed towels, dusted the rooms, and vacuumed the hallway. While washing the tall wall mirrors in one of the unoccupied second-story rooms, she pressed too hard on the glass and the mirror spun around like a revolving door.

"Whoa." Anna took a step back.

A four-foot-wide passage was now open behind the

mirror. She poked her head inside. Dusty particles swirled. Unpainted wood planks and flooring made up the passage. Turning on her phone flashlight, she stepped inside. It was claustrophobic, but she could walk through without turning sideways.

The floor creaked beneath her. Standing behind the mirror, she could see into the adjacent room. It was the young honeymooners fooling around on the bed. Anna felt dirty seeing it. She continued through the corridor and reached a T-intersection. She followed the path to the right, coming to a stop in a little pocket behind the second-floor storage office.

Sprawled out on the floor was a human skeleton. She wore a tattered, moth-eaten dress. A knife hilt jutted out of her forehead.

9

ALLEY

*L*ike the wailing of a terrible beast, police sirens sounded in the distance. Clouds covered the coal-black sky. All around, autumn-kissed trees stood like creepy silhouettes in blackness. Under the light of the large club sign, Anna stood. She wore a thick jacket over her long-sleeve shirt. She hugged herself.

The squad car zoomed through the forest-lined path and braked harshly outside of the hotel. The two overly-familiar cops from last time exited. Anna bothered to read their name tags this go around. The muscular, dark-skinned one—Officer Parkman—led the short and squat Officer Dana toward the hotel's front door. Anna matched their brisk pace. "It's this way."

She led the officers to the second floor. Like last time, they insisted on going alone. This time, they came back quickly and were more interested in the case than Anna's womanly figure.

Dana asked Anna, "You've not touched her, right?"

"No. I called you right away." Anna fidgeted, thinking

about her patrons. "Is there any way we can do this without getting the entire department involved?"

Parkman said in his deep voice, "Protocol is protocol. Are you aware of any other passages like this?"

"Mr. Ferguson never told me anything about this," Anna said. "So no, I'm not aware."

Dana said to his partner, "We might have to canvas the entire property."

"I'll see what I can do about a warrant," Parkman said.

"Not happening," Anna said.

Dana said, "Ma'am, this hotel is a crime scene. It's our job to search for clues."

"It's my job to respect my patrons' privacy," Anna argued.

"A woman is dead," Dana reminded her.

"But my patrons aren't. They have rights," Anna said. "This room and that corridor are your crime scene. If you want any more than that, you'll have to talk to my lawyer."

Dana grumbled. "Lady, let us do our jobs."

"As soon as you let me do mine, sure," Anna said.

Dana boiled.

"It's cool, man," Parkman said to his partner. He turned his attention to Anna. "We're asking for your cooperation."

"Every room here is considered its own residence. You wouldn't search an entire apartment complex if there was a murder in one. Same rules apply," Anna said.

The officer didn't like being told no. Neither did Anna. She'd fight tooth and nail before she'd let her establishment be raided by the cops. Her reputation meant everything at this early stage.

Move cops arrived. Then the detective and the forensics team, including photographers, and the coroner. The second-floor hallway became a madhouse. One by one, Anna's handful of patrons stepped out of their rooms and watched the chaos unfold. The female honeymooner wrapped her arms around her spouse. They both seemed intrigued by what was happening. Lance, the creepy blond man who had oily skin, was mortified. He stood by the old gentleman named Andrew Warren and said, "I can't believe it."

Asher was confused and lingered next to his mom, asking her a million questions that she didn't know the answer to. "Who died? When? What's on the other side of the passage? Are there more bodies? Are we in danger?"

Justin wore a hard face, annoyed the cops were around.

There were a handful of other residents that had been staying for the night. They gasped and spoke quietly amongst one another. The only person Anna didn't see was Agent Cameron. Granted, he lived on the third floor.

After the skeleton was extracted, the police dispersed and, soon after, the fanfare. Anna apologized for the inconvenience. She followed Officer Dana and Parkman out of the lobby.

Dana asked Parkman, "What about this Ferguson character?"

"He is our number one priority," Parkman said. "No one knows this place better than him."

Dana cursed softly. "That means…"

"Yeah, all those stories must be true," Parkman said.

They pushed open the double glass doors and walked out into the brisk, autumn air. It smelled of salt from the nearby ocean.

Parkman glanced over his shoulder. "Do any of the old employees still work here?"

"I wish," Anna replied. "It's just me and my sons. The rest quit when I took over."

"We'll find them," Dana said.

"Thank you, Officers," Anna said.

Parkman said, "Don't thank us. Our superiors denied the search warrant."

"How come?" Anna said.

Dana replied, "Club Blue has a lot of history. The local color doesn't like to air it out in the open. The old bloods are especially sensitive when it comes to past mistakes."

Parkman said, "But don't get too excited. We'll find a way into that horror house of yours. The truth won't stay buried forever."

Hearing this from the more reserved of the two officers shook Anna.

"Stay safe," Dana said.

The officers got into their squad car and drove away.

Head hung low, Anna returned inside. She bumped into Cameron. "Sorry, I didn't see you."

"Quite the night," Cameron said.

Anna nodded. "It reminded me of how much I miss sleep. I swear I've had more problems in the past two days than I have in my entire career."

Cameron said, "Maybe it's the hotel. The place might be cursed."

"Well God, send a priest," Anna mocked.

Cameron smiled.

"What?" Anna replied, peeved, "You need a towel or something?"

"You're funny, that's all."

"Yeah, my life is a series of unfortunate events. It must be hilarious to a spectator."

Cameron replied, "You look like you could use a drink."

"I'd prefer a bubble bath… and a pizza. That would be nice." Anna's stomach growled.

Cameron said, "I have one."

"A bubble bath?"

"A pizza. I got two on a discount. I can lend one to you."

"It's pretty hard to lend a pizza."

"You know what I'm saying. You want it?" Cameron said.

"Yes, but I can't stay up with you. I'm exhausted."

"I understand," Cameron said. "I'll bring it down."

"Bring it to my room. I'm closing early tonight," Anna replied.

Cameron went his own way. Anna stayed at the desk until eleven-thirty. She put her closed sign on the door and locked it, then returned to her room. She felt the day's labor in her bones. Cameron knocked on the door, holding the pizza box.

He said, "You want me to bring it in or…"

"Nah, I'll take it from here. Thanks, though." Anna took the box.

"Have a good night."

"You too," Anna closed the door, curious why he would like to enter her room. Did he like her? Anna thought of all of James's romantic gestures when they first started dating in college. The memories left a bittersweet taste in her mouth. Dating after James would be… problematic. There were too many emotions she didn't need in her life right now.

The next morning was hard. Her boys were off to school. Lance called her up to his room. The nearly forty-year-old man dressed in twenty-year-old clothes showed her the broken sink. The fixture was loose. It wasn't anything Anna couldn't fix with a wrench. She grabbed her tools and crawled underneath the sink. She felt the man's eyes on her. Anna shuddered and worked quicker. She tested the sink. No more leak.

Anna said, "Anything else I can do for you?"

"That about does it," Lance said. "Say, have you been able to reach Ferguson yet?"

"I've not heard a word," Anna replied.

"That's strange for the man to run off like that," Lance

remarked. "And that skeleton too. The whole situation is horrible."

Anna agreed.

Lance said, "Well, at least you got it handled, right?"

"I do," Anna said, sounding convincing.

"Good, good," Lance mumbled to himself.

Anna went about her business.

That night, she brought her boys to the bowling alley and locked the door.

"Why are we eating in here?" Asher asked.

Anna set aside the glass, grabbed the ball, and rolled it down the lane. It knocked over three pins. "That wasn't as dramatic as I hoped."

Justin asked, "What? You want to play or something?"

Anna shrugged. "I don't know. Do you have what it takes to beat me?"

"Psh." Justin set aside his plate and joined her.

Always the competitive one, he started bowling spares and strikes. Asher entered the game and got swamped. They played two games.

It ended with Justin as the victor. 138 to 129. Asher had 81.

Anna high-fived her sons. "Good game." She sat on the plastic bucket seat. "I should probably get back to the front desk."

Asher sat opposite of her. "I feel like we're not getting any new people."

Anna felt the anxiety building in her chest. "Yeah, we need to be more aggressive in our marketing. I haven't gotten around to it."

"I could help," Justin said.

"You're already doing a lot," Anna said.

Justin said, "Let me work full-time."

"Justin, you can't do that and school," Anna reminded him.

"I wouldn't," Justin replied. "School sucks. It's not getting me anywhere."

Anna said, "You used to love it."

Justin replied, "Not really. Besides, that was before everyone thought I was a rapist. My teachers won't even look me in the eye. Everyone moves when I sit down. Asher knows. He's seen it."

Asher nodded. "It's messed up. I tried to sit next to Justin, but he wouldn't let me."

"Because it's gay to sit next to your freshman brother," Justin replied.

"Enough of that, Justin," Anna said. "You're old enough that you shouldn't be calling your brother names."

"Yeah," Asher added.

"I didn't ask for your insight," Anna said to him. She looked at Justin. "I know it's hard, but everyone goes through it."

"You don't understand, Mom," Justin said seriously. "Everyone hates me. Every. One."

"That can't be true," Anna said.

Asher said, "It is. Even people in my grade spread rumors about him. That McKenzie chick doesn't even come to school anymore. Apparently, she hasn't said a word since that night."

"Geez," Anna remarked.

Justin said, "And I didn't touch her, okay? She's the one who left claw marks on my back."

Anna could've gone her whole life without knowing that. She sighed. "You really can't manage, huh?"

Justin said, "You need me here. I want to be here. Let's just do it."

Anna pondered it. She thought about her son a lot. To be

accused of such a horrible thing must be unbearable. If he stayed full-time, she'd save money and time, but her motherly side wanted to give him a good education. "How about this: I let you stay, but after a few months and we start paying off some of this debt, you take online classes."

Justin groaned. "Online sucks."

"Throw me a bone here, Justin. I can't have you going through your life as a loser," Anna said.

Justin seemed conflicted and annoyed.

"I could transfer you to another school if you'd prefer."

"No, no. I'll be fine doing the online stuff," Justin said.

"Awesome," Anna said, "We'll see your principal first thing tomorrow."

Anna gave him a hug.

10

REDEMPTION

*A*gent Cameron Ryder sat on the chest by the large bedroom window. The view of Sebring, the surrounding woods, and the Atlantic was stunning. Night had already fallen, but the beacon on the old, distant lighthouse shone on. Cameron's right knee was bent and his foot rested on the chest. His left leg hung off the side. He held the phone to his ear.

"The skeleton was female. I suspect it was Alana Brown," Cameron said.

"Is that the one that went missing in '86?" asked Jesse Coleman, Assistant Director for the FBI's criminal investigation branch. He was an Englishman who'd been at the agency for decades, and Cameron's mentor.

"Yep. Another one of the runaways," Cameron said.

"The police suspect this Ferguson fellow?"

"He's the obvious candidate."

"Occam's Razor, Cameron," Jesse said, very teacher-like.

"But there's more here," Cameron said. "The fire. The missing bodies. It could've been any one of the past patrons or a local for that matter."

"I suspect the truth will come to the light when Mr. Ferguson is found," Jesse said.

Cameron said, "I'm just asking for a little help."

Jesse replied sympathetically, "You know I can't."

"I lost my temper one time and now I'm thrown to the wolves? There are agents who've done a lot worse than me," Cameron complained.

"You nearly killed an innocent man," Jesse said. "He'll never walk. Never make love."

Cameron pinched the bridge of his nose. "Jesse, I can't keep living like this."

"You're a smart man. You'll find a suitable career."

Cameron said, "I need to have my job back. I said I'd do anything, and I meant it."

"If the agency found out that I helped you—"

"They won't. Trust me, when your superiors find out about all the names tied to Club Blue, they'll have their hands full. Give me a little latitude, Jesse. I won't let you down."

Jesse said, "You're not an agent anymore."

"Not in title," Cameron replied. "Help me. Please. I'm begging here."

Jesse's line went quiet.

"Are you still there?" Cameron asked.

"… If I do this, you better not mess up. One wrong suspect and we're over. Clear?"

"Crystal," Cameron replied.

Jesse said, "I must get going. I'll call you back when I have the files on those missing persons."

"And their next of kin, please," Cameron said.

"Very well. Talk to you soon, Cameron."

"Thank you, Jesse. I owe you."

"Yes. Quite a lot, actually," Jesse replied.

The call ended.

Cameron tossed his phone aside. He got up and paced. He

thought back to that creepy pedo freak that ruined everything. The man wouldn't talk. Cameron had to be persuasive. Years of strategic career planning was worthless thanks to some misinformation.

He didn't want to resort to this Club Blue case, but something this big would put him back in position. He'd grown accustomed to being an agent. To revert back into his father's peasantry wasn't an option. Thinking of the old man infuriated him. Overcome by a sudden flash of rage, he punched the wall. His fist didn't break the wood, but a portion of the wall a few feet away popped open an inch.

Cameron approached the hidden door that had been seamlessly blended into the wall. He pulled it open, revealing the dark corridor. A path strayed away from the windows. Bent nails hugged the inner walls. Dusty cobwebs streamed down from the room.

Cameron stepped inside.

11

WOKE GIRL

*L*ate at night, Asher heard a knock on his door. Half-asleep, he dragged his feet to the looking hole and peered into the hallway. Widened by the fish-eye lens-like view, Raven stood with a blank expression and her hands behind her back. "I know you see me."

Alarmed, Asher glanced down his bare chest and boxer shorts. He quickly put a pair of pants and shirts on before opening the door a crack. "What are you doing here?"

"Geez, you don't have to be so suspicious of everything," Raven replied.

"I'm not," Asher backpedaled. He spoke quieter. "Has something bad happened?"

Raven laughed.

The girl's reaction confused Asher.

"Everything is okay," Raven said.

"Right…" Asher replied, still unsure why she was visiting at 1 am.

Raven said, "I thought we could go exploring."

Asher buried his hands in his pockets. "It's a little late…"

"Scared your mom's going to get mad at you?" Raven playfully taunted.

"I'm worried about you and your dad," Asher lied.

"Dad will be up all night working on his book anyway," Raven said. "I had to get away from his typing. I was afraid I'd go postal."

Asher glanced back at his bed. The idea of sleep sounded really good right now.

Raven said, "Come on. It'll be fun. Maybe I'll even tell you about this place's dark secrets."

"Like what?" Asher asked.

A cheeky smile formed on Raven's pale face. "Now I have your attention."

"Does this have to do with the skeleton?" Asher asked.

"It has to do with everything." There was something ominous yet intriguing about Raven's tone.

Asher stood quietly for a moment, conflicted between a good night's sleep and following the creepy girl on one of her adventures. He folded to her request and agreed to follow her.

"Awesome," Raven replied. "Come on, and be quiet. Certain walls are thinner than others."

Asher slipped on his shoes. He used his fingers to comb his hair as he trailed behind Raven. They reached the internal balcony at the center of the second floor. The lights around the balcony and hallway were on, but not the ones in the ballroom. Raven pointed to the eye-shaped symbol above the center of the middle wall.

"What do you think that is?" Raven asked.

Asher studied it. "I don't know. It looks like what you see on the back of the dollar bill."

"Correct," Raven said. "It's the Eye of Providence."

"Like God watching us. It fits with the Jacob's Ladder theme," Asher said.

"It's also a reminder to Freemasons that they are being watched and have a higher standard they must live up to. Like recipients of the fire Prometheus brought to man, they must be good stewards of their knowledge," Raven explained.

She impressed Asher. "Sound stressful," he remarked.

"Look closer though," Raven said, leaning her torso on the railing.

Asher stood next to her. It took a few moments, but he realized the eye was inverted. "Is it supposed to be like that?"

Raven smiled at him. "Not at all."

She spun around and walked to the photos on the wall. They mostly showed old white men dressed in odd outfits. "These are the Masons that used to lodge here."

Asher stayed fixed on the inverted eye.

Raven said, "They're unnamed, but that's okay. It's the tradition they carried on that mattered more than fame. Funny enough, it is only by the good name that order gets its proper recognition."

"How do you know all this stuff?" Asher asked, joining her by the photos.

"My dad," Raven replied.

"Is he a Mason?" Asher asked.

"Nope. Just a researcher," Raven said. "There is something bigger I want to show you."

"Why do I have a feeling I'm not going to like this?"

"Little risk, little reward." Raven led him down the stairs and across the checked floor. The darkness didn't bother Raven. Asher used the light on his phone to guide their path. Raven took him out the back door.

Crickets and other night critters chirped. The wind rustled the trees. Asher felt uncomfortable but didn't complain. He wanted to see what secrets Raven had to share. The girl seemed to hold a wealth of knowledge about seemingly random things. Compared to her, Asher felt inadequate. Sure, he was good at school and learned quickly, but he didn't possess the ability to just draw up random facts out of nowhere. Raven knew more than him. That insight pressured him to be better.

They walked alongside the brick walls. Vines grew up the sides. Their leaves had started to brown as the season changed. They reached the metal ladder suspended eight feet above their heads.

Raven said, "Find a stick to get that down."

Asher shined his light across the grass earth. He walked below one of the nearby trees and found a broken branch near a stone bench. He lifted the crookedly shaped branch. "Would this work?"

"Let's give it a try," Raven said, still standing behind the ladder.

Asher held the stick above his head and snagged the bend at the end around the bottom rung. It had a weak hold, but a small knot on the stick held it in place. He pulled. His thin arms failed him.

Raven grabbed ahold of the stick too and counted back from three. On one, they yanked as hard as they could. The rusty metal screeched as the ladder came sliding down. It stopped falling an inch above the dirt.

Asher tossed the stick aside. "Thanks."

"I knew you had it," Raven said and started to climb.

The small compliment grew a smile on Asher's face. He followed after her. The rusty rungs scraped against his palms. He glanced down, realizing how far he'd gotten. Heart racing, he kept his eyes on the rung above. The moonlight was his best source of light.

"Are you sure this is a good idea?" he asked as he neared the third story.

"Trust me. You're going to want to see this," Raven replied.

Asher continued the ascent. One mistake and he'd be in the hospital. He tried not to think about it. Raven reached the last rung and vanished over the corner of the roof. Asher quickened his pace. He reached the top and crawled onto the roof. He created a few feet of distance between himself and the edge before standing. His light reflected on the large glass pyramid before him. Seven feet from the roof's edge, the pyramid capped the roof. It stood eighteen feet tall. The fogged glass panes were three-by-three feet.

Asher gawked.

Raven said, "Now you get to see the cool part."

They jogged around the side of the pyramid, eventually reaching a rusted metal door. It had a number lock instead of a traditional keyhole. "Can you guess the password?" Raven asked.

"Uh, 1,2,3?"

Raven made a buzzer sound. "Try 3,3,3."

Asher turned the number dial. The lock clicked. He turned back to Raven, shocked it worked. "How did you know?"

"My dad," Raven said.

"And how does he know?"

"Old letters to the Order's members. They opted for a number lock because keys could easily be lost. Once someone was initiated into the higher degrees, they'd learn the codes and have access whenever they pleased. Most of their gatherings here were under the cover of nightfall, away from prying eyes," Raven said. "Go ahead. Open it."

Asher pulled on the door handle. Despite the rust, it opened without a sound. He walked down a flight of seven steps and onto a checkered floor. Two marble columns topped with marble spheres stood near the wall opposite of the door. A throne-like chair stood between them. Its red leather gave it a sinister appeal. Other chairs lined the walls.

The moonlight shined over the fogged glass and illuminated the entire pyramid. Though an outside light source was still necessary, the glass's glow provided enough light to see the silhouettes of those around you. If every seat was occupied, it would look like you were standing in a council of shades.

Raven closed the door behind her. "Welcome to the highest place in Club Blue. Only a handful of people have stood where you stand, Asher."

She held her hands behind her back and gracefully spun around.

"The floor reminds me of the ballroom," Asher said.

Raven walked around the room, circling Asher. "The checkered floor is a means for spiritual access to a cross dimension."

The girl's quick, methodical movements made Asher nervous.

Raven said, still moving. "It's a place of sacrifice."

"Sacrifice what?" Asher asked, suddenly becoming sweaty. He wished he'd remembered his inhaler.

"What do you think?" Raven asked, something sinister in her eye.

Asher swallowed his spit. "They couldn't have killed people up here. How would they hide the bodies?"

"They'd take them apart limb by limb and put them in trash bags. They'd toss the parts off the edge of the roof and burn them deep in the woods. A little mop and bleach took care of the tile here," Raven explained.

"Maybe we should get going, Raven." Asher's voice cracked. "It's getting late and I have school tomorrow."

Raven asked, "Aren't you curious why they killed people?"

Asher shook his head. "No, because you're making this whole thing up to scare me."

Raven kept pacing. Asher turned to keep up with her.

Raven said, "True, I don't have any way to prove this is true. After all, the cops never arrested anyone from here for serious charges. Nevertheless, it's easy to hide a crime when everyone is in on it. That's what the Order at Club Blue was all about, Asher. Turning Masonic traditions and metaphors into actual practice. The dark arts." There was something deeply disturbing about Raven's fascinations.

Asher said, "Look, I'm gonna go. Okay?"

He felt dirty just being in this place.

Raven blocked his path.

Asher tried to slide by her right side. She blocked him. He tried her left. She blocked that way too. Asher frowned. "Move, please."

Raven shoved him.

Asher's bottom hit the cold floor. Pain shot up his tail-bone. "What was that for?"

Raven walked over him and lowered on top of his thighs. "I lied about my dad just being a researcher."

Asher squirmed, intensely uncomfortable being this close to the girl.

"He was a Mason," Raven said. "Not of this order. Oh no, what went down in Club Blue was a bastardization of years of tradition. Not that Masons are saints, either. A favorite motto of theirs is Ordo Ab Chao – order out of chaos."

"Doesn't sound so bad," Asher said, wanting everything to get this girl off him, but not wanting to be rude.

"Not unless if they're the ones staging the chaos," Raven said. "Secretly set someone up to fail. When they do, sweep in and save the day. Suddenly, you're the hero."

"I want to go back inside," Asher complained.

"Rumor has it that in this room, they'd test their members' loyalty. They'd find a helpless woman or boy, probably drugged, and bring them in here." Raven put her hands on Asher's shoulders. "They'd pin them to the floor, cut them open, and use their blood to reach out to whatever was on the other side. They'd invite that spirit to dwell inside of them, and then they'd have the courage to make bigger sacrifices in society." Raven lowered her head and whispered into Asher's ear. "It's all bullcrap."

"What?" Asher asked.

Raven giggled and sat up. "Yep. There's no way to prove any of this, or that ghosts, spirits, or whatever they were trying to reach out to were real. Their rituals mean nothing at all."

Asher felt relief.

"Or are they?" Raven asked.

She stood up just as Asher's legs were going numb. She extended a hand.

Asher took it and allowed her to help him stand. Annoyed, Asher asked, "Do you like scaring people?"

"I just think it's kinda cool to think about this stuff," Raven said. "I mean look at this place. There are so many secrets and symbols. Who knows the real reason behind any of it? Part of me wants all of it to be true, like I've stepped into a world outside myself. The other part of me wants to run from it and bury my head in a pillow."

I agree with that second one. Asher thought.

Raven said, "Either way, I'm just glad I got to show you all these things."

Asher was rather shocked.

"Like my dagger," Raven lifted up her black pant leg and brandished the curved blade from her shin sheath.

Asher cursed. "Put that thing away!"

Raven pretended to jab it at him.

Asher ran away. "Stop it!"

Raven playfully chased him. "You've got to go faster than that!"

"Is that thing real?" Asher asked.

"Duh," Raven replied.

They ran a few laps around the room before running out of breath. Raven laughed. She spun the dagger around her hand. "You want to hold it?"

"No!" Asher exclaimed, really wishing he had his inhaler.

Raven said, "I thought boys liked this kind of thing."

Asher shook his head. "Can we go now?"

Raven slid the weapon back into the shin sheath and covered it with her pant leg. "I won't bring it out anymore if that makes you happy."

"Thank you," Asher said exasperatedly.

They walked hand and hand to the ladder. Asher would be happy never to see that place again. Going down the ladder was scarier than going up it. Asher reached the bottom. They both grabbed the bottom rung of the ladder and pushed it up. It didn't get to the same place it was before they pulled it down, but it wasn't low enough for someone to reach with their hand. Returning inside, Asher found himself glancing over to Raven. Despite all the weird dark stuff she was into, there was something enigmatic about her. She was like a well-made horror movie: haunting yet beautiful. It was the type of film that you can't get out of your head even years after watching it.

As they walked through the second-story hallway, they heard a sudden scream coming from a nearby wall.

Both of them froze and listened.

Silence.

Raven walked to the wall and pressed her ear against it. Asher knew there was no one staying in the room nearby.

Raven pulled her ear away. She shook her head. "What do we do?"

Asher replied, "I-I..." he didn't have a clue. She heard the scream too. He wasn't crazy. He thought about the thumping he heard the other night. Maybe there was something in the walls. Maybe it was trying to reach out to him.

No noise followed the strange scream. Instead of waking his mother, Asher decided to lock himself away in his room. If something truly bad had happened, everyone would know tomorrow.

12

CHECK OUT

*A*t the start of her day, Anna found a sealed envelope and a room key on the lobby counter. The key belonged to the honeymooners' suite. Using her finger, she opened the envelope and found cash, but no note. She went to their room and knocked. After announcing her presence, she entered.

The covers snuggly hugged the mattress. The trash can had been emptied. Everything was neat and tidy apart from the pile of dirty towels on the bathroom sink. She'd have Justin clean those up after he started his shift, which should be thirty minutes from now. She turned off the light and shut the door as she entered the hall.

Lance was heading to his room, holding a bag of ice. He smiled at Anna. She smiled back.

At the lobby counter, Anna noticed more of her pens were missing. The vanishing of various items had grown annoying. She was inclined to believe that a guest was playing a prank on her. Or maybe Asher.

At random parts of the day, she felt cold chills. First was when she was standing at the desk and another time when she was preparing her lunch in the large kitchen. While in the lobby bathroom, she heard whispers in the stall next to her. As she washed her hands, she glanced in the mirror. Through the cracks in the stall behind her, there was no one. *The quiet is getting to you*, she thought as she dried her hands.

In the afternoon, a delivery truck arrived and dropped off a bouquet of flowers.

"Which room?" Anna asked.

"None, ma'am," the deliveryman said. "The instructions just said to bring them here."

Anna examined the flowers. A red string fashioned a mini note around the stem of the flowers. Anna opened it. Written in cursive was the question, *Do you still offer special services? – L*. Anna said. "I don't know who that is?"

"Someone has to sign for them," the deliveryman said.

Anna agreed to do so. She put the bouquet on the countertop. She opened the guest registry on her laptop. The only guest that had a name that started with the letter L was Lance. Perhaps the flowers were for him? If so, what *special services*?

A while later, Lance exited the elevator and started toward the lobby's front doors. "Nice flowers."

Anna asked, "Thank you. Did you send these?"

"Maybe you have a secret admirer." Lance winked.

Anna laughed politely. "Thank you, but is it you?"

Lance shrugged playfully and pushed out the front doors.

He had to be the sender. Anna felt uncomfortable. She'd have to find a way to tactfully decline.

Around 4 pm, Asher came home from school.

"How was it?" Anna asked as he approached the front desk.

"Alright, I guess," Asher said. "Everyone is asking about Justin. They think he was arrested."

"Where did they get that idea?"

"He's not coming to school anymore," Asher explained. "How is he anyway?"

"Good, he'll be taking over the night shift so we can stay open later," Anna explained. "I've also started building a website, but I need some creative input."

"You should market it as creepy," Asher said.

Anna laughed. "Not in a million years."

"You'd get a lot of people like Raven and her dad," Asher said.

"Who?" Anna asked.

"Raven. She's staying in Suite 212," Asher said.

"Huh," Anna replied, "I'm not sure I met her. Is she into some creepy stuff?"

Asher nodded. "She knows all about weird rituals. I thought she was super weird, and she is, but…"

Anna said, "Sounds like you have a crush."

"No!" Asher said. "That's, that's gross. She's not my type."

"Uh-huh."

"For real," Asher said.

Anna said, "Well, just don't get too attached. No one stays here forever."

13

BLOOD, SWEAT, AND TEARS

*T*he wheels made a thunderous noise as the skateboard raced down the third-floor hall. Justin kicked faster. The glass cleaner and bleach spray fit in his tool belt. The hip-hop's heavy bass rumbled in his headphones.

He thought back to his York house. He used to climb out his window and sit on the slanted roof to light up a joint. He'd spend a lot of late nights up there where no one could see him and the wind would take the smell away. No longer part of the school here, he couldn't score any more weed. Not that he cared. He enjoyed drinking more and his mom hadn't changed the lock on the bar's booze cabinet. Thinking of home reminded him of Dad. Justin came home late one night and his father was waiting up for him in the living room. The old man's glassy eyes and gentle swaying were signs he'd been drinking. The antique lamp cast a glow on half his face. The other side was drowned in darkness like the rest of the living room.

Justin headed for the stairs.

"Come over here," Father said.

Hesitant, Justin walked to him.

"*You been drinking?*" Father asked.

"*No, sir,*" Justin replied.

Father replied, "*Don't lie to me. You think I don't know you're still hanging out with those skater punks?*"

"*We just went the park,*" Justin said.

"*That's all?*"

"*Yes, sir.*"

Father picked up a book from the lampstand. He mindlessly flipped through it, a sullen expression on his face.

Justin said, "*I'm going to go to bed...*"

Father launched the book at him. It hit Justin in the nose. The fourteen-year-old staggered back. Father jolted out of his seat and grabbed the neck of Justin's shirt. His bloodshot eyes locked on Justin, who was terrified. "*You're not going to amount to anything just like your loser friends. They're all ungrateful deadbeats.*"

Justin's eyes watered. "*That's not true.*"

Father raised his fist.

Justin recoiled.

"*Did I say you could talk?*" Father shook his head in spiteful shame. "*You're worse than your mother. I oughta belt you too. Maybe that will knock some sense into you.*"

Justin yanked off his headphones, enraged by the memory. It was almost as bad as finding his mother naked and weeping on the bathroom floor. Bloody welts painted her back.

The thought infuriated Justin. He felt disgusted, sad, and ready to explode. He opened up the door to one of the rooms and stepped inside. Justin's father had only gotten worse toward the end.

He shut the door behind him. Putting his skateboard on the floor, he pulled out his window cleaner and the rag from his backpack. He turned to the corner of the room.

Standing on the bed, the Hispanic woman held her stomach. Her glossy, tight green dress hugged her skinny body. Like blossoming flowers, blotches of blood on her belly expanded from the half-dozen stab wounds. Both her eyes were partly rolled backward. She tilted back her head ever so slightly. The long cut on her neck yawned, releasing a waterfall of blood down her breasts. She screamed, shaking the room.

The cloth and cleaner dropped from Justin's hands as he darted in the opposite direction. The door stood in front of him. His foot landed on the skateboard and slipped. The board launched behind him while Justin flung forward. His head smacked against the door. Thud!

Limp, he slid to the floor, leaving behind a thin crimson streak on the door's face and on his busted forehead. He lay on the floor, unmoving.

The woman turned, her feet bowed in like a cripple and her movements twitchy. The sound like a creaking door escaped her parted lips. She stopped a foot away from Justin's body, her eyes fixed in the same upward and cocked position. Her hand, sticky with blood, reached for Justin's collar.

Justin awoke.

Sucking air through his teeth, Justin swiftly rolled to his back.

The ceiling fans whirled softly.

The little hall into the suite's living room was empty. Justin's heart raced. A throbbing pain surged on his forehead. He carefully got to his feet. The world around him tilted. He blinked. The walls returned to normal. His skateboard rested against the wall away from him. The only way to get it was around the blind corner. Justin twisted around and bolted out of the room.

He sprinted to the elevator, violently jamming his finger against the button.

Ding!

He rushed inside. The elevator door stayed open.

A tear of blood trickled down Justin's forehead and rolled along his nose. He breathed rapidly. He waited, expecting something to step out of the faraway suite.

The elevator door started to close. For a brief second, Justin saw the woman take a step out of the suite.

Trapped in the elevator, Justin wiped away the blood on his face. The pain worsened. He arrived in the lobby. Anna stood behind the counter, her attention locked on her phone screen.

Moving briskly, Justin neared her. He glanced back, paranoid.

Anna looked up momentarily. "One second."

She did a double-take, and her jaw dropped.

Fear had flushed all the color from Justin's face. Blood leaked from his swelling gash.

"Oh my—" Anna rushed around the counter and grabbed his upper arms. "What--what happened?"

"Woman," Justin said. "She was… and blood. And…"

"Shh, it's okay. One sentence at a time," Anna said, struggling to keep her composure.

Justin said, "There's a dead woman upstairs."

He watched dread sink his mother's horrified expression. Hand trembling, she dialed 9… 1…

Justin caught her hand and yanked away her cellphone. "No."

"But—"

"She was dead," Justin explained.

"We need to contact the police," Anna said.

"You don't understand. She tried to—"

Ding!

The elevator door opened.

Justin and Anna stood completely still. Not even the smallest breath escaped their lungs.

The elevator was empty.

The door shut.

Anna tried to snatch her phone back. Justin pulled his arm away from her and held it behind him. He had the height advantage over her.

"Give it," Anna hissed.

"The woman's not real," Justin said.

"You're not making any sense." She tried to grab for the phone again.

"She was dead, but she was standing! She screamed at me!"

Anna stopped trying to reach for her phone. "Is this... is this some kind of joke? I swear, Justin, if you're playing me--"

"I swear on my life," Justin interrupted. "There was someone in Suite 309. Her throat was cut open. Her stomach--" A tear fell down Justin's cheek. He wiped it away. He whimpered a curse and cried more.

Anna wrapped her arms around her boy. She held him, just as terrified. "Wait here, okay."

"You can't go up there," Justin said.

"I'll just be gone for a moment," Anna said.

"Mom, please," Justin pleaded.

"Stay put," Anna hurried toward the elevator.

Justin watched her vanish inside. His teeth chattered. A cold rush shook him. He held the phone so tight his knuckles turned white.

It was nightfall outside the glass doors.

Ding!

The elevator door opened.

Justin's pulse pounded.

Anna stepped out. Her expression was unreadable as she approached.

"Well?" Justin asked anxiously.

"How hard did you hit your head?"

"I don't know. Did you see her?" Justin asked.

"There's no one up there, Justin," Anna said. "Not even Agent Cameron is around."

"But the woman."

"What woman?"

"With the—" He rubbed his neck.

"Justin," Anna said as if speaking to a child. "You got hit. That's all."

"No, no, no. She was there, Mom."

"It was a dream," Anna said.

"It wasn't!" Justin wanted to tear his hair out. "What about that do you not understand?!"

Anna sighed. "Justin, don't believe me. See for yourself."

"Screw that!" Justin slammed her phone on the counter. "And screw this place. I'm done. Okay?"

He headed toward the front doors.

Anna yelled. "Where are you going? Your work is not done. What about your head?"

Justin pushed out of the double doors and raced into the darkness.

14

THE KINDNESS OF A STRANGER

*T*hunder crackled.

Heavy rain pelted the glass doors.

The power flickered.

The chandelier lights in the lobby hummed as they returned to life.

Anna stood behind the lobby counter, her thoughts on her runaway son. *He'll come back*, she told herself. Thinking that he was out in the rain worried her. He was a capable boy, but to be scared like that wasn't normal. She hoped that he wouldn't have to get stitches.

Her mouse cursor hovered over her most recent blog post. The article chronicled her journey as a single mom and hotel manager. She wrote about the pitfalls, stresses, challenges, and rewards, trying to inject humor where she could. If the blog got enough hits, it would be an invaluable marketing tool. Everyone loves a fixer-upper story. She'd leave out the part about the skeleton in the wall, McKenzie's breakdown, and the injury that knocked Harry the handyman into a coma. She kept the blog relatable and friendly.

Despite working long hours, she had a lot of downtime between check-ins. She got a few new residents over the last few days. They only stayed for a night. Anna hardly noticed them. She plucked away at her blog, talking about raising a rebellious son. She kept herself vulnerable. It would be more real that way.

She'd tossed a few other irons in her marketing oven. There was a billboard right off the highway ready to be rented. She'd also been reviewing social media advertising services. On her various social media pages, she had posted detailed pictures of the hotel's light fixtures, the beautiful artwork on the walls, the strange star-shaped symbols above the entrance, and the more appealing features that made Club Blue exciting and different. Having Justin doing most of the manual labor freed her up for this. His position was unpaid until the five thousand given to McKenzie's parents was paid in full.

Anna typed the end of her post. The soft clack of her fingers echoed through the large room.

Lighting flashed outside.

Thunder followed right after.

Anna stared at the front door. She anxiously chewed the inside of her cheek. She texted Justin, asking him to come back so they could talk. What if what he saw was real? Impossible. Anna didn't believe in the supernatural.

The corded phone on the counter rang. Anna put aside her worrying for a moment and answered. "Club Blue, this is Anna speaking. How can I help you?"

"Hey," the man said with a friendly tone.

"Who is this?"

"Lance from Suite 207."

"Hey, Lance. How can I help you?"

"One of my lights burnt out. I think the bulb is fried," Lance said.

"That might be from the storm. I'll come up and take a look," Anna said.

"Thanks… is your boy around?" Lance asked.

"Not at the moment. Is there something you need from him?" Anna asked.

"It's not right he left you all alone," Lance said.

Anna faked a kind laugh. "You don't need to worry about me, Lance. I can handle myself."

"Still…" Lance's voice drifted.

The conversation quickly turned stale. Anna said, "Okay, well, I'll be up shortly."

"I look forward to it, Anna."

"Bye now."

Click.

Anna put her *"Be Back Shortly"* sign on the counter and grabbed the short ladder and a few bulbs from the supply closet. She wore a pencil skirt, a suit jacket, a windowpane bodice top with a leather stretch belt at her bellybutton, and monochrome snake-cut high heels. Needless to say, it wasn't the best outfit for the job.

She knocked on Suite 207.

Lance quickly answered. The lamp on the side of his bed was the only source of light. The storm raged outside. Large raindrops pelted the window. Lance stepped aside and gestured for Anna to enter.

She set the three-step ladder under the ceiling light and took off her heels.

Lance glanced out into the hallway before shutting the door.

She felt the cold rungs through her socks as she reached the second to last. "When did they start giving you problems?"

Lance lingered behind her. "Like you said, it was probably the storm."

Anna made a mental note to check the other rooms.

Lance asked, "How long were you married?"

Anna replied, "Nineteen years."

Lance whistled, "That's a long time to stay with someone."

"Tell me about it," Anna replied. "I had some good years sprinkled in there, though."

Anna grabbed the ceiling bulb and gave it a spin. The light flickered on, momentarily blinding Anna. "Huh?"

"What?"

"It was loose," Anna said.

Anna backed down the step.

She felt Lance's hand on her hips.

"Hey," she said but wasn't in a position to pull away from him.

"Careful," Lance said.

"I can get down by myself," Anna said.

Lance let go.

Anna kept an eye on him as she pulled the ladder below the next burnt-out light.

Lance said, "I like your skirt."

"Thank you," Anna said awkwardly, hiking the steps.

"Makes you look hot."

Anna looked over her shoulder at him. "It might be easier if you wait in the hall while I finish this."

"Whoa," Lance said, getting offended. "No need to get aggressive."

"I'm not," Anna replied. She grabbed the bulb. "I would prefer some space, that's all."

Lance said, "You like the flowers?"

Anna tightened the lightbulb in its socket. It worked. *Loosened again.*

Lance asked, "You still offer the special services?"

Still on the ladder, Anna turned back to him. "Please, sir. I'm a professional."

"You never answered my question," Lance said.

Anna descended the ladder. "I don't know what you're talking about."

"The Pop-Tarts," Lance said. "I haven't seen any around here. None but you." He took a step closer.

Anna stood her ground. "Sir. Leave the room. I don't want to call the police, but I will."

A wicked smile grew on Lance's oily face. The ceiling light reflected on his shiny, spiked blond hair. "How long do you think it will take them to get here? Six minutes? Seven?" He took another step closer.

Anna backed up. The man guarded the way out. Her heart raced. "I will scream."

Lance replied, "How fast?"

Anna opened her mouth when Lance lunged at her.

She moved back, but Lance was quicker. He grabbed her throat and slammed her against the window. Her back broke the glass pane. Anna screamed, tumbling into the freezing rain and howling wind. Lance fell with her, losing his grip on her throat.

Like falling into a spike pit, Anna crashed through a tree, through leaves and branches. The pointed ends slashed at her skin and clothes. The thick branches smacked her like clubs, breaking the momentum of her initial fall and rolling her in the air. She landed face-first on the muddy grass.

Lance landed a second later. Cursing, he rolled to his side, clenching his elbow and gritting his teeth.

Anna tasted grass and dirt. Sharp lines stung across her body from the hundreds of little cuts. She struggled to breathe. Mud clung to half her face. The storm raged around her. The raindrops hit like small stones. Anna trembled. Her shock masked most of the pain. Above her, the tempest burst through the busted window. A beacon of golden light shined out.

Lance sat up, holding his bloody elbow. "Mother f—" he said the rest of the word through his clenched teeth. He sat up the best he could with one arm.

A branch had sliced open a large cut on his cheek. The water washed away the blood and flattened his spiked hair. He waddled. Lightning flashed in the distance, briefly illuminating his terrifying features. An instant later, Anna only saw his silhouette in the inky blackness.

"No… no." Anna grabbed fistfuls of grass and dragged her torso across the mud and dirt.

Lance limped towards her. "I wanted something exciting. This wasn't what I had in mind."

Anna dragged herself a little farther and pushed against the earth, hoping to get to her knees.

Lance grabbed her hair and yanked her back. Anna screamed, feeling like her scalp was about to get torn out.

"The girls at Club Blue were always fighters. That's what made them so special," Lance said.

He lifted her by her hair and tossed her aside like a rag doll. Anna landed on her back, facing the hulking man. His drenched clothes hung heavy on his bulky frame. He was a lot stronger than he looked.

"Don't scream again," he warned.

Fear gripped Anna.

He dropped down on her.

Anna reached for a nearby rock. It was two inches out of reach.

Lance put his hand over her mouth.

Suddenly, he threw his head back and gurgled in pain. All across his body, his muscles went tense. He fell to the side, landing on his injured elbow. He curled up, gurgling so much he couldn't move. His hands and fingers curved inward like gnarled branches.

Anna followed the two string-like lines running from Lance's back and to the stun gun in Agent Cameron's hands. He held down the trigger, pumping thousands of electric volts into the rapist.

15

SILENCE

*T*he windshield wipers fought the onslaught of rain but the storm grew fiercer. Justin kept one hand on the steering wheel. Stealing his mother's SUV was an impulsive choice that he regretted the farther he strayed from Club Blue. He drove through town, barely able to see twenty feet ahead of him. He felt sickened, reminded of the woman's bloody wounds and vile expression. Eyes bloodshot and emotionally exhausted, he reconciled why he was driving and where. *Away*, he told himself. *Far away*. His conscience beat him up. His mother and brother were still at the hotel. The woman could come back. Hurt them.

His stomach rumbled. He needed food. His head pounded, but he had a high pain tolerance. He learned how to skateboard by falling hundreds of times.

Behind torrents of rain, a chrome diner lured him in.

He swiftly turned off the main road, his wheels splashing out a wave of water. He parked outside the diner. His heart nagged at him. *Go home. You can't run forever*. But that thing in Suite 309 was real, more real than anything in his life. What was reality? Was he blind to the truth his whole life? Was it just the hotel or were there things like that everywhere? He shuddered. He became acutely aware he was alone in the dark car during a dark and stormy night. He needed shelter and someplace bright. The storm had him on edge. He adjusted the rearview mirror, examining the gash on his forehead. It was smaller than he thought. The bleeding had stopped, and the skin swelled. He used his fingers to brush his bangs over it. It didn't hide the wound, but it made it less noticeable.

Going headlong into the rain, he ran to the diner. He pushed open the front door. A little metal bell on the door signaled his arrival. Water dripped from his clothes and hair. The forty-foot run left him drenched.

Keeping his head down, he moved to a booth in the back.

The waitress approached. She was middle-aged and had teased blonde hair and a rough complexion. The discoloration on her cheeks hinted at a lifetime of smoking. "Can I get you a coffee, handsome?"

"Water," Justin said, keeping his voice down.

"Looks like you got enough of that," the waitress joked.

Justin didn't look at her.

The woman said, "Alright, handsome. It'll be right out."

Justin watched her go. He reviewed the menu. It had typical diner fare one would find at an IHOP or Waffle House. Justin could eat a horse. He settled for two steakburgers, a large order of fries, a milkshake, and a slice of pie for dessert.

The waitress jotted down his order when she returned. This time, she noticed the gash on his head. "Oh my. Do you need a band-aid? Does it hurt?"

"I'm fine," Justin snapped.

The waitress backed off. She put a hand on her hip. "Okay, but don't get blood on my table."

Her sass infuriated Justin. He held his tongue. He didn't want to be eating the chef's spit.

His phone dinged. Justin checked it. It was a text from his mother. She wanted him to come home. Justin put the phone face down on the table and leaned back into the seat. A few of the patrons eyed him. His hostile glance back caused them to look away. If he got one good thing from his father, it was the ability to intimidate others.

The next ten minutes dragged on. He anxiously tapped his foot. Staying seated made him stir crazy. He had this feeling that he had to go back home. His mother was in danger, and so was everyone at the hotel. *You can't help them now,* he thought. He hadn't been able to protect his mother and brother from Father. How could he make a difference now?

The waitress arrived, holding the tray of food. She placed it in front of Justin. She reached into her waist apron and pulled out a band-aid, which she put on the table. "Anything else?"

"No," Justin replied curtly.

He squeezed ketchup on his burger patty. It sputtered out like blood before pouring normally. Justin took a large bite. It tasted like heaven. This diner might be the only thing worthwhile in Sebring.

Lingering nearby, the waitress asked, "You sure you don't want to cover that cut?"

Justin's death glare sent her away.

He took another bite.

In midchew, the diner door opened.

A gaggle of high schoolers rushed inside. They laughed, having tried and miserably failed to escape the rain. Justin noticed a few of McKenzie's friends in the mix.

Hopefully, they wouldn't see him… but they did.

They stopped joking among themselves and gossiped quietly as they looked Justin's way. His face flushed red in rage. His appetite vanished. He pulled out a twenty-dollar bill from his wallet and left it on the counter before storming out of the side exit. Shoulders boxed and eyes down, he huffed and crossed through the rain. No amount of persuading would change their perception. He'd always be the guy that ruined McKenzie Michaels, as if she was a saint before they hooked up. That girl had been a cock carousel for years. That was how Justin got her so easy.

Justin sat in the Sorento. The other students gossiped at their table. He regretted leaving his food. It was too late to get it now. He told himself that he didn't care, that it didn't matter he was homeschooled like a sheltered loser. Deep down, he felt lost, regretful, and bitter. Maybe the bloody woman was a twisted manifestation of what was inside of him. He tried not to think too much into it. He didn't want to snap like McKenzie.

A thought came to mind.

He quickly left the diner and drove through the web-like neighborhoods around Sebring until rolling to a stop outside McKenzie's house. Two cars were parked in the driveway. The kitchen light was on. The TV played in the living room. McKenzie's room was dark. He parked in front of the house next door and turned off the headlights. He set his jaw. After a long moment of contemplation, he shut off the car and got out.

The freezing cold downpour caused him to hug himself on the way to the house. There was a screened porch jutting out of the building. He could climb it if he needed and scoot his way to her window.

He looked around the grass. The darkness of night made it impossible to find any throwable pebbles. Turning on his phone light would alert the neighbors. They probably thought he hurt McKenzie as well. He blindly dug around in the bushes near the house, grabbing a few sticks and snapping them into small pieces. He walked back ten feet and chucked the broken twigs at McKenzie's window. Every time he hit, he glanced around, making sure no one had seen him.

After two minutes of waiting in the rain, Justin concluded she hadn't heard him or wasn't home. His shoulders sank and he started back to his vehicle. He twisted back one last time, seeing McKenzie's silhouette standing on the other side of her window.

Justin waved at her. He mouthed, "Can I come in?"

The rain distorted McKenzie's face.

"Screw it," Justin mumbled and jogged to the screened side porch. He grabbed onto the bars between screen squares and pulled himself up to the room. He was careful to stay on the metal railing as stepping on the screen would send him falling through. The wind pushed him off balance. He stayed hunched and walked one step at a time. Sheets of rain slapped him. He spat out water. He took the last step, reaching the wall. He rested against it.

"Open up," he said, waiting for McKenzie to get the window. She didn't, and he didn't want to be left hanging on the sill.

Much to his surprise, the window actually opened. Using her hand to guard her face from the rain, McKenzie stuck out her head.

Justin hugged the corner of the wall. "Can I come in?"

McKenzie looked confused.

Justin said, "It's about what you saw that night."

The wind screamed, tossing McKenzie's hair. The rain fell harder. McKenzie's eyes watered.

"Please," Justin begged. "I'm freezing my balls off."

McKenzie nodded.

Justin reached far and grabbed the windowsill. McKenzie grabbed his wet forearm. Justin grabbed the sill with his other hand. His legs dangled. McKenzie helped pull him through. Justin flopped on the damp carpeted floor. She shut the window, preventing any more rain from coming in.

McKenzie flipped the light switch.

Justin sat up, shivering.

She handed him a blanket.

He wrapped himself in it.

McKenzie sat at the corner of the bed. She didn't bother to wipe the rain from her make-up-less face. Her eyes had heavy bags. She wore a large t-shirt and sweats. She smelled faintly of body odor.

Her room was a cluttered mess. Clothes littered the floor. The books and notebooks covered the desk. The ajar closet door revealed a collection of childhood toys and dolls that had been haphazardly crammed inside. Old family pictures and boyband posters clung to the pink walls.

Justin pulled his knees up to his chest. He wanted to take off his wet clothes but had to avoid the wrong impression. He said, "There's a lot of rumors about us."

McKenzie twiddled her thumbs.

Justin said, "That's it? You're not going to say anything at all? I had to drop out of school because of it."

McKenzie focused on her hands. Her shoulders were bent in and her legs close together in a very guarded posture.

"What's wrong with you? Huh?" Justin asked.

McKenzie was silent.

Justin gave up. "Whatever. I didn't come by here to talk about that anyway." He took a deep breath. "I saw something at the hotel tonight."

McKenzie stopped moving her thumbs.

Justin said, "It was a woman. Her neck was cut open. Someone stabbed her in the stomach. She... she started screaming at me. She tried to get me. Is that what you saw too?"

McKenzie shook her head. "I..." She stopped herself, unfamiliar with her voice as she was speaking for the first time since the incident. "I saw..."

She shut her eyes and shook her head.

Justin said, "Tell me."

McKenzie's eyelids squeezed tight. She controlled her breathing. Regaining some control, she grabbed a notebook at the foot of the bed. She flipped through the pages. Not bothering to look at what was on it, she handed it to Justin. "Him. I saw him."

Justin reviewed the pencil sketch of a well-dressed man with his face torn off. His eyes were large and wide, having no eyelids. The cuts around his jaw and ears appeared to be surgical.

Justin lowered the notebook. "Did he try to hurt you?"

McKenzie opened her mouth, but no words came out. After a second, she managed to say, "He was still there in the corner."

"For how long?" Justin said.

"Even after you carried me out of the room," McKenzie replied. A tear trickled down her pale cheek. "I still see him."

"Where?" Justin asked. The hairs on his arms stood.

McKenzie raised her shaking finger, pointing at something behind Justin.

Justin's heart skipped a beat.

He slowly turned his head to the dark corner of the room. "I don't see anything."

McKenzie trembled. She whispered, "He's looking right at me."

Justin still saw nothing.

McKenzie's breathing quickened.

Justin stood up. He put on a brave face and walked to the corner. He brushed his hand against the wall. "Am I close?"

Suddenly, a wave of cold flashed over Justin. The temperature must have dropped twenty degrees. He quickly moved back a step.

The temperature was normal again.

The color left Justin's face. He kept staring at the corner, terrified to see what would happen if he looked away. "What does he want?"

"I don't know," McKenzie whispered. "He follows me."

Someone knocked on the bedroom door, causing Justin to jump a mile.

"McKenzie," her father said. "I'm going to bed. You need anything?"

The doorknob jiggled.

"Please open up," he pleaded. "Say something. Anything. I just want to know you're okay."

"I'm… I'm fine, Dad," she yelled.

"Baby, you're talking!" her father exclaimed.

"We'll discuss this tomorrow. I want some alone time."

"Okay, yes, I understand," her father said, confused. "I love you."

"You too."

"Goodnight."

"Night," McKenzie said.

Her father lingered.

Justin held his breath.

The father walked away.

Justin waited until he couldn't hear the man's footsteps. He said to McKenzie. "I should go."

McKenzie said, "Please don't."

Justin replied. "If he finds out I'm here…"

McKenzie stood. "I don't want to be alone anymore."

Justin took steps away from the corner, still not looking away. "I'm sorry."

McKenzie's face scrunched. She started to silently cry. "I just want him to go away." She fell into Justin's arms. "Why won't he go away? Why?"

Justin embraced her, but only for a moment.

He needed to get the hell out of this town.

16

BUTTERFLIES

"This way," Asher led Raven through the third-floor hallway.

"Will it be another skeleton?" Raven asked, intrigued.

"Uh… no," the fourteen-year-old said.

The covered lights on the walls flickered.

Raven grinned creepily. She loved the storm. She said it added to the hotel's "atmosphere." Asher wasn't sure his mother would agree. Last Asher checked, she was down at the front desk. Something was up with Justin. It was supposed to be his night to work, but from Asher's window, he saw his older brother speed away in Mom's car. Asher finished his homework not long after and decided to show Raven something cool he spotted while cleaning.

The rooms on the third floor were particularly intriguing. Each suite had its own shape and size. For a one-time visitor, you wouldn't pick up the fact the rooms had different lengths and width, and thus wouldn't know about the hidden corridors snaking throughout the hotel. Asher, having been from room to room many times, could guess where many of the passages were located, but he didn't know how to access them. Mom had not been forthcoming about how she found the skeleton, and she forbade Justin and Asher from going into the passage where she traveled. In fact, that entire suite was off-limits. They'd only rent it out if they had overflow. They haven't been that lucky so far.

Asher unlocked Suite 314.

Raven proudly said, "I've made you into quite the explorer."

Asher said, "I've always liked exploring. I just want to avoid dust allergies."

"How long have you had asthma?"

"All my life," Asher replied and walked into the room. "I spent a lot of time in and out of the hospital."

"I bet you wish you're free of that stuff," Raven said.

Asher nodded. "Who wouldn't want to be? I'm allergic to grass. Grass! Like, how am I supposed to live a full life like that."

"You'd die if you went outside?" Raven asked suspiciously.

"No, but I'd get very itchy and break out," Asher explained as he walked to the bathroom.

Raven asked, "What if you ate it?"

"I've never tried," Asher said.

"Cool," Raven lingered outside the open bathroom door.

Asher gestured for her to enter. Raven followed. She glanced around. "A bathroom?"

Asher walked to the empty space beside the shower and brushed his hand up the tile wall. "I was washing the wall, and—" His fingers brushed against a tile that depressed a quarter inch.

Click.

The wall inside the shower opened.

"Oooh," Raven said in awe.

Asher grinned. "And you said you taught me how to explore. I found this one all by myself."

Raven stepped into the shower and peered into the gap. "It's tight."

Asher replied, "I got through it."

Raven turned back to him. Her mouth was open in surprise. "You went without me?"

Asher felt bad, "No, I... I mean, yes, but only to make sure it was safe."

Raven said, "Safe? Where's the fun in that?"

Asher said, "Well, I was just looking out for you."

"No. You wanted to go alone. Admit it," Raven said, arms crossed.

Asher protested, "No."

It was an obvious lie. He had to make sure there was something cool before reporting back to Raven. He stepped into the shower with her. "Follow me. I'll show you what I really wanted you to see."

He pulled his shirt over his mouth and squeezed into the gap. He walked sideways. The light on his phone guided him. Raven squeezed in after him, not caring about breathing the dust.

They followed the corridor to a T-intersection.

"These are interconnected with other rooms," Asher said, "You can look through mirrors and peepholes into the bathroom."

"That's perverted."

"I'm not the one who built it," Asher defended himself.

Raven posed the question. "I wonder if they had a real torture chamber somewhere in here?"

Asher didn't want to think about that. It was creepy enough everyone on the third floor could spy on each other. This tunnel covered one side of the floor. There was another tunnel on the odd-numbered rooms he didn't know how to access.

He followed the left path twenty paces before turning

down a similar corridor that had a window where the bath-room and wall were located. Obviously, the person inside could see the observer. At the end of the hall was a ladder built into the wall. A latch covered the top. Asher climbed the wood rungs, reaching the ceiling latch. He turned the switch and pushed up, opening to the fourth floor. He crawled into a charred room. Raven climbed out after. Asher had already swept the floor on his last visit. Unlike most of the rooms on the top floor, this one didn't suffer much damage. The hidden latch was near the front of the room and in a corner.

Raven brushed the dust off her black dress and leggings.

An old rusty bedframe was pressed against the opposite wall. The lampstands were in disrepair. The storm beat against the boarded window.

Asher shined the lights over the walls. Behind the burnt and curled wallpaper were massive paintings of Monarch butterflies. Most of them suffered damage from the fire, but a few survived.

Raven approached one of the walls and touched the butterfly painting. "It's beautiful."

Asher followed her, illuminating portions of the wall with his light. "I thought you'd like it."

Raven turned around. "You know what this is, right?"

"An artist's masterpiece?" Asher asked.

"No, silly. MK Ultra. Monarch Programming."

"Uh, what?" Asher asked, extremely confused.

Raven said, "It's a secret government program... well, not so secret now. Monarch Programming was a type of mind control. They'd break down their subject's will and fracture their mind into different alters, much like altered person-alities."

"H-how?" Asher asked.

"The handlers would torture their subjects and break

their will through trauma. Fun fact. It seems to be a technique satanic cults use on their victims."

Asher regretted asking.

Raven said, "You dig deep enough, you could tie this stuff to Nazis, but that's a different story. For millennia, mankind has been practicing how to enslave one another. Even Pluto talked about the shadow in the cave. One group of elites controlling society through sleight of hand and ritual… like the stuff I showed you before."

"Yeah, that was not fun," Asher said.

"Some say this stuff ties back to Egyptian times. Maybe even older." Raven turned back to the butterfly mural. "For the CIA, the Monarch acronym was used because the victims felt a butterfly sensation in their stomach. They'd have a number of alters. Some would get triggered by certain words or images."

Asher said, "That's horrible."

"Oh, you don't know the half of it," Raven said. "These alters would be used for sex slaves and murders. Sometimes the people with them don't even remember what they did or to who. Imagine living your whole life not realizing you were brainwashed. You know some say this stuff ties into demon possession."

Asher shook his head. "I don't know about all that."

"It's true."

Asher said, "Then why isn't anyone talking about it?"

"Most people can't handle stuff that dark," Raven replied.

Asher said, "I don't believe it."

Raven said, "You might one day."

"Did your dad tell you all this?"

Raven replied, "He spent years digging into this stuff. He knows what he's talking about."

Asher asked, "Has your dad ever stayed here before?"

"A handful of times," Raven said. "He wouldn't write about all this stuff if he didn't believe it."

Asher thought to himself, *What if her father was the one who was living in the unburnt room? What if he knew about the skeleton in the walls?*

Raven walked to the boarded windows. She peeked through the crack. Asher stood next to her.

"You must think I'm really weird, huh?" Raven asked.

Yes, Asher thought. "No," he said.

Raven said, "You're lying."

Asher looked down at his feet. He felt nervous. "You're different than anyone I've ever met."

Raven said cynically. "I thought so."

"I never said that was a bad thing," Asher backpedaled. "It's just..."

"Weird."

Asher felt like he was trapped. Out of frustration, he asked, "Do you want to be normal?"

Raven said, "I don't know. My mind is always running. I used to think everyone was like that, but I know they're not."

Asher said, "Normal is boring."

Raven said, "But it's kind of romantic. If there is such a thing as love. And I'm not saying there is, but it seems to just be for normal people."

Asher didn't know what to say to that. He never thought about love.

Raven said, "I don't get how we can know so much about all the bad stuff and still enjoy the little things."

Asher didn't have the answer to that either.

Raven sighed, "One day I hope to find the balance. I'd live in a big Victorian mansion and have a bashful lover just as sinister as I am. We could have our little dark-eyed children running around and host these amazing Halloween parties."

"Halloween is coming up soon," Asher said, not sure how to get into the conversation.

Raven said, "You should dress up."

"Nah."

"Come on." Raven poked at his side. "I want you to surprise me."

"Hey!" Asher scooted away from her poking.

"Ticklish!" Raven said.

Asher shouted and ran from her. Laughing maniacally, Raven chased him around the room and tickled him.

"Stop—ahahhaha—S-stop! I'm serious, hahaha! Oof!" Asher's foot snagged on the leg of the bed frame and he crashed on the floor. Unable to stop running fast enough, Raven tripped and landed on top of him.

She quickly rolled off, holding her belly and laughing.

Asher rubbed his head. "Ow."

He fixed his glasses. He felt his lungs get tight and he started coughing.

Raven's laughter died down. "Are you okay?"

Asher sat up, pulled out his inhaler, gave it a shake, and blasted a jet into his mouth. His airways felt like they opened again. He lay back down the floor. His stomach rose and fell.

Raven said, "Thank you."

"Huh?"

"For listening to me ramble," Raven said. "My dad says I talk too much. That's why he likes me out of the room."

Asher said, "Well… I'm glad to listen."

It sounded cheesy. He internally cringed.

Resting in ash and dust, the two of them looked up at the ceiling.

What now? Asher thought. *Is it too quiet? It's getting awkward. The inhaler must have made me look like a wimp.*

Raven rolled to her side and pecked Asher on the cheek.

Asher froze.

Raven laid on her back.

Asher gently touched his face. It was like he had a million thoughts and none at the same time. *Did she just...* Asher put his hand back on his belly, trying to downplay the whole thing. His mind was consumed and enticed, but there were butterflies fluttering in his stomach.

EMF METER

*J*ustin left McKenzie's house through the bedroom window. He dangled from the soaked windowsill as fat raindrops stoned his back. He moved to the screen roof railing and regained his balance. McKenzie's sorrowful expression tempted Justin to spend the night. Beautiful women hypnotized him more than any other vice. However, he was soon coming to the realization that he needed to live his life for himself.

He dashed to his vehicle. His foot nearly slipped on the muddy front lawn. McKenzie watched him speed away.

Drenched and shivering, Justin drove back to Club Blue. He noticed a large tarp over one of the second-story windows.

He parked on the side of the building. He rubbed his freezing hands together but failed to conjure any heat. Keeping his head down, he dashed for the car and into the front lobby doors. He pulled on the handles, but the doors didn't budge. A dim light illuminated the room. The front desk was unoccupied.

Staying under the awning, he walked until he could see

the tarp-covered window. Though pinned down from the inside, the blue covering flapped. Confused, Justin pulled out his front door key and opened the lobby. He locked it behind him. "Mom?"

His voice echoed.

Tracking water across the tile floor, he walked behind the front desk. The door to the office was locked as well. He used his key for that and checked his mom's office. She wasn't there.

Justin hugged himself. His wet clothes clung to his pasty skin. He pressed the elevator button rapidly before it opened. He quickly moved to the second floor. The hallway was long and empty.

Justin approached his mom's door and knocked.

No reply.

He hammered his fist on the door. "It's Justin. Open up."

Still no reply.

He rubbed his hand down his mouth. Being back inside the hotel, his heart raced. Though he didn't see the faceless man, the idea of an invisible force lurking about terrified him.

Justin hit the door harder. "Mom. C'mon. We need to talk."

The door opened a creak. A sliver of his mother's face was visible. Her bloodshot eye glared at Justin. There was a scratch on her cheek.

"You alone?" she asked.

"Yeah," Justin said, annoyed. "What's going on? What happened to the window?"

Anna opened the door.

She wore a bathrobe. Her hair was wrapped in a towel. Small scrapes and cuts painted the left side of her face. There were more scrapes and splinters on her hands.

Justin opened his mouth to speak.

Anna embraced him, hugging him tighter than a life raft. "Mom..."

Anna let go. She glanced out in the hallway. "Get in. Hurry."

Justin followed her inside, shutting the door behind him.

Anna's wet clothes were bundled in the hamper. She walked Justin into the center of the room.

Justin said, "Tell me what happened."

Anna grabbed the bottle of vodka from the lampstand and took a drink.

Justin was appalled by the action. He grabbed the bottle and yanked it out of her hand. "We don't have time for that."

Anna glared at him.

Justin said, "We need to get Asher and get the hell out of Sebring."

Anna yanked the bottle back from him. "First of all, don't touch my drink. Secondly, where have you been?"

"I needed to clear my head," Justin replied. He reached for the bottle.

Anna pulled away. "You weren't here, Justin."

"Duh. This place is cursed," Justin said, feeling crazy saying it.

"I was attacked," Anna said. "And you care more about some stupid ghost thing. Give me a break, Justin. If you don't like here, you don't have to lie."

"Attacked?"

"There was a rapist in my hotel!" Anna shouted.

"Calm down," Justin said forcefully.

Anna took a swig.

Justin said slowly. "Start from the beginning."

"While you were *clearing your head*, I was assaulted at my hotel. My hotel."

Justin put both hands on his head, unsure how to handle

this information. "Assaulted—What? Have you called the cops?"

"No, I gave him a free room voucher and a bottle of champagne—of course I called the cops! What kind of a dumb question is that?"

"Well, I don't know what's happening!" Justin shouted.

"You would if you stayed!"

The conversation fell into silence.

Justin brooded, angry, frustrated, unsure if he should hug his mother or punch the wall.

Anna walked to the window and sipped her drink. She winced at the taste and looked at the black storm outside.

Justin calmed himself, remembering that she was the victim here. "Are you okay?"

Anna chuckled and shook her head. She had another drink but didn't swallow. She looked at the bottle with disgust and set it aside.

Justin said, "This place is bad for us, Mom."

Anna stared outside. "I was pushed through a window."

Justin's eyes widened.

Anna continued. "I fell two stories. The tree broke my fall. I got bruises all up and down my back and butt. Cameron said it was a miracle I didn't need to go to the hospital. The paramedics suggested that I go, but who is going to pay for that? We have enough debt already. Add a couple of thousand and we'll never get out of this pit... I suppose it's my fault. I should've been wiser with our money."

Justin said, "Did this man that attack you... did he..." his voice trailed off. The rest of the question scared him.

"No, thank God. Cameron showed up before he could do more than rough me up. None of this would've happened if I wasn't alone."

Justin balled his fist. "Okay, sure. Blame me. I'm the cause of all your problems. The high school dropout. The loser. Raped a girl. I'm just as bad as that guy, is that it?"

Anna glanced over her shoulder. "I never said that."

"It's what you're implying. First, I wasn't strong enough to stop Dad, and now I'm not strong enough to keep you safe here. I'm the screw-up child. What about Asher, huh? When does he start taking some of the blame?"

Anna turned back. "He's fourteen!"

"I was running the house at fourteen while all he did was play his stupid games. That's all he ever does. Where was he tonight?"

Anna said, "I don't know." She cast down her eyes. "I haven't checked on him."

"So he's probably playing his stupid game." Justin wanted to punch the kid's teeth out. "When will he grow up? When he will he take some of the responsibility?"

Justin's bitterness towards his brother had deep roots.

Anna said softly. "Asher's a fragile boy. He can't know about what happened tonight."

Justin set his jaw.

Anna approached him, swaying slightly from her drink. She grabbed Justin's wet sleeves to keep her balance. Her hand squeezed the cloth and water poured out. "Please, Justin. He can't know."

Seeing his mother's desperation softened Justin's heart. Nevertheless, his expression was still hard as stone. He said, "We need to leave."

Anna let go of him and backed up a few steps. She wiped her leaky nose and rubbed her finger on her thigh. "We can't just walk away."

Justin said, "Our lives are in danger."

Anna replied, "We have bills to pay. I have mouths to feed."

"Settle for bankruptcy," Justin said.

Anna replied, "And screw up our lives forever? We can't go back to York."

"We'll stay at Grandma's," Justin suggested.

"That's not a long-term solution," Anna said.

"It's life or death, Mom," Justin replied.

Anna shook her head. "I won't go."

"You were almost raped!" Justin exclaimed.

"This hotel is all we have," Anna replied.

"It's a death trap. This place is garbage, anyway."

Anna's eyes watered. "Don't you dare say that. All your father's fortune is tied into this place."

"So what? It's a building, Mom. That's all it is. In a few years, we'll get another," Justin said.

Anna's face turned red. "If you hate it so much, go. You're old enough to make it on your own. I'll pull Asher out of the school and he and I will run the place."

Justin crossed his arms. Annoyed, he said, "You'd take Asher out of school for this dump?"

"Don't call it that!" Anna snapped.

Justin said, "You're obsessed."

"This isn't just a building. It's our home. Our dream," Anna replied, passion in her voice.

Justin replied, "Whose dream?"

"Ours," Anna said firmly.

"Is it?" Justin asked. "You're sure?"

"Justin, I swear..." Anna warned.

"What?"

"You make me want to tear my hair out." Anna grabbed the vodka bottle.

Justin hugged himself tighter. His teeth chattered. "I'm gonna take a shower."

Anna sat at the corner of the bed and didn't say anything.

Justin stopped midway to the door. He turned back. He

felt an apology at the tip of his tongue. He turned back to the door and left, not saying another word.

Justin closed the door behind him and stormed to his room. The moment he entered, he threw off his clothes and entered the shower. Hot water splashed over him. A large part of him wanted to pack his bags and leave tonight. Anna was right about him surviving on his own. He believed himself to be resourceful. But who would take care of his mother?

He was good at making it seem like her words didn't hurt him, but his soul ached knowing his mother was attacked. After Father passed away, he'd promised himself to never let another man hurt her, and yet he was gone in her most desperate hour. Afflicted by a sudden jolt of rage, he punched the inside of the shower. Pain shot through his knuckles to his wrist.

He should've stayed, but instead, he fled like a coward. He hated cowards. He'd die before he let himself become one. A battle waged in his mind. Logically, leaving was the best option, but he knew Anna. She wouldn't change her mind. And where she went, Asher followed. The other option was to stay. Justin wouldn't be a coward, but at any moment, the faceless man or the woman in the green dress could come for him. The only thing that scared Justin more than them was the loss of his family. Yes, they annoyed him and made stupid decisions, but they survived under Father's iron rule together. Any one of them could've run away, but they endured the horror together. When Anna had every right to leave, she stayed behind for her children, knowing that James would kill them all if they tried to flee.

Justin turned off the shower dial. He stood bare in the shower. Maybe there was a way to leave and keep them all together. An idea came to mind. It was foolish and not thought out, but it might just convince the others he was right.

The next morning, he woke up before sunrise and booted up his phone. Finding what he needed online, he took the Sorento to town and parked outside of the local tech shop. The moment the owner unlocked the door, Justin moved inside.

With a perplexed expression on his face, the cashier rang up his items. Justin collected the large tab. Mom wouldn't be happy, but it was a small price for safety. He returned to the hotel and unboxed the camera, audio recorder, motion trigger, and an EMF reader. It was a remote-like handheld device designed to detect electromagnetic fields. Spikes in the frequency suggested a change in electrical current, and thus a spirit being.

Working the day shift, James pushed his cleaning cart through the halls and kept the EMF reader within reach. He watched the little needle, waiting to see a spike in energy. Getting no results, he decided to wait until evening to hunt for the woman in the green dress. If he could catch her, he might just have enough proof that ghosts were real. The moment Anna saw it, she'd want to leave. Until then, Justin just had to stay alive.

18

CITY ON A HILL

A week had passed since the incident and Agent Cameron... well, Cameron had been a godsend. Anna liked to call him by his name now. He had offered to fix the window with the promise of being reimbursed by the insurance company. Anna agreed and Cameron got working. He knew a lot about the hotel's window design and where to buy similar glass panes. Anna assumed it was his investigative skills that led him to that discovery.

Meanwhile, Anna worked at the desk. She cut back on her drinking after the major hangover the morning after Lance's attack. The police carted him off. They found pliers, disposable gloves, and other tools in his travel bag. The cops told her that she wouldn't have to worry about him again. She chose to leave the past behind her and focus on her job.

Working the front desk took a certain type of patience and imagination. She had a lot of time to herself and dedicated it to social media marketing, blogging, and reading saucy romance novels. After the attack, she needed to have something more loving to dwell on and hoped the novels would be her balm. Unfortunately, they were way too graphic and made her feel uncomfortable having them around.

A grey-haired man and his beautiful twenty-something daughter arrived one evening. At least Anna thought they were father and daughter until they kissed each other after getting their keys. Let's just say it wasn't a peck on the cheek.

Anna went back to reading her book.

The end of October neared, and the weather grew colder. Colorful leaves painted the trees around Club Blue and Sebring. The wind swayed their branches. Justin raked the leaves every few days. Anna forced Asher to help, though the fourteen-year old's allergies proved problematic.

Towards the end of her shift, Anna got a call from Andrew Warren, the older gentlemen from the second floor, asking about his broken heater.

Anna sent Justin to check on it. He wasn't happy, but that was a given. Her son was adamant about wanting to leave, but eventually followed Anna's way of thinking. He didn't talk anymore about the crazy supernatural stuff either. Frankly, he was suspiciously quiet about it since that horrible rainy night. Meanwhile, Asher was in his own world. She gave him more time to complete his homework. Despite Anna threatening to take him out of school if Justin left, she couldn't bring herself to do it. It would be a crime to let a smart kid like that waste his talents cleaning hotel rooms and doing general repair. That type of work was better suited for Justin.

Justin sent Anna a text, saying that the heater wasn't started. Anna decided to head to the boiler room. She descended into the basement. The concrete floors and grey corridors were unappealing and maze-like. Every step, her heels clacked on the floor. As she neared the boiler room, the temperature climbed. She entered the room, seeing the large boiler, pipes running all across the wall. Steam filled the

THE HAUNTING AT SEBRING HOTEL

room. It was part of the old design and fogged the entire space. Anna entered. She grabbed the worker's manual placed in a wall-mounted box. Anna flipped through the pages, scanning over content and info-graphs until finding the section labeled room heating. Holding the book at her side, she braved the steam.

The heat caused her to sweat like a pig. She reached the back of the boiler, reviewed the chart mounted on the wall, and found the valve to Warren's room. She touched it and yelped at the sudden contact with scalding hot metal. She opened and closed her hand a few times. She slipped her hand into the sleeve of her blouse and turned it that way. The valve resisted her and the heat leaked through her thin sleeve. Muscling through the pain, she turned the valve. Victorious, she called Justin.

"Any luck?" Justin asked.

"Try it on your end," Anna said.

She waited, the heat bearing down on her.

Justin returned to the phone and said, "It's working now. It just took a while to warm up."

Anna said, "It could've been a lot worse."

"What was the problem?" Justin asked.

"The valve was turned off," Anna said. "Were you down here at all?"

"Nope. Maybe it was Asher."

"Unlikely," Anna said.

"Anything else you need?" Justin asked.

"That's all. See you up there," Anna replied.

The call ended. Anna slipped her phone into her pocket. She had suspicions that someone had turned off the valve. No one could get down the basement without the elevator key. She imagined that the same person messing with the valve had stolen her pens, broaches, and earrings. So many small things had gone missing in the last few weeks, Anna stopped counting. Either she was becoming incredibly forgetful or there was a thief in her midst. Anna dreaded both reasons.

She stepped back into the fog, slowly making her way out of the room when she saw the figure silhouetted in the steam.

Anna stopped.

The figure was fifteen feet away. Their features were lost in the white fog. By their shoulders and height, Anna could tell it was a man. Her hand found her cellphone but kept it in her pocket.

She waited for the person to move. He must've seen her too. There was no way he couldn't.

"Justin? Were you down here the whole time?"

A loud jet of steam burst out of the pipe nearest Anna's head. She staggered, blinded temporarily. Regaining her balance, she turned her attention back to the fog.

The figure was gone.

"H-hello?" Anna asked.

She hugged the book close to her chest.

"This isn't funny," she said.

More steam flooded the room. The hot and damp air blanketed her. She continued forward, glancing into every blind corner. She reached the end of the room undisturbed. She put the manual back in the wall-mounted box and waited to see if anyone would step out of the steam. After a long minute, she turned off the light and headed to the elevator at a brisk pace. It must've been in her head.

She reached the elevator and recognized her need for another handyman. Her strengths lay in management and hospitality, not gritty, sweaty work. Justin was a huge help, but he was a novice. Anna returned to the lobby counter. She took a seat on her comfy chair and fixed her frizzy hair. She needed the money and extra employment to keep the hotel afloat. New people visited every week, but Anna was still in the red.

Stress caused her head to throb. She contemplated going on a mini-vacation, but that wouldn't help her. Weighed down by the million little things she needed to do, she rested her head on the counter. It was meant to be a little nap, but the moment she got comfy, she was out.

She dreamed about walking the halls of the hotel when suddenly it caught fire. The doors to various rooms burst open as residents dressed in flames ran. They screamed and cried for help, but dropped like flies all around Anna. A man shrouded by smoke and shadow watched her from the end of the room. He was silhouetted against the back wall. He held a scalpel in his hand. Anna knew she needed to run, but she stepped towards him. The small flame nipped at her heel and caught her pantyhose on fire. She continued down the hall. The flame grew greater and soon engulfed her body, but she walked forward, unaffected.

The mysterious man said, "It's your home. Let's share it together."

Suddenly, the flames became real and licked her skin. Excruciating pain exploded all across her. She screamed as her body started to liquify. She expected to wake up, but the fire burned hotter.

A cold hand touched her shoulder.

She awoke and nearly fell out of her chair. Anna panted. The dream felt so real that she patted down her body, making sure she wasn't still burning.

"Ma'am, are you alright?" the Catholic priest asked. He was a short man with soft features. His eyes were a lively blue and there was a shaky smile on his lips. His priestly garments were traditional black and he had a white collar.

The priest looked at her, both curious and empathic.

Anna apologized. She wiped the drool from the corner of

her mouth. "This is embarrassing," she said, trying to get into the right mindset.

The priest said, "You look troubled."

"No, no, I'm... um, I'm fine. My name is Anna. Welcome to Club Blue." She forced a smile. *Falling asleep on the job. You know better than that,* she berated herself.

"I'm Stephen," the priest said, smiling.

"What can I help you with today, Stephen?"

He fished out his wallet. "I'd like to stay for five weeks."

"Really? Business or pleasure?" Anna asked.

Stephen replied, "A bit of both. Is it okay if I pay in cash?"

"Be my guest," Anna said.

Stephen pulled out a bank envelope of large bills. "That should cover the cost."

Anna opened the envelope and pulled the bills halfway. She counted them. "This is way too much."

"You can keep the extra," Stephen said.

Anna said seriously. "I can't do that."

Stephen said, "You need it more than I do. Please. I insist."

Anna wasn't going to say no to free money at this point. She opened the register and put it inside. "Thank you, Father. It's a major blessing."

Stephen chuckled lightly. "It's not *Father* anymore."

"Oh," Anna replied, usually much better at hiding her surprise, but the drowsiness made her much more emotive.

Stephen didn't provide any more details.

Anna grabbed a key from the case before her.

Stephen said, "Actually, can you put me on the third floor instead?"

"Of course," Anna grabbed the key from a higher hook. *For the money you're paying me, I'd let you have my suite.*

"Suite 303," Anna said proudly. "Is there anything else I can do? Extra towels? Delivery."

"I just want space. That's all," the priest replied.

"I'll tell my sons not to disturb you," Anna said.

The priest nodded. "Thank you, Anna. Have a wonderful evening."

"Enjoy your stay," Anna replied.

Stephen grabbed a small travel bag from the cab outside, spoke to the driver, and returned inside.

"Would you like any assistance carrying anything in?" Anna asked.

"No, ma'am," Stephen replied. He raised the little bag slightly. "This is all I have."

He entered the elevator and left the lobby.

Anna wondered how he could survive five weeks from a bag only big enough for an extra change of clothes.

19

DARKEST HOUR

*T*he alarm blared.

Justin quickly reached over and turned off the alarm clock on his phone. Silence filled his lightless room. It was almost 3 am. Witching hour.

He rose from his bed and glanced around, waiting for his heavy-lidded eyes to adjust. He pulled on the lamp string. The sudden introduction of light blinded him for a moment. He squinted and yawned. Already dressed in jeans and a long-sleeve shirt, he slipped his feet into his shoes resting at the foot of his bed. He stood up knowing that if he stayed in bed any longer, he'd fall back asleep. He approached the kitchen counter, pulled the camera battery off the charger, and put it in his GoPro camera. Next, he grabbed the audio recording device and clipped it to the lip of his pants. Not wearing a belt, his skinny jeans sagged slightly and the top of his boxers muffined out. Lastly, he grabbed a cheap flashlight to go above the GoPro and EMF reader.

He admired himself in the mirror, impressed by his gear and his due diligence to get up for the last five nights at 3 am to ghost hunt. He stepped into the lit hall and quietly shut his door. At this time of night, the hotel was deathly silent. Keeping every step as silent as he could, he turned on the EMF reader and scanned. Simply imagining another encounter made his heart race. Keeping a mental list of unoccupied rooms, he unlocked the first suite and stepped inside. He kept the lights off. He listened to his own breathing as he navigated the room using his headlamp, carefully opening the bathroom and closet door. Getting no results, he returned to the hallway and tried the next room.

The second floor was a bust. He took the stairs to the third. The atmosphere felt different on this floor. Tenser. Justin believed it was just his mindset, but there was a little thought bubble that said it was much more. He started with Suite 301. It was a dead lead. He moved to 302 and then 304. Entering Suite 306, the needle on the EMF reader wobbled but quickly returned to normal. Justin was on edge, waiting for something pop out as he searched every nook and cranny.

He left the room unsatisfied and continued down the hallway, checking each suite until reaching the one where he first encountered the woman in the green dress. Suite 309. He hesitated to open the door. *You're not a coward*, he reminded himself, using his own convictions to force him to step inside. He didn't let the door close fully behind him. His pulse pounded. He kept the EMF reader in his hand. The needle stayed steady. He slowly turned the corner where he could see the bed. No woman. No change in frequency. Justin doubted that the device worked. He finished exploring the third floor before going down to the lobby.

He walked through the bar and kitchen before entering the ballroom. The room was pitch black. Justin's flashlight shined over large pillars and dozens of tables forming a U around the dance floor. At the far end, he saw the grandiose staircase that was center with the room until it reached its first flat area and then split left and right into the balcony. The second-floor balcony had dim lights on the wall that allowed for some visibility.

As Justin walked through the ballroom, he heard a woman scream.

Immediately, Justin dipped behind the pillar and turned off his headlamp. On the balcony, he saw a woman dashing out from the second floor's main corridor and for the stairs. From Justin's point of view, he could only see her upper body. She wore a dress. Her long brown hair flowed as she ran. She had olive-colored skin.

Someone out of sight grabbed her wrist and pulled her from Justin's view.

The woman's scream was muffled by the attacker's hand.

Justin watched in horror. Staying in the shadows, he pulled out his cellphone. He hated the cops, but he called them anyway.

The muffled scream died down.

Justin told the woman on the other end, "I just witnessed a murder…. Yes, Club Blue. Hurry."

Justin stayed behind the pillar. The ballroom fell silent.

He took deep breaths. *That woman was just killed.* It didn't feel real. The killer was in his hotel. He needed to stay quiet and out of sight. In a few minutes, help would arrive.

SOMEONE KNOCKED on Anna's door.

She awoke from her nightmare and pulled her covers up to her neck. A loose strand of hair glued to the corner of her mouth.

The person knocked again, louder.

"Sebring PD. Open up," the cop said in a muffled voice.

"What the…" Anna mumbled. She swiveled her legs out of bed and put on sweatpants and a large t-shirt. She combed her fingers through her messy hair as she reached the door's peephole.

Officers Dana and Parkman stood on the other side. Their faces were stretched and distorted by the fisheye lens.

Anna removed the metal bar lock before opening the door. "What's happened?"

Dana, the short, ugly mug cop, said, "Someone reported a homicide here."

Anna cursed.

Parkman said, "Yeah, but there are no bodies or blood."

"Who called it in?" Anna asked.

Parkman said, "Your boy, Justin."

Anna rubbed her brow. "Okay. Show me where."

She followed them out. It must've been around 4 am. The cops looked more miserable than Anna.

They walked her over the ballroom's balcony

Dana said, "He said it happened here."

There was no sign of struggle. No blood. No homicide.

Anna really didn't need this stress right now. "Where's Justin?"

"Outside," Parkman said. "He said he had GoPro footage, but the file was corrupted."

"What? Why was he filming?" Anna asked.

Parkman shrugged.

Dana said, "I think he was ghost hunting."

Anna tilted her head, confused.

Dana said, "We get calls about the young guys busting into condemned properties and trying to capture a spirit on camera. Most of the time, they scare themselves silly."

Anna sighed. *Justin, what am I going to do with you?*

Dressed in their pajamas, the couple stepped out of their room. The grey-haired man kept his hand around the twenty-something-year-old's waist.

"What's going on?" the man asked.

Dana replied, "We'll be right with you, sir."

The man nodded. His woman yawned.

Parkman said, "Just in case your son's claims are true, we're going to have to interview your guests."

"Is that really necessary?" Anna asked.

"For your safety, yes," Parkman said.

Anna asked, "Can you do it tomorrow?"

"I'm afraid not," Parkman replied.

Dana added. "We'd like the guest list from you. If a woman is missing like your son described, we need to know about it."

Parkman said, "We'd check the security cameras, but it appears you haven't installed them."

Annoyed, Anna led them to the lobby and gave them the guest list.

Justin sat on the curb outside.

It was going to be a long night.

20

AMENITIES

"*T*hank you for staying," Anna said to another disgruntled guest.

The businessman heaved his luggage out of the lobby.

Anna plopped down her seat, a heavy frown set on her tired face. The incident last night sent half of her guests elsewhere. Most of the extended-stay visitors remained, but it was still a noticeable stain on the hotel's reputation. She expected to read bad online reviews over the next few days. With the winter months nearing, she didn't imagine many people would drive north. She thought about rebranding the entire motel. It would kill the historical charms that she delighted in but would hopefully replenish her clientele list. The idea sickened Anna.

Justin entered via the stairs. His work polo was tucked into his slacks. His unwashed long hair rested on his shoulders. He approached, wearing his typical blank expression.

Anna glanced around the lobby, making sure it was empty. It was only the two of them.

Justin stopped at the counter. "What do you need me to do today?"

"No apology?" Anna asked.

"For what?"

"Last night, you idiot," Anna seethed.

Justin broke eye contact and ground his teeth.

Anna said, "We lost a lot of money because of that stunt. After the whole skeleton and Lance thing, I'm surprised we still have a business."

"I thought someone died," Justin explained.

"Who, Justin? Who? All of our guests were accounted for," Anna said. "There wasn't any evidence."

"It must've been—" Justin stopped himself.

"Been what?"

Justin spoke quietly. "I'm telling you. There is something very wrong happening here."

Anna wanted to slap him. She kept a lid on her emotions. "I want you to take that GoPro, recorder, and all that other junk you bought and return it today."

"But—"

"Justin, it's over," Anna interrupted. "You're going to work and you're going to study for when we enroll you in the online classes next year. No more late nights, no more buying stuff on my credit card, and no more car."

"That's a load of crap," Justin bickered.

"Until you earn your keep around here, you're grounded," Anna said.

Justin balled his fists. His face flushed red. "You can't do that. I'm not a kid."

"Then stop acting like one," Anna replied.

Justin shut up.

Anna grabbed a list of recently-vacated rooms. "Start with these."

Justin yanked the list from her hand. "How will I take back the GoPro if I can't use the Sorento?"

"Figure something out," Anna said.

Justin stormed out of the lobby.

"Teenagers," Anna mumbled.

That evening, Anna sent out invitations to the last remaining guests, offering them discounted drinks at the bar. Much to her surprise, every one of them accepted. Yes, even the priest.

She set Justin in charge of the front desk while she managed the bar.

Anna wore a tight white blouse, skinny black slacks, and low heels. Her hair was put up in a bun. She wiped the bar top. One by one, the guests funneled inside.

The first was Agent Cameron. He sat at the far corner of the bar, allowing him the best vantage point of everyone who entered and exited. He wore a collared shirt, dark jeans, and leather boots. His hair was recently cut, making him exceptionally dashing tonight. He set his iPad on the table and asked for a beer.

Anna brought him a Yingling and placed it on a little napkin. "The window turned out nice."

Cameron smiled. "I'm glad you liked it. And thank you. It was a pain in the butt to fit."

"I should be the one thanking you," Anna said. "It's nice to have a man around who knows how to fix things."

"Where would you be without me?" Cameron asked, a wry smile on his handsome face as he took a sip.

"Lost and confused, probably," Anna flirted. "Your drinks are on the house by the way."

"I won't say no to that," Cameron replied.

"Just for tonight," Anna said.

Cameron said, "I'll make sure to get my fill."

Anna returned to the bar, a little pep in her step. It had been a long time since she bartended.

The impeccably-dressed Andrew Warren arrived holding a rolled newspaper under his arm. The older gentleman took a seat at the middle table. He ordered an orange mimosa.

Anna apologized for the disturbance last night.

Mr. Warren said, "You don't need to worry about me. I'm up early around that time. Anyway. Hey, have you had the chance to meet my granddaughters?"

"I'm afraid not," Anna said.

"Hmm. I suppose that makes sense. Your son was working at the front desk at the time. Anyway, they are two lovely young girls."

"How old are they?"

"Seven and ten, and, boy, are they smart," Mr. Warren said. "Their mother has them both taking piano lessons."

"That's wonderful," Anna said politely.

Mr. Warren leaned and spoke softly. "Between you and me, it's a little much for girls their age, but they are adapting. Do you have girls?"

"Just my two sons," Anna said.

"Yes, I had a son once, too," Mr. Warren said. "We don't talk much anymore."

"I'm sorry."

"You've done nothing wrong. It's that I wasn't around enough," Mr. Warren said. "I have a lot of good memories in this place, but it consumed much of my time."

For the first time, Anna noticed the Freemason signature square and compass on the old man's ring. Anna smiled. "I'm sure you know all the secrets, huh?"

"Only a few," Mr. Warren replied slyly.

"My eldest son seems to think the place is haunted," Anna joked.

Mr. Warren replied, "There are many things we don't understand about this world and the one after."

Anna digested his ominous remark. She put up a mental wall. "But ghosts though?"

Mr. Warren said, "Nothing is out of the realm of possibilities."

Anna didn't like his seriousness regarding the topic.

Mr. Warren smiled kindly at her. "I'll take that drink now."

The next guest entered and Anna had little knowledge about him. He was a tall, lumbering man. His neck was slightly hunched and his broad shoulders gave him a box-like appearance. Thin bristling hairs sprouted from his shaven head. He had a lazy eye and wore a mechanic's jumpsuit, grease stains and all. His name tag read *Fritz*. He never entered the hotel through the lobby, and rarely left his room when he was around. Sometimes, she'd hear classical music playing loudly through his door. Fritz sat at the bar and ordered a gin and coke. He drank with his head slightly down in a posture that didn't invite conversation.

Roughly thirty minutes later, the couple arrived. The grey-haired man and his young companion were joined at the hip like always. She giggled at a quiet joke he said into her ear. They were both dressed casually. The spunky girl had blonde hair and the lithe body of a ballet dancer. The man was of average height but also toned. He'd started to grow a grey beard and had a long nose that seemed unusual for his attractive face. His silver hair was brushed back. He had a lively grin and a joyful countenance. They sat three stools away from Fritz.

Anna told them about the half-off drinks and listed her suggestions.

"What would you like?" the man asked his lady.

"Hmm. Something fruity," the girl replied.

The man ordered her an appletini and observed the bar. "You should keep this open more often."

"I'm currently looking for a replacement bartender," Anna admitted.

The girl said, "You should get someone with a curled mustache. I think it would add to the whole theme of the place."

Anna chuckled. "I'll look into it."

"I'm Rosy, by the way." The girl reached her hand across the bar.

Anna shook her supple hand. "Anna."

"Christophe," the man introduced himself.

"I'm glad to have you here," Anna said. "I hope you've enjoyed your stay so far."

Christophe said, "It's been an adventure. Sebring has so many hidden shops and undiscovered landmarks. Every day we find something new. Tell her about the lighthouse, Rosy?"

"It's gorgeous," Rosy said. "There are these little paddle boats all around the beach you can rent."

Christophe added, "Sometimes they leave them overnight. Rosy and I have made a few trips over to the island."

Rosy said to him, "Don't tell her all our little secrets."

Christophe kissed her. "She won't tell anyone. I'm sure she has some of her own."

Rosy eagerly waited for Anna to say something profound. Anna didn't have anything to add.

She asked Christophe. "So, what brings you all the way to Sebring?"

"Christophe loves to travel," Rosy interjected.

He agreed. "There are so many hidden gems all across the East Coast. Every chance I get, I make a trip somewhere new. This is my first time to Sebring actually."

Rosy said, "We discovered it by accident. I'm glad to see you're starting to promote Club Blue more. It's such a special place."

Christophe said, "I agree, but its lack of promotion is

what gives its appeal. You don't want the place to become commercial, do you?"

Anna said, "If I can get the right clientele, I'd be more than happy to keep hidden."

Christophe said, "I like your honesty."

Anna mixed their drinks. "So how did you two meet?"

Rosy and Christophe looked into each other's eyes.

"You want to tell her?" Rosy asked him.

"I'll let do you the honors," Christophe said.

Rosy said to Anna. "Christophe is my dance instructor."

Now things make sense, Anna thought.

Christophe said, "I own a small studio in upstate New York. Rosy is one of my better students."

"Just one of your better students?" Rosy fished for a compliment.

Christophe denied her. "Well, there are certain areas you could improve."

Rosy's self-confidence was shot down.

"But," Christophe said, bring hope back to her face. "With a little more practice, you'll be the next Anna Pavlova."

Confidence restored, Rosy pecked him on the cheek.

Christophe spoke to Anna. "Anyway, I've been meaning to get the studio more funding, but I'm afraid of it becoming too big. I won't have as much time to spend with my students. After all, so much learning comes from private practice."

Rosy said, "That's how Christophe and I got so close. I'm going to help him run the studio after I finish my Liberal Arts degree."

"Oh, you're in college?" Anna asked.

"I know. I look much older," Rosy said. "There's always a younger, pretty girl I have to compete with, but Christophe has my back."

The dance instructor sipped his drink.

Anna felt like she was talking to living clichés. Part of her felt bad for the girl. Her dipsy personality got her paired up with a man double her age.

The Catholic priest entered next. He awkwardly stood at the entranceway, unsure if he should proceed. He wore his priestly garb and collar. After a moment of hesitation, he found a seat in the middle of the bar.

The sleep-deprived author David Hunt and his fifteen-year-old daughter quietly entered after him and sat at a booth in the back. David shut his tired eyes. He wore a twine jacket, t-shirt, and jeans. Raven was clad in black. She had straight black hair as well. Anna didn't notice them.

She approached the priest. His hands were folded on the table. His face lit up when he saw her. "Anna. How are you?"

"Wonderful, Stephen, and yourself?"

"Joyful," Stephen replied happily. "I've been having a great day."

"The clergy is not harassing you to come back?" Anna joked. The moment the words left her mouth, she was hit with remorse.

Her remark saddened Stephen. "I, uh, should probably be forthright about what happened between me and the clergy."

Anna listened, uneasy about what she was about to hear.

Stephen said, "See, I've spent my whole life learning the proper practices, reciting liturgies and shepherding a large body of believers. It was a good lot. I had everything I ever wanted. But I didn't feel anything. I was an empty cup. You ever feel that way?"

"Sometimes. What did you do?" Anna asked.

"I started digging into Scripture. I fasted. I prayed. I wept for too many nights. And, suddenly, as fast as a flash of lightning, I heard the Lord speak to me just as we are now."

"Wow," Anna said, keeping her doubts hidden.

"Yes," Stephen said, a spark of life in his eyes. "Phenomenal. The scripture opened up to me like never before. I understood the Holy Spirit, and I saw the hypocrisy of my brethren. I thought the pomp and circumstance was a way to honor God, but it was a veil keeping us from knowing Him, truly knowing Him. My whole existence was about tradition and formula. Yet, I'd finally found intimacy with Father God. No, wait, better said, he found me." Stephen smiled ear to ear. "I took this revelation to my mentors, thinking they'd all see the truth and we'd move into celebration and reformulation, but instead, they ridiculed me. I was branded a heretic. A villain of the church. They excommunicated me, and stripped me of my title and church."

Anna felt uncomfortable talking about religion. She wasn't sure what to say. God and faith had never been a part of her life. She prayed when the going got bad but was never sure to what god or force.

Stephen said, "That's a long story. I'm sorry to bore you."

"I'm always happy to hear about my guests," Anna replied.

Stephen said, "I have much to say then."

Anna smiled awkwardly. "First, let me get you a drink."

"Water is perfectly fine," the priest replied.

Anna returned to the bar.

Cameron joined the couple at the bar. They chatted about their travels. Mr. Warren invited Fritz to join him. Fritz did so. The two men didn't speak much. Fritz seemed especially uncomfortable. The priest observed them. He was jolly after sharing his story. Anna may not believe all his God-talk, but he may have good advice for handling her children. Perhaps he could help straighten out Justin. Anna could hope.

As the hour waned, the power cut off and all the guests fell silent.

21

SLASHER

*J*ustin stood perfectly still in the darkness.

His forearms rested on the lobby's cold counter.

Not even the faintest bit of moonlight escaped through the glass entrance doors and windows. His heart raced. He felt something coming toward him.

His phone buzzed.

He answered.

"Are you okay?" Anna asked from the other end.

"Fine," Justin said.

"I think a fuse may have blown. Can you check the basement?"

Justin despised that idea. "Let's wait outside until it returns."

"Justin, I'm serious," his mom commanded.

"Ugh, can't Asher do it?"

"...No. Call me when you get it back on." Anna hung up.

Justin groaned.

He turned his cellphone flashlight on. He grumbled about

how stupid this was and wished he had time to put on his GoPro.

He pressed the elevator button. It didn't work either. The outage must've affected everything in the hotel. He entered the stairwell and shined his light down the gap between the stair sets.

Justin shivered briefly for no reason. He took one step at a time.

He continued his descent. He blinked, seeing the woman in green appear in front of him. Blood poured from her neck. Her eyes were cocked and partly rolled back. Her legs were bowed. The vision ended in a flash.

Justin shook his head rapidly. He whispered, "It's not real. It's not real."

He'd taken the coward's way out last night. He swore he saw a woman die, but the evidence was against him. Part of him believed he was insane. Another part believed McKenzie's testimony. *Maybe we're both crazy*, Justin thought. He continued to the bottom of the stairs and unlocked the door to the basement corridor.

The more he thought about it, the more he believed he witnessed a real murder. There were secret tunnels all around the hotel. The killer could've stashed the body inside and the police would be none the wiser. What if it was the killer that cut the power? Justin swallowed a glob of spit. *If he's here, this ends tonight.*

Full of fear and determination, he pushed open the door and entered the basement. His light beam only revealed twenty feet in front of him. The heavy door shut behind him, locking from the outside. He could still leave, but no one could enter without the key.

As he walked, he felt a sudden wave of cold. The hairs on his arms stood. He heard a soft whisper, but the words were lost, indistinguishable.

Mustering his courage, he shouted. "I hear you! Come out!"

His voice reverberated through the dark corridor.

He continued deeper. One hand stayed on his concealed pocket knife. The moment the killer or spirit got close, he'd cut them.

He blinked, seeing a millisecond vision of a woman being beaten by a shadowy assailant.

Justin trembled.

He went eight more feet.

His foot splashed in something. He shined the light down on the crimson puddle.

He cursed and jolted back. His light shined over the walls that were now splattered with gallons of blood.

The image disappeared a second later.

He drew out the knife and held it in his shaking hand. He continued forward.

Adrenaline raced through his veins.

He felt something tugging at the back of his shirt. He twisted around and slashed. There was no one.

Fighting the urge to flee, he forced himself to continue. He walked by the steaming boiler room, not noticing the silhouetted figure in the foggy steam.

He reached the back closet and entered the generator room that had the breaker box.

He heard something shivering in the corner.

Justin turned that way. Nothing. He cursed loudly. "Just come out already!"

Silence.

Justin shouted, "I know you see me! Come on! Are you scared?"

Annoyed by the lack of response, he marched over the breaker box and yanked open its door. All the switches were set to "on." He toggled them off and then on again.

Light returned to the basement.

Justin sighed loudly.

The generator hummed.

Anna sent him a text. *"All good up here. Thank you."*

Justin pocketed his phone and knife. Perturbed, he hurried out of the basement. Maybe it was all in his head. Maybe he was crazy after all. He had blackouts during sex. That strange quirk was bleeding into the rest of his life. No one else saw the visions. No one cared. He returned upstairs.

As he repositioned himself behind the lobby counter, the limber mechanic named Fritz exited the bar. He avoided eye contact and headed for the elevator. Justin searched his name on the guest database. He was staying in Suite 211. That was near the balcony. Justin didn't trust him.

The old man was the next to leave. Andrew Warren. He nodded curtly at Justin before heading upstairs. *What is his angle?* Justin asked. *Why are you here?* It dawned on Justin that he knew none of the guests. Any one of them could've been the killer. If they know about the secret passageways, they had to be a reoccurring visitor.

The couple left two hours later. They laughed and stumbled, both drunk out of their mind. The young woman's bracelet slipped from her wrist. The man picked it up. "You don't want to lose that."

The woman put the bracelet on. "Yeah, my mom would kill me."

Unless they had split personalities, Justin was sure they weren't the killers.

Justin didn't see the writer and creepy girl Asher liked exit the bar, but they weren't there when he peeked inside. Cameron and Anna sat on stools next to each other. Anna laughed at one of his jokes. Justin wondered what sort of relationship they were cultivating. He knew his mother. He knew how manipulative she could be if she wanted.

Over the next few days, Justin observed the guests. During the day while he cleaned, he'd take extra time in the room and look over their things. He never touched or moved any of their belongings. He still had some shred of kindness in him. The couple was the most interesting. They had moved most of the furniture against the wall and opened up the floor of their suite to dance. They had leotards hanging in their closet and ballet shoes they kept clean. They also had wetsuits to dive into the freezing Atlantic.

Andrew Warren's room was tidy and neat. There were a plethora of books he'd packed into the shelf and he had a small table with a tea kettle. The old man planned on staying at Club Blue for the long run. Maybe even until he died. Justin perused his bookshelf, seeing historical texts, books about symbols, and classic novels he had marked with hundreds of notes. Unlike most of the guests, Andrew was around the hotel most days. He'd spend much of the time in the woods behind Club Blue. There were benches and nice walking paths through the trees.

Fritz owned little. He had a few changes of clothes, a TV he ran constantly, and a small work station at his desk. He'd whittle little birds out of wooden blocks. He had a brush set used to paint fine details on the figurines. Each was its own work of art. On his bathroom mirror, he'd taped a picture of a woman. She had large glasses and a slightly unattractive face. Creases were all across the photo. Fritz must've brought the picture everywhere. He was gone from 6 am to 9 pm almost every weeknight. He worked as a mechanic near one of the local shops. His minifridge was packed with beer and leftover food.

The priest came and went randomly. He lived out of a single suitcase and may have only had one set of clothes outside the priestly garments. His room was bare. The TV remote and channel surfing guide collected dust. He had not touched them since he arrived. A Bible was open on the floor beside the window. The passage was about Jesus and the adulteress woman. It read, *"Let anyone of you who is without sin be the first to throw a stone at her."*

The priest also owned a Bluetooth speaker and nothing else.

After replacing the bedsheets, Justin exited his room, confused. With so little, what did the man do all day?

Agent Cameron was in his room when Justin brought new towels. The agent scrolled through the news on his laptop. A lot of open tabs cluttered his internet browser. Justin couldn't read the title of any of them. Cameron acknowledged Justin with a brief "hello" but continued reading. The agent had packed his clothes into the dresser. He made his bed every morning. His closet door was shut. Justin didn't have a chance to look inside. He had a few books on forensic sciences near his bed as well as books regarding surgery and construction. Justin left the room not knowing much about the agent.

None of the guests did anything suspicious over the next few days and Justin had a lack of supernatural encounters. Halloween was coming up shortly. Anna had bought tons of decorations, nothing distasteful though. Asher helped hang spiderwebs and string orange and black banners through the ballroom. He isolated himself as he worked and didn't speak to Justin. Justin suspected something was up with him but didn't really care to investigate. At least his brother was doing something. *It's about time.* The decorations for Halloween were a lot of work, but Anna aimed to make it perfect.

The sun fell and darkness spilled over Sebring.

At 1:30 am, Justin finished his shift at the lobby. He locked the doors but lingered by the entrance. He was still grounded, and though there wasn't anything for him to do outside, the lack of freedom made him yearn to take a drive. He fought the urge. He needed to repair relations between him and his mother. His mission was to capture a spirit or killer on camera. Despite Mom's wishes, he kept his gear. She was too caught up with other expenses to notice Justin hadn't gotten the refund.

Exhausted, Justin returned to his room. He crashed on the bed, though he didn't sleep. His dreams had been horrible for the last few nights. He never remembered them, but he'd wake up in a cold sweat. Around 4 am, he sat up. His eyes stung. His head throbbed. He felt hot and cold at the same time. He splashed his face in the bathroom sink. His face was haggard. As someone who prided himself on his good looks, he hated seeing himself turning pale and sickly. He thought someone would take notice, but no one did. Maybe it was just another aspect of his growing insanity. His father was insane. Not clinically, though. Just violent and paranoid. Perhaps it was genetic. Tired of staying cramped up in his room, he stepped out into the hallway. He kept his pocket knife and walked to the second-floor balcony. He rested his hands on the rails and peered down at the checkered ball-room floor.

He walked to the wall next to him and rubbed his hand across it. The killer might've pulled the woman through a secret door. He studied the framed painting. He tried to move them, but they were attached to the wall. *Strange*, he thought. The portrait showed a few former Masons seated in a row. The eyes of one were black pits. They peered deep into Justin's soul. He backed away and checked the floor. There was no breach in the carpet. He walked down the steps and returned to the post where he hid during the woman's murder. He forced himself to remember. She had hazel hair and olive skin. She wore a pearl necklace and jade earrings. Her dress, from what little Justin saw from his vantage point, had shoulder stripes and was a glossy green.

The revelation hit him like a bus. It was the same woman who had the slashed throat and bloody stomach. He hadn't witnessed a recent murder. He saw a moving image from the past. No wonder why the police didn't find anything. The murder could've been years ago.

Justin's mind raced. The gore must have blinded him to the woman's beauty. She was trying to communicate with him. Maybe she wasn't the threat after all. Maybe she was warning him. Justin charged up the stairs. It seemed so obvious now. The spirit wanted his help. Looking back, she never tried to hurt him. She tried speaking, but her cut throat destroyed her vocals. As he speed-walked by to his room, he heard a loud thump in one of the suites.

Justin froze. He approached the suite where the couple was staying. He pressed his ear against the cold door.

Silence.

He waited.

Nothing.

He returned to his room and locked the upper latch on the door. He rested on his bed and locked his fingers behind his head. He needed a way to communicate with the dead woman. He needed to learn who she was.

He got up the next morning, put on his work uniform, and headed down to the lobby. His mother was already at the counter, dressed nicely and wearing a push-up bra. She must've been trying to impress someone.

"Morning," she said as Justin approached.

"Sup," Justin said. "I think I learned something last night."

"Is it another one of your crackpot theories?" Anna asked.

Justin's shoulders tensed up. "Never mind."

Anna said, "Oh, the couple in Suite 204 checked out."

Justin was intrigued.

Anna said, "Yeah. Their keys were on the counter when I got here this morning."

"But you didn't see them though?" Justin asked.

Anna shook her head. "Clean their room today."

Justin pushed his custodial cart to their room first thing. Their bed was tidy and their closet clean. Everything was spotless apart from the small dent in the wall. Justin vacuumed. Something got sucked up that made the vacuum make a grinding noise. Justin turned it off and opened the bag. He reached in and removed a bracelet. It belonged to the young blonde.

Justin pocketed it.

After cleaning the rest of the rooms, he returned to the lobby and asked Anna to tell the couple they forgot something.

Anna scanned through the ledger and gave them a call. Justin kept the bracelet in his pocket. His fingers brushed against it.

Anna said, "Hey, Rosy, this is Anna from Club Blue. My house cleaner found something of yours and wanted to know the best way to deliver it to you. Thank you. Call us back soon."

"Call them again," Justin said.

"Not right now. It wouldn't be professional. If they don't respond, we'll try in a few more days," Anna said. "What did you find anyway?"

"It's nothing," Justin said. He returned upstairs and knocked on Agent Cameron's door.

The agent answered the door. He was dressed in a white shirt and cheap jeans. He eyed Justin, unsure why he was here.

Justin pulled out the bracelet and showed it to him.

Cameron asked, "What's that?"

"It belonged to Rosy. The blonde chick down on the second floor."

Cameron replied, "Are you wanting to give it to her or…"

Justin glanced around. There was no one on the third floor. He said, "She checked out late last night and left this behind."

"Have you tried her callback number?"

Justin shook his head. "I heard something in their room last night. It was a loud knocking sound. There was a dent in their wall too."

"Why are you telling me this?" Cameron asked.

Justin's palm sweated. "I think something happened to them."

Cameron raised a brow.

Justin handed him the bracelet. "She wouldn't leave this behind."

Cameron studied the little gemstones.

VANISHED

After the teenager left, Cameron shut the door and returned to his desk. He set the bracelet beside his computer. He knew this would be the case that would get him back into the agency. He'd have to tread carefully, however. He didn't have the proper authority to conduct formal interviews or search people's homes. His former FBI director would lend him some assistance, but not until Cameron formed a compelling case. That meant he needed suspects. More specifically, a prime suspect with a strong motive.

He clicked through his open internet tabs and stopped on the Swan Song Ballet Studio webpage. The front image showed Christophe Michaels gracefully leaping across the stage. He starred in over sixty percent of the photos. The rest were beautiful young women. Cameron called the number listed.

A kind woman answered.

Cameron inquired about Christophe and his return.

"Hopefully next month. He tends to take prolonged vacations to travel. I can't give you an exact date," the woman apologized.

Going over his social media, he had a picture with his teenage son, but no wife. He must've been divorced. His son's profile was private, but the boy was eighteen and living in Florida. There was a chance no one would look for Christophe.

Rosy Julian wasn't as a loner like her partner. Much of her social feed consisted of night clubs, theaters, and other places she could dance. She appeared to love it all but was listed single under her profile description. Her tryst with her instructor must have been hush-hush. There was no link to her parents on any of her social media sites. Christophe might've been the only one to know about her stay at Club Blue. The police probably wouldn't come looking for them for a while. It would be easy to say they checked out and were lost on the road. After all, Christophe's dinged-up car was no longer in the parking lot.

Justin texted Cameron the number Christophe listed on the ledger. Cameron called and went straight to voicemail.

Late that night, Justin knocked on Cameron's door.

"I'll show you the room," Justin said anxiously.

Cameron replied, "Thanks, but I can do it alone."

The seventeen-year-old looked annoyed. "I'm the one who told you about this."

"And I'm the professional," Cameron replied. "Let me see the key."

The teenage boy sulked. He dropped the key in Cameron's palm and said, "I want it back tomorrow."

"Let me ask you something, kid. If you think these people were killed, how come you haven't called the police?" Cameron asked.

Justin brushed his hair out of his face and replied, "I don't trust them. Besides, one more scandal and this place will collapse. My mom can't handle that. Not after what happened with James."

"James was your father, right?" Cameron asked.

"In blood, yeah," Justin said bitterly.

"My dad wasn't perfect either," Cameron said, putting it mildly. "Yours died in the bathtub. I heard the police suspected foul play."

"Screw you, man," Justin said.

"I was just making a little conversation."

"Talking about James is off-limits," Justin replied. "Now, can I help you investigate or what?"

"No," Cameron replied sternly. "I can't have you tampering with evidence."

"I'm not an idiot," Justin replied, getting mad.

"Then you're smart enough to realize that one false move could derail this entire case. Fewer people. Fewer variables."

Justin crossed his arms. He set his jaw to one side. "Fine," he finally conceded. "But you keep me involved."

"We'll play it by ear," Cameron said.

Despite his frustrations, the boy left Cameron to his own devices.

The FBI agent entered the room. It had been cleaned two times over. Cameron slipped on his own pair of leather gloves just to be safe. They were soft and fit snugly over his veiny hands. He saw the small dent Justin had mentioned when he first told him about the killings. It was a snug fit for a forehead. There were no blood or hair follicles. They'd been meticulously removed. The agent pulled a blacklight from his pocket. He turned off the light in the room and found bleach stains across the entire hardwood floor. A mop had been dragged across it too. It could've easily been a custodial practice to mix bleach and mop water.

Cameron searched the bed and around the corners. The boy had found a bracelet somewhere out of sight. It remaining in the maliciously-cleaned room was an oversight. After exploring the room, Cameron exited into the hallway. He continued his search using the black light. He couldn't turn off the power in the hallway, but the black light still worked up close. He followed the hallway in the trajectory that the hidden corridors led and eventually ended up in the stairwell beside the elevator. The black light highlighted a few droplets of blood trickling down the steps. It wasn't much, but it was far more than a nosebleed. It must've leaked all the way out to the parking lot.

23

SCORCHED

*A*sher stood outside Raven's door. It was late. His homework wasn't done, but he couldn't stop thinking about her. He had avoided her since the kiss. It was just a little peck on his cheek, but he'd never experienced something so earth-shattering. Part of him thought it was wrong. He was fourteen. He should be focused on his studies and video games, not a future wife. Would they get married? How would he go about that? He didn't know a thing about women or kids. Was he in love? He didn't expect it to be so confusing and stressful. He had to speak to her and find what she really thought of him. His body temperature was through the roof. Gathering what little courage he could, he knocked his bony knuckles on the sturdy wooden door.

He quickly put his hands in his pockets. Not wanting to seem nervous, he withdrew them. Somehow, he felt more awkward and exposed. He put his hands back. *Get over yourself*, he thought. *She's just a girl. You've talked to girls before. Nothing has changed.* Except it had. Raven liked him and he wasn't sure if he liked her. Frankly, she still scared him a little bit.

"This is stupid," he mumbled and turned to run away.

Creeeak.

The door opened.

Asher's stomach dropped.

"Hey," Raven said in a monotone voice.

Asher turned back to her. He was burning up. There were stains under his armpits. "What's up?"

He clenched his fists in his pockets.

"Are you okay? You look nervous," Raven pointed out.

She knows. Oh geez. Play it cool. You're a cool guy. She likes you. You're already winning. "Me? Nervous" Asher chuckled awkwardly. "W-what are you talking about?"

"Something is definitely up with you," Raven said suspiciously.

"Y-you're funny," Asher deflected. "So are you going to invite me in or..."

"Sure," Raven said and walked into her suite.

Asher used his inhaler and stepped inside.

Click. Click. Click. David Hunt plucked away at the classic typewriter's metal keys. He finished a page and added it to the rising stack. The novel must've been over five hundred pages at this point. David hunched his back and continued writing. He scratched the back of his head furiously.

Asher closed the door behind him. A sudden wave of cold splashed over him.

"Hello, Mr. Hunt," Asher said.

Click-click-click! David typed faster.

"Mr. Hunt?"

David stopped and slammed his fist on the table.

Yelping, Asher jumped back.

The grouchy middle-aged man swiveled his chair around. He had dark circles under his eyes and extremely greasy bangs stuck to his creased forehead. He glared at the nerdy little boy. His expression softened and his shoulders deflated.

Giving the boy a pitying, pursed-lip smile, he turned back to his typewriter and continued his novel, typing much slower now.

Raven rested on her belly on the twin bed closest to the window. A book was open before her. She swayed her legs. "I heard your brother was ghost hunting."

"Huh?" Asher asked. "Justin doesn't believe in that dumb stuff."

"Well, I didn't actually hear about it." A wry grin formed on the girl's pale face. "I saw it with my own eyes."

"No no no," Asher said as he stood awkwardly by the corner of her bed. "Justin has much better stuff to do than that."

"I think he may know about the MK Ultra stuff too."

"Justin!?" Asher said astonished.

Raven shrugged. "Probably not. He's not really the brains of the family. His hunting equipment is amateur at best. An EMF reader? *C'mon.*"

Asher rubbed the back of his neck. He didn't have clue about any of this stuff. Maybe he should spend less time on his computer. Lately, he'd gotten hooked on Real-Time Strategy games. His brain fired off different ways to improve his resource management in StarCraft.

Raven kept talking about ghosts and stuff. Asher was caught up in the best way to maximize his states. *Focus,* he thought, returning his attention to the girl in front of him.

"...You just got to open your soul up to them. They'll do the rest, you know what I'm saying?" Raven asked.

"Yep," Asher lied.

"You weren't listening to a word I said," Raven said.

"Uh, no, not really." Asher grinned nervously.

Raven got an idea. "You know what?" She got off the bed, excitement in her big blue eyes.

I don't like where this is going.

Raven said, "I bet you we can do a lot better job than your brother."

"How would we do that?" Asher asked. He secretly hoped it would be something so impossible so he could shoot down her suggestion.

"Just trust me," Raven replied. "I know things."

Raven headed for the door. "Hurry. I'll show you the way."

"Okay," Asher said hesitantly. "Goodbye, Mr. Hunt."

The man was too caught up in his story to acknowledge him.

The moment the door closed behind Asher, Raven grabbed his wrist and ran down the hall.

"Whoa!" Asher exclaimed, the black-haired girl pulling him quicker than he could process what was happening.

Raven hushed him. "Not so loud. We don't want anyone to hear us."

Raven pulled him up the stairs and to the third floor. Asher was winded by the time they reached the suite with the hidden bathroom wall.

Asher rested his palms on his knees and caught his breath.

"Open it up," Raven said anxiously.

Asher surrendered the master key and let her do the honors. She pulled Asher to the bathroom and opened the secret door.

Peering into a dark, dusty corridor, she smiled gleefully. "You first?"

"Why me?" Asher said, catching his breath.

"Because you went first last time."

"Shouldn't it be the other way around?"

"Don't tell me you're scared," Raven taunted.

"I'm not!" Asher replied and stepped into the skinny tunnel. He turned on his phone flashlight.

Raven followed behind him, keeping her hands on his shoulders.

He felt tense.

Play it cool. He took a deep breath, inhaling a lung full of dust. He coughed into his sleeve.

Raven said, "Don't die on me yet."

"I'm—" Asher coughed. "Fine."

He pulled the neck of his shirt over his mouth and continued through the corridor. He reached the T-intersection. "What way?"

"To the fourth floor," Raven said.

Asher hated the idea, mainly after hearing Raven's theory behind the butterfly room. Nevertheless, he put on a brave face and soldiered on. He reached the ladder, opened the overhead latch, and arrived at his destination. Raven followed him. The painted butterflies captured her attention.

"Now what?" Asher asked.

Raven locked her elbow in his. "We find out who's staying here."

Asher strengthened his resolve. Raven's close proximity forced him to ditch his fears. He didn't have the luxury of being nervous. She'd already called him out on his lies too many times.

They stepped into the scorched hallway. Asher's flashlight was the only source of light.

Raven said, "Imagine being trapped up here when this place was on fire?"

"I'll try not to," Asher replied.

Raven ignored his comment. "It must've been horrifying."

Asher walked with her. His little heart pounded against his ribs. He glanced at her a few times but could hardly see more than her silhouette in the dark. "So, uh... are we, like, uh... together?"

Raven asked, "Right now? Yeah."

"No, I mean, *together* together. I just need to know so..." Asher didn't know where he was going with his train of thought.

Raven asked, "Would you like to date me?"

Asher stopped.

"What?" Raven said, alarmed. "Did you see one?" She squinted, scanning the darkness.

"N-no. I-I-I didn't see anything."

They kept walking.

Pressure pushed down on Asher to answer her question. He watched his feet as he went. Finding some words, he said, "I've never had a girlfriend."

"Well, I've never had a boyfriend," Raven replied.

Asher was relieved. It seemed obvious thinking back to the last conversation where Raven talked about being a weirdo. It was nice to know he wasn't living up to an impossible standard.

Raven said, "How about this: if you'll be my boyfriend, I promise I won't kill you in your sleep."

"What!?" Asher exclaimed.

Raven giggled. "I'm joking... or am I?"

"Alright," Asher said, "Just no killing."

Raven nestled her head against his shoulder and smiled softly.

I guess I'm dating now, Asher thought. He couldn't stop grinning like an idiot.

The decaying walls and pitch-black setting suddenly didn't seem as terrifying.

"So, uh, how do we track these ghosts?" Asher asked.

Raven said, "We wait. They're out here."

"Have you seen them before?" Asher asked.

A noise came from one of the suites. The color in Asher's skin flushed away.

Raven tugged at him. "Over there."

Excited, she let go of his arm and rushed to the room.

"Careful," Asher said. They lingered outside the suite and shined the flashlight through the hole in the wall from the hallway. A rat scurried under the collapsed dresser.

Asher sighed exasperatedly.

Raven was disappointed.

Asher caught a whiff of smoke. "You smell that?"

"What?"

Asher sniffled. The smell became stronger. "I think something is burning."

Raven shook her head. "I don't think so."

Suddenly, a cold hand grabbed Asher's ankle and yanked him backward.

He toppled hard, slamming his chin on the hardwood. "Raven!" he screamed as he was dragged across the floor.

The phone landed at Raven's feet, casting its light up her horrified face. Her big, terrified eyes were the last thing Asher saw before he was pulled into the nearby room.

The door slammed in his face.

He screamed and cried. "Please, noooo!"

The thing released his ankle. His leg hit the ground. He scurried to the door and tried the knob. It didn't turn. He banged on the door. "Help! Help!"

The door didn't budge. The smell of smoke intensified.

Asher shouted louder and threw his body against the door. He bounced off, not causing any damage. Shoulder throbbing, he twisted around and backed up. He hit the door. His glasses sat lopsided on his face. His eyes started to adjust, but the darkness still masked the threat.

He grabbed his inhaler with a shaking hand. He put it into his mouth and pressed down on the medicine. It didn't work. He shook it and tried it again. He noticed there was a crack on the side of his inhaler. He put it back in his pocket. Tears trickled down his cheeks.

"A-Asher?" Raven said on the other side of the door. "Are you in there?"

Asher whimpered and sank to the ground. He pulled his knees up to his chest.

"Talk to me." Raven's voice cracked. "Please."

Asher silently cried. His tears were fat and constant. His face became ugly with drool and snot. He shut his eyes. *Wake up. Please, just wake up*, he told himself.

His chest tightened.

The smell of smoke was suffocating.

Asher coughed.

Something moved in the back of the room. It was just far enough out of sight that Asher couldn't see, but he knew it was there.

The thing's feet pitter-pattered.

Asher squeezed himself.

Raven called his name from the other side. Her voice was broken and desperate.

The thing walked into view.

It was a man, or the shape of one at least. His features were masked by darkness.

Asher pulled his knees close to his chest.

The figure reached out. Its movement went from slow to insanely fast, taking Asher's shirt before he could react.

Gripped by fear, Asher let the thing drag him up the wall and use one hand to pin him there. He leaned his head in, only inches from Asher's face. He had no breath. His face was without skin. He held Asher tightly.

His mouth opened and a horrifying, throaty rattle filled the room.

Fear froze Asher.

The faceless man whispered into Asher's ear. "Help..."

"W-who?" Asher asked, wanting to get out as fast as possible.

The faceless man said, "Help... us."

The door burst open and Raven dashed inside.

Motionless, Asher rested on the floor.

Raven stopped quickly. She covered her mouth. Her eyes watered. "Asher!"

She rushed to him and shook his shoulder. His body rolled to his back. His glasses were crooked. He stared at the ceiling. Tears trickled down the sides of his face. He breathed slowly.

"Can you stand?" Raven asked.

Asher didn't react.

Raven called his name and shook him again. He blinked but refused to move.

"We've got to get out of here," Raven said. She scooped her arm under the boy and helped him sit up. "You can't make me do all the work."

Asher hunched over and almost fell to the floor.

Raven helped him stay upright and gritted her teeth. "*Really?* Really?"

Grumbling, she tucked her arm behind Asher and helped lift him. He propped against her. If she failed to hold him, he would fall. Raven guided him out of the room and hurried down the scorched hall.

24

DOUBTS

*S*eated at the corner of the mattress, Anna put her hand on Asher's forehead. He didn't have a fever, but the boy was silent, sickly pale and sweating profusely. Anna withdrew her hand and turned her anxious gaze to the window. The morning sun cast its golden rays across the unlit suite. The fourteen-year-old had been bedridden for days.

Anna sensed something wrong when he failed to be outside on a school day. She found him on the floor in his suite. Anna thought he was playing around, but her son was trembling and silently crying. She managed to get him into bed. He refused to eat. Justin had taken over parts of Anna's shift so she could check on him. Guilt flooded her heart because she'd refused to take him to the hospital.

She brushed aside Asher's bangs. "Please talk to me."

Asher stared at his reflection in the black TV screen.

"I just want to know what happened," Anna said.

The boy's emotionless expression sucked the life out of the room.

"Let me in, Asher," Anna pleaded. "Whatever it is, we'll get through it."

She stayed by his side for an hour before returning to her duties. Justin worked the counter. Anna wasn't in the mood to deal with people. She left him to complete that job while she took over custodial work. The rooms were already spotless, but she wanted something to do that wouldn't require much thinking. She was getting sick of being in her head all the time.

She re-cleaned mirrors and windows, straightened pictures, and dusted the heating vents. As she cleaned one of the suites on the third story, she discovered a button shoved in the corner. She lifted it, holding the blue button between her finger and thumb. The cute button must've belonged to that McKenzie girl. The thread on the back of it was frayed. It must've been torn off. If Justin never hurt her, why was there a sign of a struggle?

She pocketed the button and pushed the cleaning cart back into the hallway. Dressed in running clothes, Cameron walked down the corridor. He smiled at Anna. "Hey."

Anna pursed her lips.

"How is everything?" Cameron asked.

"Fine," Anna replied. He didn't know about Asher, and Anna really wasn't in the mood to discuss it.

Cameron said, "I wanted to thank you for the other night."

Anna was confused.

Cameron clarified, "Talking to me at the bar."

"Oh."

"I haven't had a chance to make any positive human connection since I got here. I was starting to feel a little stir crazy," Cameron joked. "In all seriousness though, it was a good time. I hope we can do it again."

Anna replied half-heartedly, "I'm sure we will."

Cameron couldn't tell she was distant. He put his hands in his short pockets. "I should probably get going. There's this new gym I want to try out."

Anna smirked. "Now you're really trying hard to impress me."

Cameron replied, "Maybe, but I have a feeling that it will take a lot more than a gym membership to woo you."

A small grin formed on Anna's distraught face.

Cameron said, "Anyway, I'll see you around."

He walked in the opposite direction. Anna rubbed her forehead, but it did little for her headache. Feeling the button in her pocket made her heart hurt. Stressed, she bit into her inner cheek. The pain didn't do anything to redirect her thoughts. The choice was clear: confront Justin about the button and learned what really happened that night. The truth terrified her though. She took the cleaning cart back to the janitor's closet and took a walk.

A violet gust swept dead leaves across the browning grass. Over a third of the woods was barren. The rest were gradually losing their leaves. Wearing a jacket, Anna crossed her arms to stay warm. A thirty-minute walk through the woods ended at the rocky beachside. A handful of people strolled along the water. Large waves crashed against shale. The lighthouse stood in the distance. It looked perfect against the rich blue sky.

Anna's hair blew across one side of her face. She brushed it away. She stood at the edge of the raging water. The breaking waves a few feet below sprinkled water on her shins. It seemed months since she'd taken a step out of Club Blue. She left to get groceries and other necessities, but that was goal-oriented. Standing at the edge of the water wouldn't help her sons or her hotel. As a workaholic, the idea of getting fresh air rarely crossed her mind. She worried that if she got into a leisurely mindset, it would affect her output. Momentum was her friend and in the last few months, it was the only thing that had gotten her through. Losing two staff members, hearing allegations against her son, being pushed from a window, and the million other problems she faced would've broken her if not for seeing the bigger picture: creating her own little paradise where people could lodge and forget about their problems, even if only for a night.

She removed the button and rolled it between her fingers. She stared out at the choppy waters.

"God bless you! Have a wonderful afternoon!" Stephen the priest waved at an old couple walking away from him, looking to get as far away as they could.

Making a split-second decision, Anna tossed the button into the water.

Stephen lingered near a park bench. He noticed Anna heading his way and waved at her.

Anna glanced at the couple walking away. "Getting new converts, I see."

"Sowing seeds," Stephen replied.

"Ah," Anna said, standing by him.

The priest eyed the various people around them.

"Who are you looking for?" Anna asked.

"Sorry, I have to—," He didn't finish what he was saying as he hurried to a young man and his elderly mother a few dozen feet away.

"Excuse me," Stephen said to them. "Sorry to interrupt. This may sound strange, but I feel like God has a word for you two."

The elderly woman was intrigued. The man was guarded.

Anna couldn't hear the rest of Stephen's words, but it ended with the three of them holding hands. The young man glared at Stephen as he prayed.

Anna chewed on the inside of her lip. It appeared even

God had more important people to worry about. Feeling cold, she returned to Club Blue.

She entered the side entrance and headed to Asher's suite. She wanted to ask what he'd like for dinner. The moment she stepped inside, her heart broke. Her baby boy hadn't moved since the morning. Anna lingered by his bed.

"Hey," she said softly.

Asher didn't reply.

Anna said, "I was thinking about getting Chinese food for dinner. I know it's your favorite."

Asher didn't respond.

Anna begged, "Please, Asher. We really don't have the money to take you to the hospital. I need you—this family needs you to wake up."

Asher's lips moved.

Anna moved closer. "What was that?"

He mumbled.

Excited, Anna put her ear near his mouth. "Speak louder."

Asher whispered, "He told me what happened to him."

Anna's heart pounded. "Who?"

Asher whispered, "He was still alive when he took it off."

"Baby, you're not making any sense."

Asher turned his bloodshot eyes to her. "He wants freedom."

Anna took a step away. "Who?"

"The faceless man," Asher said. He reached over and grabbed his spare inhaler from the nightstand. He blew a jet into his mouth.

"I-I don't understand."

"He was on the fourth floor," Asher said. "I spoke to him—"

"What the hell were you doing up there?" Anna exclaimed.

Asher said, "We needed to find him."

Anna wanted to tear her hair out. "You know I expressly forbade anyone from going up there. Remember Harry? He's still in the hospital. Why did you wait to tell me this?"

"Something…" Asher lowered his head. "Something very bad happened here, Mom. A lot of bad things."

"You sound like Justin," Anna said frustratedly.

"It's real. Why else would I be in this bed?" Asher said. "I was too afraid to move."

"So, it was a big act?" Anna asked.

"No, I-I-I spoke to him," Asher shuddered.

Anna knew something had happened to Asher and perhaps he did see something horrible on the fourth floor, but he was uninjured. There was no one coming after them. "Asher, I really can't deal with this right now."

They went back and forth a while longer, but Anna eventually had enough. She left the room and headed to her office. Passing through the lobby, Justin sensed she was distraught.

"Asher okay?" he asked.

"It seems like you're not the only one who thinks the place is evil," Anna went to the office and slammed the door. She sat at her desk and buried her head in her palms. She was pissed that her son would pull a stunt like that. Pretending to be sick. In some ways, she believed it. Maybe Asher saw a fleeting shadow or got scared by something in the upper rooms. What mattered was that he wasn't truly injured. Maybe it was time to sell the hotel. It had brought her nothing but grief.

She couldn't believe she was having such thoughts, but what else should she do? Everyone hated it here. She didn't have a solution for that issue, and selling would only cause more problems. Where would they live? Who would buy the property after all the potential lawsuits? How would they pay off their massive debt? Love it or hate it, Anna was in this for the long run. Though for the first time, she truly had doubts about her purchase. She only wished things would've improved since escaping her abusive husband. At what point would she catch a break? She could hope something good would come of this. No, she couldn't just hope; she *had* to believe good things would happen. She wasn't a bad person. She didn't deserve this. Everything she'd ever done had been for her family... or had it?

25

NAMES

$\mathcal{L}$ ate at night, Justin rapped his knuckles on his little brother's door.

"Leave me alone," Asher shouted.

"It's me," Justin said.

"I don't want to talk," Asher said.

"Stop being gay and let me in," Justin replied.

A few seconds later, the door opened.

Asher's eyes were puffy. His hair was a mess. His body odor was horrible. "What do you want?"

Justin pushed by him. "Shut the door."

Angered but always the pushover, Asher closed the door.

Justin sat at the two-person table near the kitchen. He commanded Asher to sit.

"I don't want to talk right now," Asher said.

"Just do as I say, okay?" Justin said.

Hesitant, Asher sat at the table. He locked his fingers together and rested his hands on the tabletop. An ugly frown hung lopsided on his round face.

Justin said, "You saw one of them, didn't you?"

"Yeah…" Asher admitted. His anger began to subside.

Justin said, "The one that keeps coming after me is a woman. I've been trying to get pictures of her."

"What good will that do?" Asher asked.

"If Mom sees that this place really is haunted, she'd let us pack our bags and leave," Justin said.

"She'll never believe us," Asher said. "Besides, I didn't see any woman."

The information alarmed Justin. "Was it the man without the face?"

"You know him?" Asher asked.

"No, but McKenzie does. That's why she snapped," Justin replied.

The comment sickened Asher.

Justin felt a righteous fire. "We have enough witnesses to convince Mom."

"Don't be stupid," Asher said. "She saw what happened to me and still didn't want to go."

"You think we should just leave then?" Justin asked. "She'll follow us. I know she will."

Asher replied, "That won't fix anything."

"It'll save our lives," Justin said.

"The faceless man doesn't want to hurt us. He desires to be free. We need to let him out," Asher said.

"Why?" Justin asked, "What makes you think he won't try to kill you?"

"He spoke to me," Asher said. "He told me how he was trapped here until he's avenged."

"If every murdered person was forced to walk the earth until their killer was stopped, we'd see a lot more ghosts," Justin said.

"This place is different," Asher said. "I know you can feel it. The cold chills. The strange sense of being watched. Nightmares. It's all tied to this location."

"Are we on some sort of Indian graveyard?" Justin asked.

"Don't be an idiot. It's because of the rituals," Asher said.

Justin seemed really confused now.

"How can you not know?" Asher asked. "Geez, you must be living under a rock. Can't you see the symbolism in the paintings and on the walls and roof? Even the tile floor has meaning. There is an Eye of Providence over the ballroom if you look carefully."

"You're making stuff up."

"I'm not! The Freemasons made this place... well, a rejected sect of the Masons that took their traditions to the extreme. Whatever sacrifices they performed cursed this place. Why do you think there's been so many accidents and bad people coming here? They're drawn to this place."

Justin didn't believe him, but he forced himself to keep an open mind. At this point, anything was possible. "Okay, so how do we break the curse?"

"Break it? Heck if I know," Asher replied. He got up and paced. "Did you know that the fourth floor was home to MK-Ultra experiments? They were using certain mind-breaking methods to make slaves."

"Where are you getting this information?" Justin asked.

"The butterfly paintings on the wall," Asher explained matter-of-factly.

"That's retarded," Justin said.

Asher shrugged. "Believe what you want, man. Truth is truth."

"Show me, then," Justin said.

"I'm not going back up there," Asher said.

"We'll go together," Justin suggested.

"No way. I thought I was going to die last time. That freak grabbed me. I couldn't do anything to stop him."

"But you said he didn't want to hurt you."

"I said he wants to be free, but I don't want to make him angry by messing around in his domain," Asher said.

"If we want to break this curse, we have to learn the truth about this place," Justin said.

Asher gawked. He collected himself. "I thought you wanted to leave."

"McKenzie is being tormented by this thing, people are getting hurt, and there is a killer lurking around here. If it's all tied to the curse, we have to understand what we're dealing with, and we can't do that unless we get our hands dirty. Long story short, if we break the curse, it won't matter if we move or not. Everyone will be okay," Justin said. He'd run for too long. Agent Cameron had rejected his help just like everyone else. This was his declaration against his cowardliness. He had nothing to lose. Well, nothing but his life. *The life of a stupid high school dropout*, he thought bitterly.

Asher said, "You can do whatever you want, bro. I'm not going up there again."

"Then, I'll go myself," Justin declared.

Asher crossed his arms and averted his gaze. "You're going to get hurt."

"So what?" Justin said. "Something needs to change, Asher. We can't keep going around in circles. I'm going to put an end to this, one way or another."

If that means confronting the faceless man, then so be it, Justin thought.

"Look, I'll help you, but I'm not going up there."

Justin stood. "Well, if I don't come back, at least you'll know what to tell Mom."

Asher asked, "Tell her what?"

Justin spoke defiantly. "That we were right."

He left his little brother and snuck into his mother's suite. She was working the night shift. Justin grabbed the fourth-floor key from the dresser. He returned to his own suite and grabbed his equipment. Fully decked out, he adjusted the GoPro strap on his forehead. Taking one last look at himself in the mirror, he marched out of his suite. He followed the stairs to the fourth floor and unlocked the door.

He stepped into the scorched hallway. The floor creaked below his skater shoes. The headlamps resting above the GoPro cast a circle of light down the black corridor. The needle on the EMF meter trembled. He checked various rooms and peered into the clogged secret passages in the wall. It looks like someone had purposefully piled debris inside. The broken walls groaned like a dying old man.

The EMF needle spiked when passing by one suite. Sweating, he pushed open the door and took a few steps back. The room lacked furniture. A tall and skinny wall mirror had a large crack down the front. A part of the ceiling had broken, leaving a small pile of burnt wood on the floor.

Justin approached, seeing his shattered reflection. He could see the hollowness of the wall behind the crack in the mirror. Justin picked a burnt wood plank from the floor and slammed it against the mirror. The glass shattered, revealing the hidden corridor. Justin pulled the EMF reader back out and stepped inside. The passage here was clear of debris. He followed it, either having to crawl in the space under the windows or climb up a ladder that would lead to a cramped space above the door. Justin found old film cameras set in different bathroom mirrors. Their film rolls were missing and the cameras were non-functional. He found peepholes in the bathrooms and behind burnt picture frames.

He followed the seemingly random spikes of the EMF reader. Eventually, it led him through a crawl space which ended at the elevator shaft. He looked down at the pit below him. The elevator was currently on the ground level. Directly across from him was a second crawl space. A rope net had been strung up across the upper wall of the elevator. Similar to what you'd see in a ship mast, you could use this web-like rope to move across the shaft and arrive at the crawl space.

That's just what Justin did. He took hold of the rope and moved to the hole. He crawled across and found a little room too small to stand in and only wide enough to have an old sleeping bag. There was a shelf nailed into the wall. Old jewelry and weddings rings rested on it like a shrine. A list of names was carved into the wall above the jewelry. The EMF reader went wild.

Not relying on his video camera to save the footage, he pulled out his phone and snapped pictures of the names. There were fourteen in total. The first and last name was listed.

The EMF reader stopped going crazy.

This appeared to be what the dead wanted Justin to find. Just in case the police needed to get involved, he didn't touch the jewelry.

Justin returned to Asher's suite. His brother was impressed by the find.

Asher reviewed the list of names. He researched them online. It took a long time, but eventually, he found them on the Missing Persons list spanning over the last thirty-five years. The last one went missing fifteen years ago.

Asher and Justin traded looks.

Asher said, "I think there was a serial killer."

With the sudden disappearance of Rosy and Christophe, Justin knew the killer was still active.

26

PAST SINS

*A*nna was at the lobby desk. More of her pens were missing. Other things were missing too. It was really getting old fast. After Asher's recovery, her head had been in a bad place. She'd started looking into hotel costs and perhaps a time to put Club Blue on the market. Someone would argue that she should've given up on Club Blue months ago when Lance attacked her, or after the discovery of the skeleton, something she'd not forgotten but actively chose not to think about. However, to understand why she kept the hotel so long, one had to look into her past.

As a child, she never had much going for her. Her parents were supportive but rather distant, and she wasn't the most attractive or the smartest in her class. She was average all the way around. It was that general *blah* attitude of life that sparked her need for escape. She loved reading romances and adventure stories set in exotic locations like the Nile or someone's old house in the middle of an ancient European home. Her parents had an affinity for travel and whenever they would go on a road trip, Anna would come along and pretend to re-invent herself. On the cruise, she imagined herself as a rich socialite with the world at her fingertips. In Japan, she imagined she was a girl on a quest for spirituality and would spend long hours walking alongside shines and graveyards. That little escape was freeing, not because she had a bad life, but because she had a mundane one.

One day, she decided she wanted to travel the world alone. She dreamed of taking a single suitcase going through the Alps or staying in a lodge on top of the Himalayas. She had this romantic vision of meeting a colorful cast of world travelers like herself and discovering the little hole-in-the-wall places that she'd forever carry in her memory. Just after college, when she was about to start her grand trip, she met James. He was a young, wealthy engineer who also longed to escape the mundane. His romantic outlook drew them together. They dated, went to a few destinations around the States, and eventually got married.

Wanting to invite people to share her same experience, Anna started working at a local hotel. She learned the ins and outs and quickly climbed the corporate ladder. Her only complaint was that the hotel wasn't romantic or located anywhere special. Many of the guests were families on vacation or businessmen wanting to save some money on room cost. Anna wanted the world travelers, the quirky hippies who lived like nomads, and artists looking for their muse in a foreign land.

Before she could act on this sense of longing, Anna got pregnant. Her goals were again put on hiatus. Her unmet expectations added tension to the marriage. James was angry because of work and feeling as though Anna had changed. Being a fellow romantic, it meant he had impossible expectations of what she should be and what their marriage should look like. Anna was never good enough and because of that, James became bitter. His bitterness turned to violence. For years, Anna was a prisoner in her home. Sure, she could go to work and to the community pool, but James forbade her to leave. Her emotional numbness angered James even more. Club Blue was more than just a nifty hotel. It was the realization of years of bottled-up dreams. It was a sign of Anna's freedom, not that she hated marriage, but the prison that was hers was shut down. Leaving Club Blue would be like putting shackles on her hands and feet.

Sure, her mind would make debt or financial instability as the main reasons for staying, but the reason was abstract and probably foolish to most people who'd never felt truly unstable in their identity.

Anna stood behind the lobby counter, pondering her exodus from Club Blue, but she knew she'd always find another reason to stay put. In a sense, the place of her freedom had become her new prison.

Father Stephen exited the elevator. He wore a sweater and slacks suitable for the chilly season. His hair was neatly combed. A few bristles grew on his cheeks and neck. He hadn't shaved recently. He approached the counter.

"How are you, Stephen?" Anna asked politely.

"Good, I, uh, wanted to apologize," the priest said humbly.

"What for?" Anna asked.

"For not talking to you at the beach," Stephen said.

"That's not a big deal. I forgot about it, honestly," Anna said.

"Be that as it may, it wasn't right for me to leave you mid-conversation," Stephen replied.

"You're forgiven, Father," Anna said.

It looked like a burden was just lifted from Stephen's shoulders. Light returned to his tender face. "Is there anything you'd like me to pray for?"

Anna said, "Oh, um, I'm not really religious."

Stephen replied, "I'm not really either."

"Isn't it a sin to lie?" Anna teased.

Stephen grinned. "I'm not religious. I'm spiritual. Relational. Yes, the latter is a more apt description."

"Is that like a New Age thing or…"

Stephen looked horrified, "No, no. It's still Christianity. In the first and second century, Christians were outcasts. They'd been driven from the synagogues and outlawed by the Romans. Followers from all walks of life met in secret, but yet proclaimed their faith openly. It's very different from what we have today."

Anna knew that. She nodded along to stay interested.

"Long story short," Stephen said, "That's what I feel called to."

Anna said, "You must be very happy."

"I am," Stephen replied.

Anna stood awkwardly.

Stephen interrupted the silence. "How about you?"

"I'm fine."

"Are you saying that to be polite?" Stephen asked.

Anna nervously brushed her fingers through her hair. "I have problems like everyone else."

"Is it your children?" Stephen asked.

"That's rather personal," Anna said sharply. She didn't know why she had so much resistance toward the man of faith. He hadn't wronged her in any way, neither had the church.

Stephen locked eyes with Anna. "They've been seeing things."

"Huh?" Anna said, playing dumb.

"Demonic manifestations," Stephen said.

Anna replied, "You've dealt with this type of thing before."

"Once," Stephen replied.

"What happened?"

"I went to a woman's house. She'd been acting strange,

cutting herself, cursing, foaming at the mouth. I thought that stuff was only in Hollywood movies," Stephen said.

The story gripped Anna. "What did you do?"

"I sat her down. We started talking. She seemed normal. None of the actions her sister had described were manifesting. I had a little doubt that she really had a problem, but being outside of the institutionalized church, I allowed myself an open mind in regard to the supernatural. I started talking to her about her life. All was good until I mentioned childhood abuse. The woman snapped. She started screaming and cursing. I was praying. After a few hours of praying against specific word curses, generational curses, and leading her through the salvation prayer, she was sobbing and worshiping God," Stephen explained.

"Well, thank God my boys aren't in that state," Anna said. "They just saw some things around the hotel that spooked them."

Stephen said, "Hmm."

"I thought they were just being dramatic, but they're pretty convinced what they saw was real," Anna explained.

"Have they been going through any stress lately?"

Anna chuckled.

"I see," Stephen replied. "Might I ask what?"

"I really shouldn't say," Anna replied.

"You can trust me," Stephen said. "I promise whatever you share won't reach another soul."

Anna sighed. "Well, Justin got accused of assaulting a girl from school and dropped out. Asher saw something on the fourth floor that scared him so bad he didn't leave bed for days. Before that, he's always playing his game or running around the hotel somewhere. I rarely see him."

Stephen said, "Well, the visions that they have had might be the result of trauma. Not everything is supernatural, but not everything is psychological either. How is the relationship with their father, if you don't mind me asking?"

"He's no longer around," Anna replied.

"I see... did he ever—ah, I feel that's a conversation for another day. What I'm feeling right now is just to pray for you and your sons. Would that be okay?" Stephen asked.

"Sure, do what you want."

Stephen outstretched his hand. Anna held it. His palms were soft.

"Father, thank you for being here," Stephen prayed. "I ask you to watch over Anna and her boys and protect them from evil. In Jesus's name, amen."

Anna was surprised by how short the prayer was. She expected a talker like Stephen to go on for five minutes, not five seconds.

Stephen said, "The Lord knows what's happening. I feel Him saying that it's going to be okay."

I sure hope so, Anna thought.

Stephen said, "Is it okay if I counsel you?"

Anna said, "I don't have the money for that."

"It'll be free," Stephen said. "I know I can talk a lot, but I'm a good listener, too. You don't have to go through this alone. I don't believe any of us are supposed to."

Anna said, "Maybe I'll give it a try."

"Great," Stephen said, "I'm free anytime. Until I can get a small group going, you'll get priority."

"That's sweet, and if you need a space to run your group, you can use the ballroom on Sunday mornings."

"Really?" Stephen said, excited.

"Yeah, no one else is using it right now," Anna said.

Stephen thanked her. "I knew God called me here for a reason." He walked to his room, a little pep in his step.

Anna wasn't sure why she opened up or allowed him to preach on Sundays. She could do with a change and perhaps

Stephen could bring something special to the hotel with his group. At this point, Anna didn't have anything to lose.

She went back to work, dwelling on the priest's words. *It's going to be okay.* It was simple, cliché even, but she couldn't remember the last time she heard it. Her phone rang.

It was the York Police Department.

Confused, Anna answered.

"This is Detective Dean Casey. Am I speaking to Anna Hall?"

"Yes, Detective. What can I do for you?" Anna asked.

"New evidence has come up regarding your husband's passing. We need to talk to you at the York Police Department as soon as possible."

"I don't understand," Anna replied, feeling like the walls of her life were suddenly closing in.

"We need to discuss the findings in person," Detective Casey said. "Hello? Are you still there?"

"Yeah... Yeah. I'm here."

"Would you be able to come by tomorrow?" Casey said.

Anna shut her eyes. "That should—that should work."

"Thank you, Ms. Hall. Have a wonderful afternoon."

The call ended. Anna sank into her chair. She rested the phone on her lap and took a deep breath. She exhaled slowly. Just when she thought life was about to take a better turn, the rug was ripped out from under her. She texted her boys, asking them to meet her in the office.

Both exhausted, the teenagers arrived within ten minutes. It didn't appear as if they had gotten any sleep either. *We're all miserable*, Anna thought, almost ready to laugh if it wasn't her life that was in shambles.

The two boys stood before her desk.

Anna said, "I have to make a trip to York. It may take a day or two."

"What's going on?" Asher asked, concerned.

"I just have to settle a few things with the police."

Asher's countenance fell. "They don't think you hurt Dad, do they?"

"No, no, I'm sure it's just to review some new findings," Anna said.

"But what if they blame you?" Asher asked.

"They won't do that," Anna reassured him.

"How can you know?"

Anna gritted her teeth. "Please, Asher. I got this covered, okay? I just need you two to take care of the hotel while I'm gone. Can you do that?"

Justin nodded slowly.

Asher asked, "What about my homework?"

"You're just going to have to do both," Anna said. "You guys know how things work. If there is a problem, call me, but only if it's a big problem. I don't want to reschedule my appointment."

"All right," Asher conceded, though he wasn't happy about the extra workload.

Justin was silent.

Anna asked, "How about you?"

Justin said, "I'm fine with it."

Asher said, "Well, I have to get back to my homework." He left without saying another word.

Justin was going to follow when Anna called out his name. The seventeen-year-old turned to her. "Please, keep an eye out. If something happens to me, I'll need you to watch over Asher."

"I know," Justin said seriously. "Make sure something doesn't happen then."

SUSPICIOUS BEHAVIOR

*A*sher made the controversial decision to call the police and tell them about the list of names. The officer asked Asher's age. Upon hearing he was fourteen, the officer told him to stop making up crackpot theories about Club Blue. There were enough horror stories surrounding that place to fill twenty books. The officer's negligence shocked Asher. He brought the information to Justin at the front desk. Like always, the hotel wasn't getting many visitors. The brothers had time to talk.

Justin said bitterly. "I don't trust the police."

"Maybe if we show them the jewelry you found," Asher replied.

Justin's eyes darted around the empty lobby. He spoke in a low, angry whisper. "Keep your voice down. If the killer is around, he'll know that we messed with his trophies and we won't have anywhere to run."

"We should tell Agent Cameron," Asher replied. "He'll know what to do."

"No. He'll keep us in the dark. The moment we turn over

the information, we open ourselves up for an attack," Justin said.

"But there's a pretty good chance the killer isn't around. The last missing person was fifteen years ago," Asher reminded him.

"The last missing person he marked in that spot," Justin said. "The killer could've just moved his trophy room elsewhere."

Asher said, "You know who I think it is? The concierge."

"The what?"

"The guy who sold this place to Mom. He was super suspicious, and rumor has it that no one has been able to reach him since he sold the building. 'Sides, he would know about all the secret passages," Asher said.

Justin thought about it. "Maybe you're not so gay after all."

"I don't know what that has to do with anything, but okay," Asher said. *Besides, I have a hot chick waiting for me right now*, Asher thought proudly. He started thinking about Raven. He hadn't spoken to her since the encounter on the fourth floor. The more he thought about her, the more beautiful she became. The dark circles under her eyes aside, she had a pretty face. Blemish-free, too, which was rare for girls his age.

Justin snapped his fingers.

Asher was torn from his imagination.

Justin said, "You're staring off like an idiot. What's going on?"

"Nothing, just thinking," Asher said. "You know that Raven girl—"

Justin replied, "Have you kissed her yet?"

Asher's face turned red. "What? No."

"Then why are you talking about her?" Justin asked.

"Let's focus on the killer, okay?"

Justin said, "As I was saying, we shouldn't tell Cameron. He is a suspect too."

"How come?" Asher asked.

"Just because he works for the FBI doesn't make him the good guy," Justin said. "Let me tell you something, Asher. Never just trust someone because they're in a position of authority. There are A-holes in every layer of society. You got to look out for yourself."

"I do," Asher replied. "I'm the one who talked to the faceless man, remember?"

Justin chuckled, "Whatever happened to being too scared to go up the top floor?"

"I'm not scared. I'm smart and after a few days of thinking, I think it's pretty cool to say that I faced down a ghost," Asher said proudly.

Asher could tell his brother was impressed, even though he had his normal guarded expression.

Justin said, "I've been watching the residents for a while now. They're all suspicious if you ask me."

"And you want us to keep spying on them?" Asher asked.

"Until we can be sure they're innocent. True, people like Cameron would've been too young to have killed some of the victims, but he might've been involved in the rituals you talked about. Remember there is that old man who is a Freemason," Justin said. "Lastly, there is that strange priest and the quiet mechanic."

"We can spy on them, but how will we know who is innocent?" Asher asked. "This guy has been killing for years and may know the layout of the hotel."

Justin said, "People are their true selves when no one is watching. Use the secret tunnels to your advantage."

Asher said, "This is getting exciting."

"Just tell me what you find," Justin said. "I'll man the desk and write down who is coming and going. Perhaps we can spot a pattern."

Asher went his own way. He started by following the priest mainly out of convenience. Asher knew how to navigate the network of tunnels on the third floor and reached his room easily. Standing behind the bathroom mirror, he saw the priest brushing his teeth. Asher felt weird knowing that he could see the man and the man couldn't see him. The priest walked back to the living room. Asher scooted through the passageway. He was careful not to make any noise. He stood behind a painting hung above the TV. A tinted piece of glass covered by a thin layer of see-through paint allowed Asher to see the entire room. The priest walked to the window. He lowered himself to the floor and read his Bible.

Asher watched him for a while, getting bored rather quickly. He hoped his spying would be like a movie where all the boring stuff was cut out. That obviously wasn't the case. Asher pulled out his Nintendo DS and played his video game on mute. The hidden corridor was hot. Asher sweated like a pig.

After forty minutes of reading, the priest stood. He started to pace and talked to himself. He mumbled mostly. Asher couldn't make out the words. At one moment, he was laughing with the biggest smile and the next he was silently crying. Asher watched in horror. The man started to dance and sing like a madman before speaking in an unknown tongue.

Asher shifted uncomfortably.

The priest lifted his hands to the ceiling and loudly declared hallelujah. Asher stayed watching. After a long time of strange worship, the priest sat on the edge of his bed. He shut his eyes and his opened palms rested on top of his thighs. A large smile lingered on his face. Asher would've sworn that the man was high, but at no point did he take any drugs. The priest stayed in that catatonic state. Asher took a note of it on his phone. Wanting to see the other guests, he left the unorthodox priest alone and continued down the musky corridor.

He exited the secret passage, crossed the hallway, and discovered an access point through the janitor's small closet. It led to the secret tunnels on Agent Cameron's side of the third floor. He followed the tunnel to the last suite. He spied on the room from the other side of the living room wall mirror. The agent wasn't home. His room was tidy. Everything was immaculately organized. Unsure when he'd be back, Asher returned to the hallway.

He stepped out of the janitor's closet just as the priest exited his room. Whistling, the priest walked in the opposite direction, not noticing Asher. He entered the stairwell. Asher jogged after him. He entered the stairwell, seeing the outside door closing. The priest was fast. Asher hurried down the stairs. He pushed open the outer door and watched the priest walking in the rain. His heads were in his pockets. His head was in the clouds. He welcomed the rain as he strolled through the woods.

Asher stayed in the doorway where it was dry.

The priest walked around for five minutes before turning back to the door. Asher closed it carefully. He raced up the stairs and peered down. He waited.

Wet from the storm, the priest entered. He ascended the steps. Asher watched him return to his room. Asher went to the second floor and entered the room where Anna had discovered the skeleton. He wasn't sure where the secret door was, so he spent a solid thirty minutes pushing on different walls and touching various objects. He pressed one of the tall wall mirrors near the closet. It spun around like a revolving door.

Asher entered and squeezed through the tight corridor.

He landed behind a mirror in Andrew Warren's room. The old man sat at a chair by his window listening to a twenty-something-year-old talk about her job. Her eight-year-old daughter played with dolls on the floor. The man was quiet, polite, and wholesome. The twenty-something-year-old must've been his daughter or granddaughter. She was pretty, young and wholesomely dressed. Judging by her age, she must've had her daughter when she was a late teenager.

Asher spied on them for a while. The old man was an expert listener. When it was time for his guests to leave, he hugged them and escorted them to the door. He spent the rest of the afternoon watching TV and napping. Bored out of his mind, Asher decided to take a break from scouting and walk through the hotel. He snuck into the bar, hoping to play his game without anyone noticing.

Much to his shock, James Hunt was seated in the back booth and typing on his classic keyboard. An unlit cigarette hung out of the unkempt writer's lip. He appeared to be so caught up in his narrative to light it. Impressively keeping his cigarette in his mouth, he sipped a glass of bourbon. He didn't acknowledge Asher's entrance.

He shouldn't be in here, Asher thought. The bar was closed until Mom got back. Asher didn't have the guts to confront him. Also, he didn't want to make Raven mad by throwing him out. Leaving the man to his own devices, Asher went to the ballroom and got lost in his video game.

His phone dinged.

Fritz is home, Justin wrote.

Asher put his phone away and proceeded upstairs to his last suspect. He watched Fritz through a peephole behind the bed.

Wearing his grimy jumpsuit, the lumbering man shouted into his phone.

"Oh, you want the car too? The house wasn't enough?"

Bitterness laced Fritz's words. "... Uh, huh. Sure. I'm the *problem*. Your life was *perfect* before you met me... Tell Jim! I don't care. He won't do anything... Good! Do it!"

Fritz hung up the cellphone and threw it. Asher flinched, thinking it would hit him. The bed's pillow absorbed the blow. Fritz stood in place. He boiled in rage. He sat at the edge of the bed and squeezed fistfuls of the covers. He cooled down and turned on a crappy Western. He looked like he'd spend the rest of the night watching TV.

Asher sought out Raven and found her seated on the railing surrounding the ballroom. She gently swayed her legs. Her head was tilted down, looking at the tables, chairs, and checkered floor.

Asher cautiously approached. "What are you doing?" His voice wavered.

Raven patted the railing next to her. "Join me."

"Uh... That's not really that safe."

"Okay, bye then." Raven pushed on the railing, ready to jump.

"No!" Asher shouted as he ran to her.

Raven stopped herself. Giggling, she swiveled around to face Asher. "Gotcha."

Asher caught his breath. "Don't do that."

"Afraid I was going to get hurt?" Raven asked.

"Yeah. Duh," Asher fixed his drooping glasses. "Haven't we had enough near-death experiences?"

"What's life without a little risk?" A cruel smile crawled up Raven's face.

"I don't think I'll ever understand you," Asher replied.

Raven said, "You should be thanking me."

"For what?"

"Saving you from that thing on the fourth floor," Raven replied. "Also, has there been a reason why you haven't spoken to me since then?"

Asher rubbed the back of his neck. "I've been busy."

"You're a terrible liar," Raven said pointedly.

"Look, it's just a lot to process," Asher replied. "I thought my mind was going to explode after we got out of there. I didn't want to leave my room."

"Scaredy cat." Raven stuck out her tongue.

Asher said, "It's called being smart."

"If you were smart, you wouldn't have gone upstairs in the first place," Raven reminded him.

"It was your idea!" Asher explained.

Raven thought for a moment. "Oh, it was, wasn't it?" She giggled to herself.

Asher put his hands in his pockets. He glanced around the empty ballroom. Raven stayed seated on the rail but was facing Asher's way.

What do I do now? Asher thought. He had a girlfriend. Kind of. But what did that mean? Asher wasn't sure. Raven craned back her head and studied the ceiling mural. Asher felt the room getting awkward.

"I've been hunting a killer," Asher said.

Raven's eyes widened. "Excuse me?"

Asher took a few steps closer. "I can't really talk about it."

Raven slid off the railing and walked until she was a foot from him. "You've got to start from the beginning."

Standing so close made Asher feel nervous. He put on a strong face. "My brother and I found a list of names carved in the elevator shaft... well, more like in a little tunnel by the elevator shaft."

Raven was greatly intrigued.

All the attention made Asher want to tell her everything. However, he knew Justin would kill him. "I really can't say any more about it."

Raven crossed her arms. "Then I don't believe you."

"But I'm telling the truth."

"Liar."

Asher's pride flared up. "I have proof."

Raven gave him an *oh really* look.

Asher said, "The list of names matched up with a bunch of missing people. The couple that was staying here a little while ago went missing, too. Now that could just be a coincidence, but I believe it's much more."

Raven lit up with excitement. "You're tracking a real killer."

Asher nodded. "I guess I am. But, he could be someone who did all his dirty work years ago. The most recent name on the list went missing fifteen years ago."

"A cold case," Raven said. "This is awesome."

"That's all I can share right now," Asher said. He didn't want her to investigate the suspects on her own and ruin the whole operation.

Raven asked, "Have you found out how he killed his victims?"

Asher said, "No."

Raven replied, "Oh well. It's still cool."

"Not really. If he learns that I'm tracking him, he'll kill me. Please, Raven. Don't tell anyone," Asher begged.

"Who would I tell?" Raven asked.

"I don't know. Your dad," Asher guessed.

"You don't have to worry about me. I know how to keep secrets. If you knew the stuff I'm hiding, you'd faint," Raven said.

Asher wasn't sure what to say to that. He said, "I want to involve you, but I don't think Justin would like it."

"Your brother is such a buzzkill," Raven replied.

"He stood up for me when no else would," Asher said.

"I didn't know you respected him that much?" Raven asked.

"He's my older brother. The guy has been through some stuff, but he's not an idiot," Asher replied.

Raven admired his respect for Justin. She asked, "Who do you think is the killer?"

Asher replied, "I wish I knew."

Raven took his hand. "We'll find out together."

Asher smiled at her.

Not wanting to mess up the investigation, Asher convinced Raven that they should relax and investigate after they were rested. He took her back to his room and they played video games until late in the night. At 1 am, he walked Raven back to her room. She hugged him goodnight and slipped inside the dark suite.

Exhausted from the day of spying, Asher walked to his suite when someone called his name.

He turned his head. Andrew Warren stood in the hallway. He wore an ironed button-up, dark slacks, and fancy black shoes.

"Hey, Mr. Warren," Asher said awkwardly.

"Come here for a minute," the old man beckoned.

Asher contemplated running to his room. Afraid of being rude, he obeyed the man. Standing in the middle of the hallway in the dark of night left Asher in an awkward position. If this man was the killer, Asher's only defense would be to scream.

He came to a stop about two yards from the elderly man.

"How are you?" Warren asked kindly.

"Good," Asher replied. He buried his hands deep in his pockets.

"I didn't see you today." Warren sounded like a concerned friend.

"I was caught up in other stuff," Asher said. "Do you need a new towel or something?"

"No, I'm okay. I just thought it was strange you or your

brother didn't house clean today. Is your mother around?" Warren asked.

"Not right now," Asher said, wishing that he hadn't revealed that information.

Warren hunched over slightly, resting his hands on his knees. "You're a bright young man, Asher."

"Thank you, sir," Asher replied.

Silence lingered between them.

Asher said, "I should probably get to bed."

"Of course." Warren straightened up. "I just wanted to tell you that you have a bright future ahead of you. A young man that learns the value of hard work at a young age is destined to go far."

Asher smiled awkwardly.

"I'll let you get back to it then," Warren said.

Warren returned to his suite. As he stepped inside, Asher said, "Mr. Warren."

The elderly man turned his head to him.

Asher asked, "Are you really a Freemason?"

A smile grew on the side of Warren's mouth. "What do you know about the Masons?"

Asher glanced down. "I know they do a lot of rituals. Some of them used to live here."

Warren stepped out of the doorway to his suite. The door clicked shut behind him. "There's a lot of rumors about the Masons these days. Some of them are quite disturbing."

Asher wasn't sure what he'd gotten himself into.

Warren said, "The Masons aren't a secret society. They are a brotherhood. A fraternity, some might say. Do you know what is?"

"It's like a club," Asher replied.

Warren nodded. "Yes, a very special club. I've been at this lodge most of my life. Some of my fondest memories are within these walls."

Asher thought. *Literally within the walls or figuratively?*

Warren continued, "My brothers have moved on, but I keep the torch lit. What we have shouldn't be forgotten, but passed down into the next generation of bright young men."

"But don't you kill people in your rituals?" Asher asked, instantly regretting he let his tongue slip.

"Where did you hear that nonsense?" Warren asked.

Asher shrugged.

"Listen carefully. Whatever lies the internet or other sources are trying to fill your head with are ill-founded. Only the initiated understand our modus operandi."

"But what about your sacrifices and all your cryptic messages?" Asher asked. He knew he was digging his own grave, but curiosity got the better of him.

Warren asked, "Do you wish to have wisdom?"

"Yes," Asher nodded. He got ready to run if the man took a step closer.

Warren said, "You can't transmute gold into lead. Why?"

"Because they're two different things," Asher guessed.

"Good," Warren said. "But some great men have claimed to have done that very thing."

"What does this have to do with sacrifices?" Asher said in a loud whisper.

Warren said, "You'll see. Answer me this, how would you produce gold out of lead?"

"You can't. I just said they're two different things," Asher said. "I guess you try painting one, but that wouldn't be real."

Warren replied, "Exactly. Can a pear tree grow pomegranates?"

Asher shook his head.

"Why?" Warren asked.

"Because plants can only grow their type of fruit," Asher said. He was uncertain where this was going.

Warren asked, "Can you expect a man to change the fruit of his life if he's caught in a certain way of thinking?"

"Maybe," Asher replied.

"He can't," Warren declared.

Asher was confused. "People change all the time."

Warren said, "Their actions, sure. But what about their heart and mind? The core of who they are?"

Asher thought aloud. "Gold can't change. Lead can't change. Man can't change, either... man, that's depressing."

"There is a way," Warren said.

"How?"

Warren said seriously. "He must become gold."

"That's impossible," Asher said. "We are who we are."

"Not if he is born again," Warren said. "To be born again, the old way must die. Completely. Only by being gold at the beginning can he be gold forever. Only by being a new tree can he produce new fruit."

Asher asked, "So you're saying that the sacrifice you perform is your identity, not actual life... right?"

Warren smiled proudly. "I knew you were a smart young man."

Asher smiled with his pursed lips.

Warren said, "The lodge where you stand doesn't follow the ways of the traditional Masonic order, but our knowledge is very much the same. We simply apply it differently." He yawned. "My, it's late. I should get to bed. My granddaughter is coming over tomorrow and I don't want to be snoring her whole visit."

He reopened his door.

"Mr. Warren," said Asher.

"Hmm?"

"What sort of fruit are you bearing?"

There was a twinkle in Warren's eye. He wished Asher a good night and vanished into his suite.

CHERRY

*J*ustin sat behind the lobby counter and scrolled through the FBI's "Most Wanted" list on his mother's laptop. There were no known killers around Sebring, Maine. Apart from the hotel fire in the 1960s, Sebring didn't have much of a known history. Justin was suspicious of anything too clean. Looking into his own life, he knew no one was perfect.

He rubbed his eyes. Lack of sleep had become his new normal. Asher was currently away for school. He was supposed to keep an eye on the guests. The strangest of the bunch was the priest. According to Asher's text, the man was on a different plane of reality.

The day dragged on. A few new guests arrived, paid for a single night, and were given suites on the second floor. Justin wasn't always good with striking up a conversation and failed to ask what they planned to do during their short stay. From what he overheard, he gleaned they were attending a wedding.

Asher got home around 4 pm. He had a lot of homework and would have to take a break from spying for the night.

Justin wasn't happy, but let his brother make his own choices. Hopefully, his little brother would realize that a serial killer was a much bigger threat than a few bad grades. Justin grumbled to himself, lamenting school. He hated it while he was there and he hated it even more now he was gone. Deep down, he knew the reason for his disdain was his own failure. If he'd been clever enough, he could've convinced his peers that he didn't do anything to McKenzie she didn't ask for. If he wasn't so concerned with the opinions of others, he wouldn't hide out in the hotel all day. If only McKenzie would step up and speak the truth about him. He hadn't heard anything since the night he visited her. The faceless man probably still stalked her. He might be trying to express his desire for freedom to her.

Justin paced around the lobby to keep himself awake for long hours. Around 9 pm, a young woman arrived. In her twenties, she had short cherry-blonde hair, a cute face, and wore a large coat to cover her tight belly shirt and short shorts. She had dark eye shadow, red lipstick, and a distraught expression. By her quick pace and the way she constantly looked behind her, Justin could tell she was in trouble.

She leaned against the lobby counter.

"Hey," she said, tucking her hair behind her ear. "I need a room."

Justin gave her the standard rate.

The woman quickly said, "I don't have any money. Please, I'll leave early tomorrow morning. No one will know I'm here."

"What's your name?" Justin asked.

"Cherry," the woman replied. "How about you?"

"Justin."

Cherry's smile didn't fit the worry in her eyes. "Justin. I'm at the end of my rope here."

"Who's coming after you?"

Cherry shook her head. "Don't ask me that, sweetie. I'll only get you in trouble."

"I'm capable," Justin said.

Cherry looked him up and down. She seemed to acknowledge his strength. Justin knew it was an act. She said, "The best thing you can do for me is let me stay."

Justin grabbed a suite key from inside the key cabinet.

Cherry watched his hand. She wanted that key more than water.

Justin placed it in her palm. "Suite 213. It's near mine."

"You're amazing," Cherry said.

"Do you have any luggage?" Justin asked.

"Just me," Cherry replied. She saw the door to the bar. "Is that closed?"

Justin said, "At the moment. You want a drink?"

Cherry raised her trembling hands just above waist level, showing them to Justin. "Just something to take the edge off."

"Go on in," Justin said. "It's unlocked."

Cherry asked, "What am I allowed to drink?"

"Whatever, just as long as you leave some in the bottle," Justin replied.

Cherry's wide smile seemed much more genuine now. Her expression quickly returned to worry. "You promise I don't have to pay."

Justin replied, "It's on me."

"Nothing at all?"

Justin put out his pinky. "Pinky swear."

Cherry locked pinkies with him. "You're the best."

"Enjoy your drink," Justin said.

Cherry walked to the dimly-lit bar. The sway of her skinny hips and paleness of her long, bare legs drove Justin crazy.

He quickly put to death his perverse thoughts. He'd had

enough trouble with women since he got here. He wasn't going to fall prey to his worst desires anymore. Still…

Justin kept an eye out on the lobby's front door. He blew his breath out of the corner of his mouth and didn't blink. His mother really needed the money the girl could've provided. The booze cost might be high too. Justin didn't regret giving Cherry a free pass. If she proved to be trouble, he could throw her out.

Around thirty minutes later, Justin's curiosity got the best of him and he walked into the bar. Cherry sat alone at the bar, drinking a hard apple cider through a straw. She glanced over to Justin, looking guilty as heck.

"Relax," he said.

"I thought you came to collect the tab," Cherry replied.

Justin lingered by the door. He wanted to keep an eye on the desk. He glanced at the wall of drinks. "Out of everything you could've gotten, you chose that?"

Cherry said, "It tastes good."

Justin glanced back into the lobby.

"Who are you looking for?" Cherry asked.

Justin said, "No one, really."

"You don't need to worry about me."

"I don't know about that. You're kind of a mess."

Cherry laughed at his joke. "Alright. I won't argue with you there."

"Where are you from?" Justin asked.

"No questions about that," Cherry replied. "You can ask about my favorite color."

"Is it red?"

Cherry clapped politely. "Well done."

Justin laughed briefly.

Cherry said, "You should probably head back in there."

"Why?"

Cherry replied, "Cause I'll just waste your time."

"It might be time well spent," Justin replied. The idea of resisting his passion waned the longer he looked at her.

"I know what you're after," Cherry said.

"What's that?"

"You have the look," Cherry said.

Justin replied, "I don't have anything."

"Uh-huh." Cherry nodded exaggeratedly.

Justin snapped back into his right mind. "I'm not that type of guy."

"Prove it," Cherry kindly challenged him.

Justin smirked. He said politely. "Enjoy your cider,"

Cherry raised her bottle slightly. "See ya, Justin."

He returned to the lobby.

A little while later, Cherry left the bar. She waved Justin goodnight and headed to the elevator.

Justin felt anxious. What if whoever she was running from decided to show up? What if they had a gun? Justin wished he had a weapon.

An hour passed. He researched local restaurants and found a Chinese place that offered quick delivery. He placed a large order. Asher would have to fend for himself. When the Chinese food arrived, he paid with his mom's business card. He put up the "away" sign on the counter and headed into the elevator.

He stepped out on the second floor.

A sudden cold chill made him shudder. He saw the woman in the green dress standing at the end of the hallway. Her head was tilted to the side. Unmoving, she watched Justin.

Taking a deep brief, he continued down the hall and passed the premonition. Once she was behind him, Justin hastened his walk. He crossed through the ballroom and to the other side of the second floor. He arrived at Suite 213 and knocked.

Cherry cracked the door open.

Justin said, "I thought you might be hungry."

Cherry opened the door. "Wow. You really are trying hard. Come on in."

Justin stepped past her. He put the bag on the table.

Cherry closed and locked the door. "I imagine you'll want some, too."

Justin pulled out the rice cartons, noodles, and proteins. He put them neatly in the middle of the table.

Cherry said, "I better not have a large bill waiting for me tomorrow."

"You don't have worry about that," Justin said.

"A lot of people say that, but then right before I leave, they always ask for a favor," Cherry said.

"They sound like crappy human beings," Justin said.

"And you're the savior I've been waiting for?" Cherry asked.

Justin didn't reply. He finished setting out the food and walked to the door. "Enjoy your stay."

"*Enjoy this, enjoy that,*" Cherry playfully mocked him. "Did they train you to be this polite or are you just led astray by a pretty face? How do you make any money? Your manager must be furious."

"Goodnight," Justin replied. "Call the lobby if you need anything."

He turned the doorknob.

"You're not going to eat with me?" Cherry asked.

Justin stopped. He knew walking away was the smart option. He knew someone should be watching the lobby at all times.

Justin returned to the table. "I can only give you five minutes."

"Breathe," Cherry said. "I was more concerned about the cab driver would do to me than the rest of them."

Justin took a seat across from her.

Cherry said, "He's one of the ones who asked for a tip."

Justin replied, "Stuff like that pisses me off."

"That's the world, hon," Cherry said, breaking her chopsticks.

"I wish it weren't," Justin said. "I'm sick of hating everyone."

"I feel ya." Cherry twisted noodles around her chopsticks.

Justin ate a spicy piece of beef. He wished he'd gotten a drink.

"So," Cherry said, chewing. "What's one thing you never told anyone?"

Justin leaned back in his seat. "That's an interesting question coming from you."

"C'mon. I'm here for one night. Whatever you say, the world will never know," Cherry said.

Justin thought on the question. He knew the answer but purposely delayed. "I... I almost killed someone."

Cherry cursed. "Why?"

Justin frowned. "He was bad. He hurt a lot of people. I was going to get him in his sleep, but..." His voice trailed. "You don't want to hear this."

"You ran, didn't you?"

"I did something worse than running. I stayed put," Justin said. "Every day, I watched him hurt more and more people."

Justin balled his fists.

Cherry put her warm hand on his. She looked him in the eyes and spoke with deep sincerity. "I understand."

Justin's eyes watered. He quickly blinked back the tears. *Stop being weak. Man up. She's watching you.* Justin pulled away his hand. "I should get going."

"You haven't heard my big secret," Cherry said.

Justin stayed put.

Cherry opened her purse. She pulled out a folded photo.

She opened it and showed it to Justin. It was a baby girl, no more than two months. "Her name is Shana."

"She's cute."

Cherry said. "The clinic doctors took her out, but she was still breathing. They offered to let her go gently. She was so tiny and pink, and moved her little fists like she was driving a car," Cherry chuckled and cried at the same time. "I couldn't let them do it. Even if they would stay hush-hush."

Justin listened intently, having never heard of such a thing happening.

Cherry smiled sadly to herself. "There would be too many questions if I brought her home. I took her to a hospital nearby and dropped her off outside. I'd stop by every few weeks, but I couldn't get near her without raising any red flags. She was with the rest of the new babies."

"Wow, could you tell it was her?" Justin asked. "Most infants look alike."

Tear-stained black mascara ran down her cheek. "When they were removing her--the clinic doctors—they got parts and pieces, but not the whole."

Justin was the one who took her hand this time.

Cherry wiped her tears. "I shouldn't be crying. It makes me ugly."

"That's not true," Justin said.

"You're a sweet guy, Justin." She gently squeezed his hand.

Justin asked, "Where's Shana now?"

"With her family. Her new family. I'm going to see them, even if they don't want me," she said with determination.

They finished their meal. Cherry teased Justin to lighten the mood. At the end of it all, Justin knew he had to return to his duties. He tossed out the empty food containers, put the leftovers in the minifridge, and double-checked the bathroom to make sure she had everything she needed.

Cherry walked him to the door.

Justin lingered in the threshold. "What time are you thinking about leaving tomorrow?"

"Early," Cherry said.

"Let me know. I want to see you off," Justin said.

"To collect my bill?" Cherry joked.

Justin grinned. "I'll see you tomorrow."

Cherry watched him as he walked down the hall. Smiling sadly, she shut the door.

29

LOVELESS

*T*he phone alarm beeped loudly.

Justin awoke quickly and shut it off.

The clock read 4 am.

Justin threw on his work uniform, combed his hair, and brushed his teeth. He took the stairs, hoping the exercise would energize him. He jogged in place behind the lobby desk. He kept watching at the elevator door. Justin's heart raced. He wanted to be there when she left.

At 7 am, Justin got tired of waiting. He walked into the kitchen, cooked scrambled eggs and hash browns, put them on a nice plate and tray he found, and carried it to Suite 213. He knocked on the door.

Silence.

Justin felt bad wanting to wake Cherry, but she told him that she was the one who wanted to leave early. He had felt more vulnerable around her than any human being, and he'd known her for less than eight hours. Sure, she was pretty, but she felt more relatable than any other woman he'd been around.

He knocked again.

He thought of ways to convince her to stay. She could hide out in the hotel. Perhaps Mom could give her a job on staff. They needed the extra help. Cherry needed the money. Everyone wins. Of course, Cherry had her baby she wanted to get back to, but what's another few months when the child was young? Justin barely remembered anything before the age of five.

Not getting any replies from the knocks, Justin decided to unlock the door. It was a super creeper move and he knew it, but hopefully, the breakfast would soften the blow. If she really had a problem with him, she'd just send him away. Justin wouldn't be pushy. He just wanted her to know that she wasn't like other girls in his life.

He opened the door and slowly opened up the dark room. "Hey, it's me. I got you some food. Can I come in?"

He stepped inside and toggled the light switch. Holding the tray in one hand, he walked through the stubby entrance hall and into the main room. The bed was empty and unmade. The bathroom was dark. All of Cherry's stuff was gone.

Justin's heart sank.

An overwhelming sense of sorrow fell over him.

She must've left around a lot sooner than Justin thought. He thought he'd see her cab pull up to the front to get her, but perhaps he was too late. He could've missed her by minutes.

Justin stood in the empty suite, holding the breakfast tray and feeling like an idiot. His sorrow turned to anger. He set his jaw to the side of his mouth. Tired and annoyed, he hurried out the door. He locked it, returned to his suite, and ate the food. He crawled into bed and passed out.

30

LIGHT AND DARK

*E*arly Sunday morning, Asher sat in the ballroom and set his laptop on the round table before him. Recently, English class was making him flex his literary muscles and now he had a strong inkling to journal about his own life. He opened a Microsoft Word document. The intimidating blank page covered the screen. The word cursor blinked. His fingertips rested on the keys. Suddenly, his mind became blank and he got his first taste of writer's block.

Yesterday, he spent the whole day writing an essay and completing his excessive algebra homework. He didn't get a chance to spy on the guests, but Mr. Warren's word about being born again stuck with him. Asher always saw himself as a gamer. He didn't have any big dreams or high ambitions. All he wanted out of life was a comfy place to sleep, some good food, and a screen to occupy his time. In light of his recent supernatural encounters, he longed for something more. He also felt lame not having any real accomplishments to show off to Raven. He needed to become something more if he wanted to solve this mystery and keep his girl. He hoped journaling would help put his life into perspective so he could see where he needed changes.

Raven was the first thing he wrote about. He described their first encounter in the bowling alley and her strange father. He talked about her extensive knowledge of the hotel's history and her fascination with sinister things. She wore black clothes that made her look like Wednesday Addams from the *Addams Family*.

Asher went on to detail his encounter with the faceless man. He described being dragged across the floor and pinned against a wall. The darkness of the room hid the man's gruesome features. "*Free me*," he said.

As he started to catalog the various guests, the priest entered the ballroom. He waved at Asher and grabbed chairs from various tables. He made a half-circle around the dance floor and set a final seat to face the rest. That was the one he chose for himself.

Fritz and Cameron entered a few minutes later and joined the small circle.

The priest greeted them kindly. "Thank you for coming by. Anna was nice enough to lend me the room on Sunday mornings."

Cameron said, "I have to admit, Father. I'm not much of a Catholic."

Stephen said, "We're all after something real. That's what matters. How are you doing today, Fritz?"

Fritz shook his head.

"Hopefully a little bible study will cheer you up. You can get the Bible app on your phone, by the way," Stephen said. "Anyway, let's open up with prayer."

The impromptu church-service-thing distracted Asher. He put on his headphones, blocking out all noise, Asher copied the list of missing people into his new Microsoft Word document. He posted links to their FBI profile as well.

He saved the document on the Cloud. If something happened to him, he hoped that the police would be able to finish the investigation. He leaned back in his chair and stretched.

Stephen's service ended. He put his hand on Fritz's forehead and prayed into his ear. After a moment, the lumbering mechanic fell into Stephen's arms and wept loudly. Cameron stayed a few feet back and observed. Asher felt awkward being in the same room as the rest of them. Stephen helped Fritz find a seat. He turned to Cameron and asked if he'd like a prayer. The FBI agent refused.

Stephen sat beside Fritz and stayed with him until the lumbering man had stopped crying long enough to leave.

Cameron moseyed his way toward Asher.

Asher took off his headphones. "Yeah?"

Cameron lingered by his table. He spoke quietly. "What do you know about Stephen?"

"He's a priest," Asher said.

"I was looking for something less obvious. Have you noticed any strange behavior?"

Seated next to Fritz, Stephen pointed to Scripture on his phone and explained it passionately.

Asher replied to Cameron's question in a whisper. "He likes to talk to himself."

"Probably praying," Cameron said. "Does he have any friends around here?"

"I haven't seen anyone," Asher said.

"Does he take a lot of phone calls?"

"Not that I know of," Asher said. "Do you think he's a suspect?"

"Suspect in what?"

"Justin told me about your investigation," Asher replied.

Cameron said, "I didn't realize your brother liked to talk. Does he still think that someone killed the couple a few weeks ago?"

"Maybe," Asher replied. "I think a lot of crazy stuff happened in this hotel before. Like all the missing people."

Cameron looked concerned. "Explain."

Asher felt uncomfortable. He should've never said anything. He replied, "A lot of people who passed through here went missing. The last one happened years ago."

Cameron said, "And you think they were killed?"

"Well, yeah," Asher said. "It's the location of their killer that scares me. The murders took place over thirty-five years."

"How can you be so sure something sinister happened?"

Asher knew the agent would be able to tell if he lied. He said, "I believe someone in this hotel killed these people."

"That doesn't tell me how you know?" Cameron grilled him.

Asher wasn't willing to give up information about the hidden tunnels. "Just trust me, okay?"

Cameron sighed. He asked, "Have you tried reaching out to the police?"

"Yeah, but they brushed it off," Asher replied.

Cameron said, "Maybe you should too."

Asher lowered his eyes.

Cameron said, "I don't want to discourage you, but this is a very dangerous situation. If your information proves to be true, you could be put in harm's way. I don't want that. I have enough junk on my conscience already."

"So you're saying that the threat is real?" Asher asked

Cameron hesitated on answering the question. He replied, "I'm telling you to be watchful, but be smart. If accusations like this come out against the wrong people, it could be very bad for everyone involved. Please, Asher. I'm begging you. Let me do my job and you worry about being a kid."

Asher avoided eye contact and nodded.

"Thank you," Cameron said as if a weight had been lifted.

"If by some chance you find something that is suspicious, let me be the first one you tell."

"Yes, sir," Asher replied.

"Wonderful," Cameron answered. "We'll talk soon."

The agent left.

Asher closed his laptop and put it in his bookbag. He headed to the lobby and told Justin about Cameron. Justin was exhausted and rested his eyes as Asher talked.

"Are you listening?" Asher said, "He shut me down too."

"I told you not to talk to him in the first place," Justin replied. "We'll have to figure this out on our own like we always planned."

"How will we do that?" Asher asked. "I can't spy on people forever. I have a life, you know?"

Justin said, "We all do, unless…" he stood from his chair. "We talk to the dead."

"No way."

"They will know. They have to," Justin said.

"You go alone and I'll be surveillance."

"It's getting dangerous. We need to stay as a pair. I'm positive you'll get killed if you stay alone."

"Me?!" Asher exclaimed.

"Are you in or not?"

Asher's heart raced. Despite the fear creeping into his mind, he chose to put his cowardliness away and make something out of himself. *Lead to gold,* he thought. Determination in his voice, he said, "Fine, I'm in."

At 3 am, they woke up, got dressed, and went hunting. Mom would home in a few hours. They hoped to bring her good news. Asher held the flashlight. Justin wore the GoPro and carried the EMF reader.

Thinking they'd have better luck in the secret tunnels, they entered the tunnels on the third floor. Asher followed Justin into the secret passage. He held the flashlight over his big brother's shoulder. Walking so close, Asher stepped on the back of Justin's shoe. His brother turned back and glared at him.

Neither of them were fully energetic. If Justin's little pet peeves were teased, he'd go off like a rocket. Asher kept a few steps between him and his brother. He didn't know why he should be so scared. The dead were on their side.

They reached a T-intersection. Justin turned a corner and was suddenly launched five steps back in the opposite way.

Asher cursed, standing at the middle of the three forking paths. If he leaned to the left to check on Justin, he'd leave his back exposed. If he leaned to the right, whatever hit Justin might attack him.

Asher squeezed the flashlight tightly. It trembled in his hand. Breathing heavily, he whispered his brother's name.

No reply.

Asher took a step forward. His foot pattered on the wooden floor.

The limbering man turned the corner. His naked fat rolls squeezed against the walls. The tie strangled his meaty neck so hard his blubber-like face had turned purple. His tongue dangled out the front of his puffy lips. His acorn pecker was lost under his folds of fat.

Asher screamed and ran back.

Gargling, the naked man dashed to the left.

Asher got five feet before hearing Justin's scream.

Shaken to the core, Asher ran to his brother. "Justin!"

He turned the left corner. The obese man's body mass filled the width of the tunnel. The light reflected on his back sweat. Justin's scream was muffled by the man's chest. Though Asher could only see his brother's feet, he could tell his entire body was being squeezed into the fat man. The stranger moved down the hallway in an alarmingly quick rate.

Asher ran after him. His mind clicked off. If he'd actually thought about what was happening, he'd urinate his pants. Asher reached out. His fingers slipped behind the necktie and the man's icy, moist skin. Roaring, Asher pulled at the man's tie and smacked him over the head with the flashlight. One, two, three good hits before the fat man purposely fell back on Asher. One moment he was standing and fighting, and the next he was underneath hundreds of pounds of cold, naked man lard. Curly back hairs scratched Asher's lip and tongue.

His chest hurt from the inside as much as the out. Asher wheezed. He reached for his inhaler, but his entire body was lost under the man, along with the flashlight. Shrouded in darkness, Asher fought to breathe, to move, to live.

"You fat son of a—" Justin's voice was quickly snuffed out by the man's chest.

Asher pushed against the back fat, but his noodle-y arms failed to move. The walls of Asher's consciousness pressed in on him. He kicked and screamed. His strength drained. He cried out for help, but no one heard him. He was drowning in fat.

The fat man sat up slow like a sumo wrestler.

Crushed, Asher was limp on the dusty floor. The light shined on his fractured, perspiration-covered glasses and bloody nose.

Justin struggled violently in the man's bear hug. Lubricated by the man's sweat, Justin slipped out from under him and scurried in the opposite direction.

Enraged, the purple-faced, swollen-tongued man gurgled. He put his meaty hands against the walls and attempted to stand.

Justin drew back his foot and stomped on the center of the man's face. "Die!"

Unfazed, the fat man grabbed Justin's ankle with both hands and pulled his feet out from under him.

Justin flopped backward. His head struck the floor and he stopped moving.

The fat man picked Justin up. Justin's head dropped to the side, resting against the man's chest. His feet dragged behind him. The fat man carried him into the darkness.

Jets of shaky breath escaped Asher's mouth. Nose blood trickled over his lips and onto the floor. Quivering, he moved his hand to his pocket and gasped in pain. He felt like his entire body had been wrung out like a wet towel. Wheezing loudly, he moved his inhaler to his lips and pressed down on the top. Like the breath of God, medicine shot life into him. He let his hand fall limp beside him. The inhaler rested in his open palm. Eyes to the dark ceiling, he lay still.

He didn't allow himself to think. There was too much at stake. He snatched the flashlight and carefully got to his feet. Keeping the inhaler in his pocket, he rested his shoulder against the wall. He aimed the light down the claustrophobic corridor. Dust particles danced in the air.

"Ju-Justin!" Asher called. The constricting walls drowned out his voice.

Full of fear, Asher whimpered. He turned away from where his brother was taken. He dragged his limp leg behind him. He kept one hand on the wall for balance. His fogged glasses rested lopsided on his bleeding nose. He breathed through parted lips. Even his simplest motion was agony. He turned the corner at the hallway's "T" and bumped into a skinny man.

Asher stumbled back a step. His light shined into the crimson muscle tissue of a faceless man.

Asher walked back until he hit a wall and sank down low. "No. Please, please, no…"

The faceless man clacked his teeth. His ball-like eyes peered deep into Asher's soul.

He took steps towards Asher.

"I'm trying to help you!" Asher cried. "I'm on your side! Don't come closer!"

The faceless man grabbed fistfuls of Asher's shirt and lifted him up.

"Why are you doing this?" Asher wept.

The faceless man set Asher on his feet and let go. Keeping his face to the boy, he lifted his left arm and pointed down the left corridor.

Asher wiped a tear away. "You want me to go down there?"

The faceless man was silent.

For the first time, Asher could see the intricacies of his exposed muscles. It was so inhuman he couldn't process it was real. "Okay."

He turned away from the monster and limped through the corridor. He turned a corner and found a doorless room in the tunnel. A table stood at the center. A film projector sat on top. Its lens pointed to the wall. This part of the passageway was undiscovered by Asher. It must've been sealed behind its hidden doors. Secrets within secrets.

Justin sat on the chair behind the projector. His back was to Asher and he faced the wall where the image would've appeared.

"Justin?" Asher took a step inside.

The projector clicked on.

Little burns spots interrupted the grainy image that took up most of the back wall.

Asher put his hand on Justin's shoulder and shook him. "Wake up, man. We have to leave."

The word *He* projected on the wall.

Asher watched.

The next word was *Is.* Then. *Here.* The film restarted. One word at a time, it showed the sentence *He Is Here.*

"Who?" Asher asked.

He saw something in the corner of his eye.

The naked fat man stood to his left.

A woman in a green dress stood to the right.

Neither of them moved.

The faceless man stepped in behind Asher.

Asher cried, "What do you want from me?! I already agreed to help you."

The video suddenly changed.

It showed a beautiful woman looking right at the cameraman. She put on lipstick. She had a slender neck, hazel eyes, and olive skin. She wore a green dress. Asher recognized her as the monstrous specter beside him. The scene abruptly changed. It was nighttime and the woman was now lying face down in the woods. The camera shook each time the camera operator breathed. He lifted a knife into view. The flashlight attached to the camera overexposed the bloody knife blade, making it appear as a shard of light. The cameraman moved closer to the woman. He rolled her over. Leaves and dirt shrouded the opening on her neck. Her eyes were half open and lifeless. As quick as the blink of an eye, the killer struck with the knife. The camera cut away before Asher could see where it hit.

The next scene played out quickly. The naked fat man lay in a shower with a necktie wrapped tightly around his throat. He was dead. The next clip showed a close-up of a surgical scalpel running down the skin by someone's ear. The video cut to a brief image of the faceless man.

Suddenly, the film roll caught fire. The projector sputtered. It flashed the sentence *He Is Here* a final time before cutting off.

The flame died a second later.

Asher stood behind his brother. All three of the others had vanished.

"Asher?"

Alarmed by his brother's voice, Asher ran to Justin's side and dropped to a knee. "Hey, hey, you okay?"

"I'm fine," Justin said. "Where are we?"

"The secret passage on the third floor," Asher said quickly. "Are you hurt, man?"

"Why are we in the passages?" Justin asked.

"You don't remember?" Asher asked. "I'll tell you later. Right now, we need to go. We're not safe here anymore."

Not that they ever were.

DEADLY CONFESSION

*S*tephen rested on the floor, his arms stretched out to his sides, one ankle crossed over the other and a smile stuck on his face. From an outsider's perspective, he looked like a jolly madman or someone who just had the best day of their life. He was neither of these things. Frankly, the morning had just begun. Nothing greatly eventful happened the day before. He had little money, an extra change of clothes as the Bible had told him to bring, and a heart sold out to Jesus. He lay there, giddy, strange and separate from the cynicism of natural reality. In his mind, he saw himself as leaning against God the Father's bosom as a little infant. He had more visions like this lately. His home was God's lap.

The morning sun grew over the horizon, casting crimson and gold rays across the darkness. Stephen opened his eyes to the suite's spackle-covered roof. He sighed like a man in love and sat up. The dim room prevented him from seeing more than shapes in the room around him. His back popped as he turned to the side. It was a reminder that his flesh was frail. He stood up and reached high. He only wore boxers and had no need to change into anything else. His feet took him to the window. He rested his palms on the sill and watched the eastern sun. His bank account was in shambles, his name was tarnished in the Catholic circle, he had no friends, no family, and no plan. Un-ironically, life was good. It had been since his great encounter.

He yawned and gave thanks for abundance. He spun around and danced. He pirouetted and leaped throughout the living room. His moves were clunky and unrefined. It probably would've gotten him a few laughs if he went on a stage. He would never dance on stage. He never wanted to dance at all until he read about King David wearing only his ephod and dancing before the Ark on its way into Jerusalem. The people loved their king and his perceived madness for his God. Watching him dance, one of David's wives resented him. Her womb became cursed and she never bore a child. Reading that was the last time Stephen silently judged another's worship.

Working up a sweat, Stephen fell back into his bed. He caught his breath but kept himself from falling back to sleep. Though he had no plans, his day would be busy.

He took a short shower and put on his priestly garments. He combed his brown hair. The few grey hairs reminded him of natural mortality. After brushing his teeth, he slipped on his priestly collar and set out into the hotel. He walked the halls before anyone was awake, speaking in an unknown language that he didn't understand. He'd crossed a threshold a while ago where his faith turned into something bewildering. He trusted that the Lord was doing something to the hotel's putrid atmosphere when he prayed in spirit.

He eventually reached the downstairs and walked into the lobby. Justin slept on the chair behind the counter. His hair was wet from a shower and his face was sickly pale. Stephen came up to the counter and cleared his throat.

Justin quickly sat up. He glanced around the room in a

panic. Seeing he was safe, he asked, "What can I do for you, man?"

"I had a feeling you'd gotten in trouble last night," Stephen said.

Justin asked, "What are you talking about?"

"In the middle of the night, I heard what sounded like you shouting on the other side of my walls. It sounded serious," Stephen said.

Justin looked dumbfounded. He said, "Yeah, no. You must've been dreaming."

Stephen said, "It sounded very real to me."

Justin looked down at his hands.

Stephen asked, "Is there something you'd like to get off your chest?"

"No, I'm good, man." Justin lied.

Stephen wanted to push the issue, but opted for, "Oh, yes, well, if you ever want to talk. Come find me."

"Thanks." Justin's tone indicated that he wouldn't take up the ex-priest's offer.

If you only knew, boy, Stephen thought. *You could be so free in the midst of the storm.*

Stephen went outside. The late autumn air chilled him. He crossed his arms, conserving as much heat as he could. Leafless trees extended as far as the eye could see. He took a whiff of nature, reminding himself it was good. He hiked through the woods. Fallen leaves crunched under his feet. The cold seeped into his bones. He reached the woods' edge and saw the endless Atlantic.

He strolled along the rocky coastline. Waves broke against the large, smooth stone. There was a lesson to be gleaned from refined rock and the endurance it earned from the constant barrage of waves.

You're coming home.

Stephen stopped in his tracks. He mumbled, "When, Lord?"

Soon.

Stephen asked hesitantly, "Earthly or spiritual home?"

No reply. Deep down, he didn't want to know the answer.

He straightened his uniform, thus flattening the wrinkles. "I'm ready."

For far too many years in his life, he'd feared change and compromised. That wasn't who he was anymore. He returned to Club Blue, uncertain of what to expect. The longer he stayed in his thoughts, the more worry started to creep in. He put such things to death and refocused his mind on joy. It wasn't joy from external pleasures/achievements, but from within.

His stomach grumbled.

Fast.

"Today?" he asked, approaching the lobby.

Fast.

"Yes, Lord."

His stomach growled again. He re-entered the lobby. He flashed a brief smile at Justin. The teenager eyed him suspiciously. He didn't trust Stephen.

Stephen wanted to ask him again what he was going through. He knew that the boy would see him as too pushy. He knew the boy would be in the lobby for the rest of the day, but there was no time like the present.

Stephen's phone dinged.

Surprised to be getting a text, he opened the flip phone. It was from Fritz. He wanted to meet with Stephen. Stephen suggested the ballroom.

Yawning, he found a table near the front of the ballroom, slightly beneath the upper balcony. He shut his eyes. He longed for his morning coffee, but the fast was more important.

Dressed in his work jumpsuit, broad-shouldered and bald Fritz Lumbart descended the fancy ballroom stairs and joined Stephen at the table.

"Good morning, brother," Stephen said.

"Morning," Fritz replied.

Stephen asked, "Workday?"

"Yeah, I got to head out in ten," Fritz naturally spoke slowly and deeply. "I've been thinking more about what you talked about yesterday."

"About your wife?" Stephen said.

Fritz nodded. "Part of me wants to kill her."

"And the other part?" Stephen asked.

"I want her to be happy," Fritz said. "She mothered my kids, you know. She even brought me to church a few times."

"These types of things are never easy," Stephen replied.

"Is that why Moses had so many strict rules about divorce?" Fritz said.

"I'd say so, among other things," Stephen replied.

Fritz said, "I wish I could go back and change it, but I don't think I could be in the same building as her without wanting to punch the wall in."

"Do you have violent outbursts often?"

"Only when I'm mad," Fritz said. "That's most of the time now. It makes me want to go back to my old habits."

Stephen said, "The Lord delivered you from those once and for all. Yesterday, you became a new man. *Behold, all old things are passed away and all things are made new.* That's what the Scriptures say. And, *His mercies are new every day.* Amen."

Fritz shifted uncomfortably in his seat. "I don't feel like it though. One more stupid thing happens and I'm going to go ape."

"Let me let you in on a little secret that might just change your life," Stephen said.

Fritz listened, ready to drink up any advice he could get.

Stephen smiled, "It's not about what you feel. It's about what He's done. That's what faith is. Do you believe it?"

"You know I do," Fritz said, taking offense.

Stephen said, "I'm talking about real faith. Not just believing there is a God, but trusting Him."

"How? He's brought me to the end of my rope. I'm living out of a suitcase!"

Stephen struggled to let out his next words, but it was the truth. "Maybe He's not the one you should be blaming. A lot of things happen that aren't in His will, but they still happen. It doesn't mean He's not the head honcho, but that we make our choices. Sin often leads to death. Thank God we have a savior in Christ."

Fritz asked, "But where's He at today? I'm still in the same spot."

"Where does the Word say He is?"

"In my heart," Fritz said, defeated.

Stephen shouted, "Hallelujah! Now, why don't you talk to Him? He'll help you get this stuff sorted out."

Fritz checked his watch. "I gotta get going."

Stephen said, "The breakthrough will happen. You got to push, get close to Him, and let Him do the rest."

Fritz nodded in deep thought. He said, "I'll see you around, Father."

Head down, he walked to the lobby and out of Stephen's sight.

Stephen took a deep breath.

Anna returned in the middle of the afternoon. Walking around the hotel, Stephen waved at her. She smiled back, but her happy expression was faked and forced. Stephen made a mental note to talk to her later. Though unknowingly, the residents at Club Blue were his flock. He wanted to nurture them, groom them, and lead them to good pastures.

Stephen turned the corner to the back of the hotel, happy to get some exercise. Andrew Warren sat on a stone bench and tossed seeds to the crows. They flocked to him, pecking around the grass and cawing at each other. The gentle-looking old man wore a checkered wool sweater vest over a long-sleeve sweater. His finely-combed hair was reminiscent of Mr. Rogers.

"May I?" Stephen asked.

Warren tossed another handful of seeds to the crows. "Be my guest."

Stephen lowered himself to the cold stone slab. He interlocked his fingers.

A crow tilted its head at him. Caw!

Stephen laughed softly. "All God's creatures."

"He's not doing a very good looking after them." Warren's voice had an edge.

Stephen glanced at his ring. "You're a Freemason, right?"

"Proudly," Warren replied.

"Why?" Stephen asked.

The question caused the old man pause. Warren turned to Stephen. "I'm not buying your crackpot religion."

Back in the clergy, a statement like that would've offended Stephen. Now, he was fascinated. Stephen said, "Okay. You made up your mind. I acknowledge that."

"Then why are you still here?" Warren asked.

"I was hoping to get to know you," Stephen replied.

Warren glared at him.

The conversation wasn't going anywhere. Stephen stood up. He smiled kindly. "Have a wonderful day, Andrew."

The old man returned to feeding the birds.

Stephen walked away. Fallen leaves crunched under his feet. He was curious about Warren's hostility toward God. Freemasons believed in God and were open to a variety of faith joining them. Still, Stephen hadn't met many Freemasons and had little understanding. Perhaps it was the concept of religion Warren despised.

Stephen returned to the lobby. Anna stood behind the counter, reviewing her laptop. Her mouth was crunched to the side and her shoulders were tensed.

Stephen approached. "Hey, how are you?"

"Good," Anna lied. She faked happiness. "You look well, Father. Is there anything I can get you? Towels? Shampoo?"

"Everything is perfect, thank you, though," Stephen said.

"I'm glad to hear you're enjoying your stay," Anna replied. She typed something. The screen reflected on her glassy eyes.

Stephen lingered. Even though he'd worked with people his whole career, he was still uncertain how to approach certain topics. He cleared his throat and said, "I was wondering if you had anything you wanted to get off your chest."

"That's very sweet of you, but I'm fine, actually," Anna replied.

"Ah," Stephen said agreeably.

An awkward silence filled the room.

Stephen said, "Your boys did a fantastic job while you were away."

Anna's face lit up. "Really? I mean, I expected nothing less."

"They're really starting to step into their own," Stephen replied. "Identity at their age is a big deal. They're constantly bombarded with where to go to college and how to make friends and what clubs to join. I, for one, don't miss those days."

"They're good kids," Anna said. "I'm hoping that we'll get a chance to spend more family time together. Not that we don't ever talk, but it's getting harder."

Stephen said, "You're not doing this alone."

THE HAUNTING AT SEBRING HOTEL

"You're talking about God?" Anna asked suspiciously.

"That, but myself, as well." A small smile grew up his face. "I'm good at keeping secrets."

Anna said, "That's nice, but I have to figure out certain things myself."

"Understandable. If you ever just want someone to listen, I'm always available." Stephen waited a moment, hoping she'd accept his offer. Not getting a reply, he started for the elevator.

"Stephen," Anna said.

The priest stopped and looked over his shoulder. "Yes?"

Anna asked, "You're serious about that secret thing."

"Full confidentiality," Stephen promised.

Anna breathed in through her nose. She tapped her fingernails on the counter's desk. Hesitant, "There's something that's been on my heart for a while. Are you available to speak now?"

"Absolutely," Stephen said, excited about what the Lord would do in the woman's life. Anna led him to her office and asked him to shut the door.

She leaned on the lip of the desk and crossed her arms, making herself tiny and guarded. She regretted inviting Stephen. He made sure to keep clear boundaries between them. He wasn't there to hurt her, but to help. Posture and position mattered in situations like these.

"What's on your mind?" Stephen asked.

"I've been..." She searched for the right word. "I guess, overwhelmed. With this job, the boys, and everything else that's been happening has really pushed me to my limit, you know?"

Stephen listened to her, extending silent sympathies.

"It's like nothing ever goes right for me," Anna said. "I work hard. I try my best to be a good mom. It's all falling apart now. Frankly, I don't know if it's me or some sort of divine retribution. Whatever this rough patch is, I'm getting sick of it." She glanced up at Stephen. "So, like, what do you think the problem is?"

Stephen thought about it. "I don't have enough information to say. When do you feel like things turned unfavorable for you?"

Anna looked bitter, but the emotion was directed at herself. "I married this guy. I thought it would be true love and... he beat me."

"I'm sorry, Anna."

"Don't be. I was the one who married him. And shared his bed for nineteen years."

Stephen said, "You were trapped. Your children might've been in danger. None of that is your fault."

"You expect me to believe that when I stood by as he struck my boy?"

Stephen said, "It's not a black and white situation."

"Isn't it your God with all the rules? I neglected my children. I submitted. I'm just as bad as James."

Stephen said, "Maybe you could've run away with them or called the police, but what happened, happened. Nothing will change that."

Tears welled up in Anna's eyes. She avoided looking at Stephen.

He took a step closer. "Anna. I understand. I mean, I've never lived through something like that, but God saw, and He knows your story."

Anna set her jaw. Her frustration and sadness turned to anger.

Stephen said, "You have every right to be angry, but the bad things in your life are not some strange, twisted punishment. Sometimes, bad things just happen. Maybe it was a demonic thing, but could've just been a trial. I don't know, but the Lord is good. The walk of faith isn't a cakewalk, and I can't promise you that every problem you have will go away. But you won't ever be alone."

"Until I screw up again," Anna remarked.

Stephen looked at her sympathetically. "We all make choices we regret. It's grace that saves us."

Anna raised her voice. "So I just believe and suddenly *everything* is okay? You don't understand what I've done."

"And you don't understand God's mercy," Stephen said gently. His own eyes watered at Anna's expense.

"I killed him, Stephen."

The air was sucked out of the room.

Anna covered her mouth. Her hands trembled. "Oh no."

Stephen stood, petrified.

Anna rushed to him and grabbed his upper sleeves. A tear rolled down her cheek. Her eyes stared deep into Stephen's. Desperation shook her voice. "Please. You can't tell anyone. They'll take away my children. They'll take away everything. Please, Father," Anna moaned in sorrow. "I should've never said anything."

Stephen gently hugged her. "Shh. It's all right."

Anna sobbed into his shoulder. She hugged him so tight he could hardly breathe. Stephen gently rubbed her back and continued to speak comforting words to her.

They stayed like that for a long while.

Stephen hadn't felt the embrace of a woman for so long he forgot how warm it felt. He focused his thoughts on the predicament before him. Anna's story tore at his heart.

She pulled away from him. Her face was red and wet with tears and snot. "Promise me you won't tell anyone."

Stephen opened his mouth, but the words lodged in his throat. "I…"

Anna pleaded, "I'll do anything. I just want to be free of this torment. I just want my boys to live a good life. That's all."

Stephen said, "I'm here for you."

Anna pushed her body closer to his. "Promise?"

Stephen's heart raced. Her face was mere inches from his. Her desperate, beautiful eyes melted him.

"No one else can know," Anna said. "They're already looking at me. One misstep and my life is over."

Stephen took a deep breath. He let go and carefully distanced himself from her, no longer allowing her body heat to dictate his decisions.

"Stephen?"

"You murdered someone," he said.

"What about grace? What about my family's safety? James would beat Justin and verbally abuse Asher. He did things to me I can't even put into words."

Stephen said, "I'm sorry, Anna…"

"What does that mean?" she asked, crying again.

"I…" He felt like he was tearing his own heart out.

Anna trembled, she was so terrified. "Stephen, please."

"I… I promise I won't tell," Stephen compromised.

Anna looked like a giant weight was lifted off her. She gave Stephen another quick hug. "Thank you, Stephen. Thank you for listening. I don't have anyone else."

Stephen pursed his lips.

Anna noticed the snot stains on Stephen's inner shoulder. "Oh gosh. I'm so… so sorry."

"It's nothing, really," Stephen replied.

"No, no. Let me clean up."

"You don't have to—"

Anna had already grabbed the tissue box from the desk and started to wipe Stephen's uniform. He waited for her to finish. She wiped her own eyes. "I should probably get back out there."

"Right."

Anna thanked him again. Taking the tissue box, she hurried to the bathroom.

Stephen lingered in the hallway. His mind was divided. He knew in situations like this, the police had to be contacted. Anna would lose everything. She returned from the bathroom after fixing her make-up.

"We'll talk soon," she said as she hurried back to the lobby counter.

Stephen replied with a smile and returned to his room.

He walked a few paces before falling on his knees. "Oh, Lord. I messed up. I really messed up."

What now?

"I don't know. I call the police, I guess, but I gave her my word," Stephen lowered his face to the floor. "God, her children. What will happen to them? Who will look after them? And this place where you've called me to settle. I thought I'd have a great purpose here."

You do.

"Not if she goes to jail," Stephen said.

Rest.

"Easier said than done," Stephen replied.

He rolled on his back and stretched his arms out to the sides. "I should've listened to you more."

The hours passed. Stephen fell in and out of rest, never coming to a clear solution to his problem. It was his duty to report crimes to the police. That was that. The Bible talked about obeying the laws of the land. Stephen's mind kept going back to grace and mercy. He cared about Anna and her family. Though they had hardly gotten to know each other, Stephen imagined this relationship going somewhere. He wasn't under the same restrictions that he was when he was part of the clergy. He could marry now. He wasn't in love with Anna, but she was an attractive woman and had a certain charm. He knew such things shouldn't change the facts of her crime. If every murderer was shown mercy just because they had a family or were well-liked, there would be anarchy. However, forgiveness was the most powerful agent of change.

Stephen believed that Anna had only killed her husband out of necessity, but she could've gone to the police anytime. He didn't judge her for her actions, but since Stephen knew about the murder, he'd be held responsible if he didn't report it. His conscience gnawed at him. His confusion made it difficult for him to make a decision. Worry drowned out the voice of God.

"Okay, I'm doing it," he said to himself.

He knew he needed to tell the police, but first, he was going to give Anna a heads-up. Also, he planned on going to the police station directly. Face-to-face, they might be more understanding when he told them Anna's motive. The eyes were the windows to the soul. That one-on-one encounter couldn't be beaten.

Shoes tied, he stood up just in time to hear a low creaking noise. Stephen looked over his shoulder. The wall mirror was open like a door. A figure stood in the darkness.

ALL HALLOWS EVE

*I*n the early morning, Anna stood on the stepladder's top rung and taped the final swirl of pumpkin-shaped "Christmas" lights to the ballroom's final support column. A small smile rested on her pensive face. She stepped down from the ladder and walked back a pace, gazing across the fully-decorated lobby. Pumpkin lanterns dangled from the ceiling. Fat orange candles stood at the center of every table. Ribbons weaved around the backs of the chairs. She'd deliberately avoided any skeletons and tombstones. Any décor centered on death was a big no-no. She brushed her dusty hands on her suit pants.

Her mind felt clearer since her confession. It wasn't a wise choice to tell the priest her darkest secret, but she felt a release. Stephen gave his word, too. If he went against it, it would be between him and God. Anna still wasn't sure about this whole faith thing. She had too many questions and not enough faith to ask. Maybe one day she'd cross that bridge. Until then, she was going to live like the new her now. Because she had no secrets, the past felt like it was finally dying and Anna planned to rise out of the ashes, guilt-free and ready to improve. Fear still crept into her thoughts. The priest could betray her. The York police might find evidence. Some sort of scandal could ruin Club Blue forever.

Justin and Asher descended the ballroom stairs. Justin wore his house cleaning uniform and Asher was dressed for school. His thumbs were behind his backpack straps. His glasses' lenses were scuffed. Both the boys had gone to bed early the night before. They hadn't gotten a chance to catch up last night. The entire family was exhausted.

Anna gestured them to approach and gave them a family hug. Keeping one arm around each one, she said, "I missed you guys."

"Mom, we need to talk," Asher said.

Anna pulled away. "Did something happen?"

Justin said, "The serial killer we talked to you about. He's in the hotel."

"Don't be ridiculous," Anna said.

Asher replied, "The spirits told us, Mom."

Justin nodded soberly.

Anna's anger flared. "You know we don't have time for these kinds of jokes."

Asher said, "We both saw them. There was a fat man, a woman with a cut throat, and a man without the face. I watched videos of them being killed before the film roll burned."

"What?" Anna asked.

Asher explained. "One of them showed the woman getting stabbed in the head."

A brief image of the skeleton Anna found flashed in her mind. A knife was found in her head. She never told the boys about that. The police hadn't released that information to the public either.

Justin said, "We were going to tell you last night, but we were too tired."

Anna turned her back to them and gathered her thoughts. The boys traded looks.

Gaining some semblance of control, Anna turned back and spoke to them again. "Did they tell you who the killer is?"

The boys shook their heads.

Justin said, "Only that he's around."

Asher added, "I think it's the concierge, but it could be anyone."

"Thank God we have Agent Cameron around," Anna said.

Asher said, "He's running his own investigation but doesn't want us involved."

"Screw that, though," Justin said. "He's only going to make things worse by withholding information."

Anna said, "He's the most competent person we have. If he wants to work secretly, we have to let him."

"That's great, but we're still in danger every second we spend in this hotel," Justin said.

Asher nodded. "Even the spirits are becoming violent."

"Serial killers and spirits," Anna laughed. "What has our lives come to?"

Justin said, "The root to all this evil is the hotel. Mom, I know you don't want to sell the place, but let's be smart and stay somewhere else until this mess is cleared up."

"We can't neglect our responsibilities," Anna replied. "We own this hotel and all the baggage that comes with it."

"Staying here is suicide!" Justin barked.

Anna set her jaw. "Justin, I'm so tired of going back and forth with you about this place."

"Open your eyes, Mom! People are going missing left and right. The police won't help us. It's us versus the world," Justin said.

"You called the police?" Anna asked.

"Not that I wanted to, but we noticed a pattern of disappearances."

Asher added, "Names were carved in a secret passage near the elevator. All of them were victims. None of their descriptions matched the spirits we saw, meaning there have been more murders since the list was finished."

Justin put his hand on Anna's shoulder. "I know I can be uptight sometimes, but I'm really asking you to see things for what they are."

"You called the police without telling me?" Anna asked.

"So what?" Justin replied.

Anna verbally lashed out. "Do you have any idea how that could've destroyed us? We are on a tightrope right now. One more scandal and we're out on the streets. I can't believe you guys would do that."

Asher said, "They didn't believe us."

"I don't care!" Anna shouted.

The fourteen-year-old lowered his gaze.

Anna sighed. "I sorry I raised my voice. If you two want to find another place to stay, go right ahead. I'll front the bill for you."

Asher asked, "You're not coming with us?"

"I can't," Anna replied.

Justin grumbled. He cursed. "Fine. Stay. Come on, Asher. We'll find a cheap motel a few miles from here. I'm going to pack my stuff."

He power-walked to the stairs. He grabbed the railing and stepped up on the first step before noticing Asher wasn't following him. Turning back, his mother and little brother hadn't moved.

"Asher," Justin barked.

"I can't leave her, bro," Asher said.

"If you don't, she'll stay," Justin said.

Anna double-downed. "I'm not leaving either way. Come

hell or high water, this hotel is a part of our family. Running away from issues isn't going to fix them."

Asher said, "Mom, if you're staying, I'm staying."

Anna eyed Justin. "Are you with us? Remember, you promised to work for me."

Justin grumbled something to himself. Finally, he said, "Fine, I'll stay and work days, but I'm not sleeping in this hotel past dark."

"Fair enough," Anna said. "Make sure you bring the car back in the morning."

Asher checked the clock on his phone. "Oh man, I need to get to school."

"I'll take you," Anna said. "Justin, work the counter while I'm gone."

Anna drove Asher through town. She glanced over at him, noticing he didn't have his handheld device. He watched the small town blur by through the window.

"It's Halloween, you know," Anna said.

"I don't know if I like that creepy stuff anymore," Asher replied.

Anna asked, "Tell me about these *encounters* you've been having."

Asher shrugged. "They're hard to explain. The spirits are on our side, but they're forceful. One grabbed Justin and dragged him to the secret filming room to show us the video."

"That really happened?" Anna asked, trying to make sense of everything.

Asher nodded.

"I'm, um, sorry it seems like I don't care about it, but I just don't have any frame of reference to deal with things like that," Anna admitted.

"I don't think anyone does," Asher said.

Anna wondered if she should talk to Stephen about it. If

both her boys were sincere about their experiences, she had to believe it was true. All that being said, how does a mortal confront something like that? She can't imagine she could hurt the spirits or force them to leave. Just like with James, it was the lack of control that scared her more than the violence. She longed for order in her life. The hotel, as unstable as it was, seemed like the only chance at achieving that goal.

"How are you holding up?" Anna asked.

"Good, I guess," Asher replied. "I feel like I gotta do more. Be better. Life is too short to be caught up on stupid stuff."

His maturity surprised Anna. She said, "I'm proud of you."

"Why?" Asher replied.

"You're brave," Anna said.

"No. I'm just too stupid to run away," Asher said.

"I want to leave too," Anna confessed.

"You don't seem like it."

"I know," Anna replied.

She pulled up to the school. There was little traffic. Asher was running two minutes late. Anna told him to text her when he finished his final class. They hugged. Anna waited until she saw him go through the school's front door.

On the drive back, her mind wandered. It had to be her own selfishness that kept them at Club Blue. She squeezed the steering wheel. She wondered if she was the real danger to her children's safety.

Returning to the hotel, she headed to Stephen's suite. The door was cracked open. Anna pushed on it. "Stephen? Are you here?"

She stepped inside. The suite was tidy. An envelope rested on the bed. Anna opened it, seeing a typed letter. She read it under her breath. "Thank you, Anna. My time at Club Blue was a once-in-a-lifetime experience, but it's time for me to move on. I wish I could've said goodbye."

A sudden cold chill filled the room. Anna shuddered. Stephen's Bible and small suitcase were gone. He'd truly left. *What if he called the cops?* Anna thought. She knew she'd gone too far by telling him about James. Anna plopped on the corner of the mattress. She sniffled. She practiced breathing and reminded herself that she hardly knew the man. Perhaps the connection they shared was one-sided. Anna longed for a good friend she could trust. He had seemed like her savior. Tearing up the letter, she got up, tossed it in the little trash can, and returned to the lobby. She inquired about Stephen to Justin.

"I've not seen him," her son replied. "Did he check out?"

"Yeah…" Anna's voice trailed off.

Justin said, "Mom, what if…"

"We don't know that," Anna replied.

"I'm just saying," Justin replied.

"Keep an eye out," Anna replied. "If something else strange happens, call me and call the police."

"What about a scandal?" Justin asked.

Anna hated flip-flopping in her opinions. She said, "We'll try our best to avoid it. Come spring, we're going to renovate this place. New name. New look. New everything."

Justin smiled. "Cool."

Anna doubled-checked the Halloween decorations. She walked from the ballroom to the bar, taking photos of all she'd done. The hotel fell empty and cold. The feeling of exploration and elegance was overshadowed by dread and superstition. She thought she heard a noise, but it was all in her head. Perhaps her children only saw the ghosts because they were young or because they were more open-minded than her. She was glad she didn't have the encounters. Rapists, taxes, and other material issues were greater threats.

She walked into the bar. Soft piano music played through the speakers. She grabbed a beer bottle from the freezer and sat on the counter. She scrolled through the photos on her phone and tagged them on social media under the hashtag #HalloweenClubBlue and #spookylowprices. She wondered if she could advertise the hotel to paranormal investigators. Even better, get a show on TV. After the word got out, she could change the brand. The new design would attract new guests while the old guests would be intrigued by what changed.

The door opened.

She glanced over, seeing Cameron step inside. His hair was recently cut, making him look more handsome. He was dressed in a sweater that had two buttons on the neck and dark pants. His shoes looked new as well.

Anna said, "Going somewhere special?"

Cameron sat next to her. He rested his forearm on the bar's counter, leaning slightly. He faced her. "I heard you had a rough trip."

"Who told you that?"

"Rumors travel fast around here," Cameron said.

"I leave for a few days and suddenly everyone is best friends," Anna remarked.

Cameron said, "I missed you."

"That's sweet of you," Anna teased.

"I'm serious," Cameron replied. "You left in such a hurry, I thought something bad might've happened."

"Just life stuff. There's nothing I can do about it now," Anna said. "Oh, my boys said they talked to you about their theory."

"Which one's that?"

Anna glanced around, just to make sure no one was listening. "They believe there is a serial killer."

Cameron looked disgusted. "Yeah. That."

"Is there any proof?" Anna asked.

"A little," Cameron replied. "People have gone missing

over the past few decades. I've been trying to get to the bottom of it."

"And?"

"I can't say what I've found," Cameron replied. "It's nothing personal, but I can't compromise the mission."

"I just want to know if my family is in danger."

"No," Cameron said confidently.

"You sound sure of yourself," Anna remarked.

Cameron gently took her hand that rested on the counter as well. "I wouldn't let anything happen to you and your boys."

Anna said, "A number of guests have checked out without seeing me or leaving ways to reach them. Is there a chance they were taken?"

Cameron replied, "Maybe, but without evidence, there's no way to be sure. 'Sides, if there was a killer still around, why would he want to harm you? You're beautiful, intelligent, and way too valuable."

"Now is not the time to be flirting," said Anna.

Cameron brushed his thumb on top of her hand. She didn't stop him. "What about the rest of the missing people, like Rosy and Christophe? They were much more attractive than me."

Cameron grinned at her, too lost in her eyes to answer her question. "I'd like us to get dinner together."

Anna gently drew her hand away. She sipped her beer. "Is that why you got a fresh haircut and new shoes?"

"You got me," Cameron said.

Anna replied, "I don't know, Cameron. I've got a million things going right now."

"How about I make it easy for you? I'll call up a chef, get some fresh grouper and crab, and have him serve it to us in the ballroom."

Anna laughed at him before realizing he was serious. "That's a lot of extra work."

"You only get to go on the first date once," Cameron said.

Anna thought for a moment. At this point, any distraction from her stress would be welcome. "You better get some darn fine grouper if you're going to be using my kitchen."

"You can count on it. Will 8:30 pm be too late?"

"I'd actually prefer 9 pm." Anna said.

"Perfect." Cameron stood up. "I better get ready."

Anna watched him walk out. The man had a V-shaped torso and was strong. She knew the dangers of hooking up with someone in law enforcement. Nevertheless, she was so over dwelling on James. She finished her photo tour of the hotel.

As night fell over Sebring, Justin packed a suitcase and asked to borrow Anna's car. She wished he'd stay, but she understood the reasons behind his fears. She surrendered her keys. "Keep your phone on and be back tomorrow morning at 7 am sharp."

"All right, Mom," Justin said. He seemed guilty leaving her alone but still chose to do it anyway.

Anna stayed behind the counter for a few more hours. No new guests arrived. She headed upstairs around 8 pm and changed. She put on a slender, dark blue dress. She hummed to herself as she fixed her hair and make-up. She wore high heels that matched her outfit and admired her reflection in the mirror. She promised herself to let go of her problems for a night. No talk of killers. No talk of work. Just dinner and whatever came next. She didn't plan on giving herself to Cameron.

She took her little black purse and slung it over one shoulder. She left her room, traveled down the hallway, and arrived at the internal balcony. She ran her hand across the railing as she looked down at the tables and chairs set throughout the room. The candles were lit on each tabletop, but the one nearest the dance floor had two tall candlesticks Anna didn't recognize. There was a red tablecloth and a bottle of red wine resting in a nice bucket. Anna smirked. Cameron had gone overboard. It felt like she was stepping into a fantasy.

She walked down the left flank stairs. Gentle jazz music echoed off the walls.

Cameron stood from his seat as Anna descended the stairs. He wore a dress shirt, sports jacket, suit pants, and Oxford shoes. He looked at Anna like she was the most beautiful woman in the world.

"Wow," he said as she approached. "You look amazing."

Anna shrugged.

Cameron met her halfway. Both of them stood on the dance floor.

"The chef is running a little behind," Cameron said. "Hopefully he'll have the food ready in the next twenty minutes." He extended a hand. "A dance?"

Anna chuckled. "I didn't realize you were such a romantic."

"C'mon. Let's enjoy the moment," Cameron replied.

Anna took his hand. He put his other hand around her lower back. They swayed to the music.

"Any update on your investigation?" she asked.

"Is what you want to talk about?" Cameron asked.

"Not really," Anna admitted.

Cameron spun her around.

Anna laughed. "When did you become such a dancer?"

"I took a class in college," Cameron said.

"I find that hard to believe."

"There was a girl I liked in there," Cameron said.

Anna asked, "If you don't mind me asking, when was the last time you were in a relationship?"

Cameron said, "Five, maybe six years ago. Work took up most of my time. I had a lot of, uh, partners, but nothing long-term. I'm at a point in my life where I'm after something with more substance."

"I get it. I wasn't interested in dating after James passed away," Anna said.

"And yet here you are."

"I think it's time for a change," Anna said.

The song slowed down. Anna danced a moment longer. They discussed their favorite books and movies. It was a simple, useless conversation just to fill in the silence. Anna couldn't remember the last time she danced or when someone held her in an affectionate way. When there was nothing left to say, she rested her head on Cameron's shoulder and let him guide her.

For a moment, it seemed like they were only people in the world.

33

UNCHAINED

wo hours earlier...

SEATED ON RAVEN'S BED, Asher held the girl's cold hand. His backpack slouched on the floor. The corner of his Algebra textbook peeked out of the open zipper. The sunset cast an orange glow over the leafless trees outside and through the suite's window.

Asher had gotten back from school and worked on his homework a little bit before seeing Raven. He hadn't done much of anything since he got to her room, but it felt safer than being alone. He'd see the faceless man and naked fat guy at different places throughout the day. He kept telling himself that they were just a part of reality. It didn't make the haunting any easier. The worst was when he was in the boy's bathroom and the woman in the green dress stood on the other side of the stall. Her feet pointed into each other. Blood dripped on the floor from her various wounds. He didn't want to tell anyone about the visitations. The whole situation freaked him out. *The man who was scared is dead. The new man is not,* he told himself, holding to true to his new identity. Video games, entertainment, and useless chatter didn't mean anything to him now. He was after purpose and truth.

"Where's your dad at?" Asher asked.

"He wanted to go somewhere else to write," Raven replied. She sighed and fell back on the mattress.

"You okay?" Asher asked.

"Bored," Raven said. "Very, very bored."

"Maybe we can bowl tonight or something," Asher suggested.

Raven groaned. "That's a lame thing to do on Halloween. We should be watching a horror movie or something."

I'm living in one, Asher thought. "Not a fan."

Asher laid on his back next to her. Both of them stared at the dull ceiling.

Raven said, "Weren't you going to dress up for Halloween?"

"No," Asher said.

"That's no fun," Raven replied.

"I'm not the one who wears the same clothes every day," Asher remarked.

Raven glanced down at her black shirt and black leggings. She frowned. "My dad doesn't have the time to buy me an outfit. I'm trapped in this stupid hotel."

"Why don't you go to school?" Asher replied. "We can probably be in the same classes."

"For one, I'm a sophomore. Two, public schools are just indoctrination centers. Look it up."

"Why not go to a private school then?"

"Sure, and end up in some skull and bones cult that will turn me into a sociopathic killer."

Asher's eyes went wide.

Raven said, "That might be kind of cool actually."

"Yeah… no," Asher said.

"You're no fun sometimes, Asher," said Raven.

Her comment damaged Asher's self-confidence. He thought for a moment before he sat up. "Okay. You want to do something? Let's go see that lighthouse."

Raven sat up, her face lighting up. "Really?"

"It'll get us out of here for a little bit," Asher said. "I just don't want to stay out too late."

"Have you been inside the lighthouse yet?"

"I didn't know you could go in there."

"Yeah, you just have to get a boat," Raven said. "This is going to be exciting."

"Whoa, whoa, whoa. Seeing it from far away is good enough for me," Asher said.

Raven kept holding his hand. "Hurry. I don't want anyone to see us sneak out."

"Why?"

"Duh, it'll be more exciting that way," Raven replied.

Raven carefully opened the door and glanced into the hallway. Not seeing anyone, she gestured for Asher and headed for the side stairs near the elevator. She dashed into the stairwell, down to the ground floor, and out the emergency exit.

It was twilight hour.

Strong wind battered Asher and shook the trees.

"Race ya," Raven said and started sprinting.

"Wait up!" Asher ran after her.

Giggling, Raven weaved between the trees and kicked up leaves.

Asher kept his hand on his inhaler. He trailed a few paces behind her. He felt invisible splinters clog his throat. He pushed himself to run faster. His knees popped. He really needed to spend more time away from his desk. He reached the rocky beach and doubled over. Raven was waiting for him, both hands on her hips and not the slightest bit out of breath.

Asher shook his inhaler and used it. He leaned back and stretched. "I haven't run like that since fifth grade field day."

Raven teased, "You did pretty good."

"How are you not tired?" Asher asked between breaths. There were still spikes in his throat. He spat on the ground.

Raven said, "Maybe I'm just the best."

Asher slipped the inhaler back into his pocket and cursed. "My phone."

"Did you drop it?" Raven asked.

"No, I think I left it on the charger," Asher said. "Dang it!"

Raven said, "Relax. We don't need it."

"It'll be dark soon. What if we get lost on the way back?"

Raven said, "Have a little faith, Asher. I'm good at navigating in the dark."

"If you say so," Asher mumbled.

They walked along the seaside. It took Asher a long while to get his heart rate back to normal. The ocean raged. Its large waves smacked against the rocks. Black thunderheads darkened distant skies.

Asher stayed close to Raven. She held his hand. A few other people walked along the coast. Most of them left at the sight of storm clouds. The lighthouse stood in the distance. Its beacon rotated slowly. Raven knelt down beside the water. There were two hundred yards of ocean between here and the jagged-edged lighthouse's island.

Raven said, "It's too cold to cross."

"Hey, I thought you said there was a boat," Asher replied, hoping there wasn't a way across.

He followed her down along the coast. They reached a small pier. A wooden rowboat bobbed in the rough waters. The white paint on the bow was chipped and worn. It was attached by a rusty metal chain.

The pier creaked under Asher's feet. It wasn't the easiest place to get into the water. The construction was old and rugged, too. It could've been here since the town's inception. Barnacles and little crabs coated the wooden support beams. Newer 2x4s had replaced certain sections.

Jogging ahead of Asher, Raven was the first to reach the little rowboat.

"Aw man," she said.

"What happened?" Asher asked, walking next to her.

"No paddles," Raven said. She lifted up the metal lock securing the chain. "And this."

"Oh, well," Asher said.

Raven lowered her head, appearing upset.

Wanting to help, Asher pulled out his wallet and removed a leather pouch holding lock-picking tools.

Raven eyed it with intrigue.

Asher gestured for the lock. It was cold and weighty, but of a simple construction. He got on a knee and got to work.

Waves crashed loudly. The wind howled.

Asher stopped midway. "Wait. We don't have any way to steer this thing."

He noticed Raven wasn't behind him.

She was near the start of the pier and pulling on a loose plank. It snapped out of place.

"Holy crap!" Asher explained.

Raven smiled at him. "Impressed?"

Asher nodded multiple times.

"Keep working on the lock," she told him.

Asher picked the lock in a few minutes. He pocketed it and held the chain like a leash. The other end of the chain was attached to a ring on the boat.

Raven held two long planks.

Asher said, "I hope no cops see us."

Raven said, "It would be exciting if they did. We'll be like Bonnie and Clyde."

"You'd make a great match for my brother," Asher said. "He likes bad girls."

"Well, I like smart boys," Raven replied.

Asher adjusted his glasses. A compliment like that would feed his ego for years. Taking Raven's hand, he helped her sit in the boat first. The boat rocked on the choppy waves. He tossed the rusty chain inside it.

No longer having anything to keep it still, the boat quickly moved away from the dock.

Raven extended one of the planks to Asher. At the last possible moment, he grabbed at the very end. He pulled the plank and dragged the boat his way.

"Hurry," Raven beckoned.

Afraid he'd miss it, Asher leaped. He landed in the boat, tipping it to one side. He quickly leaned the opposite way, almost falling out. The boat found its balance.

"Whew," Asher said.

Raven laughed.

Asher laughed with her.

She handed him one of the planks.

Together, they paddled across the gap between the shore and lighthouse. They looked at each other as they rowed. Raven's inky black hair brushed over part of her face.

The sun fell away.

They neared the little dock at the foot of the island. The waves pushed them towards the rocky cliffs nearby. Asher rowed furiously. A splinter jabbed into his thumb. He gritted his teeth, but didn't stop.

Raven reached out and grabbed the edge of the dock. "Give me the chain."

Asher took two seconds away from rowing to hand it to her. Asher paddled to make up the space they'd just lost.

Raven wrapped the chain around the little docking post. She secured it using Asher's lock. Leaving the planks in the boat, they helped each other out and followed the dock to a series of wooden steps. They hiked until they reached the grassy knoll where the lighthouse stood.

The front door was locked.

Asher picked it. "We could go to juvie for this."

They entered the building connected to the tower. It was cozy and had all the furnishings of a little house. They opened the tower door and hiked the spiral staircase to the top. The massive turning light stood in the large room. Glass windows occupied all sides. They could see far into the ocean in one direction and Club Blue standing above the trees in the other. They sat on the metal floor and watched the storm clouds in the distance.

Raven sighed. Her hands rested behind her as she looked at the view.

Asher's knees were close to his chest. He tried to ignore the uncomfortable mesh floor. He noticed Raven's uncharacteristic silence. "Hey, everything okay?"

"I… I have something you need to know."

Asher waited for her to elaborate.

His mind went to one place. Her father was the killer. It made sense. He was the right age to have been involved in the previous killings. He avoided people. He fit the profile. Asher braced himself for the truth. Why didn't he see this before? It dawned on him that he was so busy looking at Raven that he never bothered spying on her father.

Raven said, "Everything I knew about the rituals at Club Blue, I learned from my father's book."

Asher kept quiet. He wanted her to confess that David Hunt was the killer.

"See, my father started his own investigation on the hotel's dark history years ago. He talked to survivors of the mysterious fourth-floor fire, he observed the various residents, and he infiltrated the exiled Masonic order that was active there for many years. At that time, they were fractured and functioning at a fraction of their former power. Most of them had vanished after the fire. Father learned all their inside secrets. He wanted to write a book about it."

"None of that sounds too bad," Asher said.

"I'm not finished," Raven said. "Asher, this isn't the first time I've stayed at Club Blue."

Asher's heart pounded. "Okay?"

"My father brought me here before. It was years ago," Raven said.

Asher still wasn't clear what she was trying to tell him. Was her father the killer? Was Asher in danger? Were they all?

He waited anxiously for Raven to reveal the truth.

34

CONCIERGE

*T*he Kia Sorento was parked on the shoulder of the road. Its lights were off, but the engine hummed. Woods occupied both sides of the street. In the darkness of its cab, Justin leaned back in the driver's seat. He twisted the radio dial, skipping through rap, country, and alternative rock station. Finally, he found a talk show that grabbed his attention.

"Hello and welcome to KHR10 Radio. I'm your intrepid host and local historian Dean Hosier, and tonight we're discussing Club Blue."

Justin wiggled in the seat, trying to find a way to be more comfortable.

"Started in 1923, the old Freemason lodge has as always been an enigma in our little coastal town. Marco Blanc, a 30th degree Scottish Rite Freemason and entrepreneur, had a very specific vision: to build a fraternity where ambitious young entrepreneurs and old blood businessman could network, enjoy prohibited alcohol, and relax for an extended stay. Mr. Blanc made a lot of money despite his low rates.

"A few years later, he turned that lodge into an upscale

hotel. Traffic flooded into Sebring, turning it into a safe haven during the depression and World War thereafter. However, everything changed in 1962 when the top floor of the luxury hotel erupted into flame."

The radio signal fizzed.

Justin tried turning the dial, but his efforts were futile. He clenched his jaw and shut off the radio. He longed to use the money Anna gave him to find another hotel, but he needed to stay close to Club Blue. He was only two miles away.

He lifted the first handwritten ledger from the dusty stack on the passenger seat. He'd stolen these from Anna's office before he left for the night. Keeping his phone's notepad app open, he flipped through page after page, taking note of any reoccurring guest. The tedious work tried his patience, but if the killer was someone other than the concierge, they had to be a reoccurring guest. Justin cross-referenced the names and dates of guests with the missing people from the past few decades. It wasn't as simple as matching a name to a date. Some guests had extended stays, meaning Justin had to take into account the two weeks to two months they stayed to see if it overlapped any of the victim's check-out dates.

After an hour, he put the thick ledger back on the stack. He pinched the bridge of his nose between his eyes. Even if he found a potential suspect, he didn't know how he'd research them, and he hated the idea of turning the information over to Agent Cameron.

Justin toggled the headlights and drove to the beach. He parked at the easiest spot and got out. Only a small glow of the sun showed beyond the horizon. Lamps alongside the nearby cemented path lit up the darkness. With his hands buried in his warm hoodie pocket, he walked the path. A hair tie held his messy brown hair in a loose man-bun. Exhaustion and lack of appetite lightened his pale complexion but darkened his eyebags. His faint mustache added to his haggard appearance.

Lightning rippled across distant storm clouds. It would hit Sebring soon. There wasn't anyone out by the beach. The old pier had missing wooden planks. There was no boat attached to it. Justin walked for a while, hoping it would clear his head. He wished he could skateboard right now, but he had bitter problems. That darn hotel had ruined his life. He felt bitter, angry, and alone. The only thing that made Sebring better than York was the lack of his father.

Like under a spotlight, a lamp shined its glow over a man seated on a bench. He wore a wool double-breasted jacket, a scarf, and a black bowler cap. A book rested in his lap, but the man's eyes were on the raging sea.

Justin recognized the stranger from somewhere. He moved closer, getting a better look at the side of his face.

"It's you," Justin said.

The concierge turned to him. White stubble painted his cheeks, chin, and upper lip. His steel-gray eyes examined the boy. "Ah. Ms. Hall's son."

Justin stood in front of him, ready to strike and flee if he felt his life threatened.

"I heard there's been a little trouble at the Club," the concierge remarked.

"Yeah, but I think it started long before I showed up," Justin replied, disdain in his voice.

The concierge stood up. "It's getting late. Maybe you should get going."

Justin held his ground. He remembered the man's name. "I'm not going anywhere, Ferguson. Not until you tell me what the hell is going on."

"I don't have time for this." Mr. Ferguson pushed past him.

Justin grabbed the man's wrist and held it at chest level.

"Let go," Mr. Ferguson warned.

Justin squeezed harder.

"I will call the cops," Mr. Ferguson threatened.

"And I'll tell them about the killings. Though it's not big news anymore, they're looking for answers about the skeleton in the hidden wall. You're number one on their suspect list."

Mr. Ferguson frowned. "What do you want from me?"

"Who's killing people in my hotel?"

Mr. Ferguson chuckled. "You're crazy."

"I know about the sacrifices. I know about all the hidden corridors. I found a list of names carved into a hidden wall of fourteen people that have gone missing over the last four decades. To top it off, we have had a number of mysterious checkouts in the last few weeks," Justin bent the man's wrist back.

Mr. Ferguson gasped in pain.

"You're going to give me answers or you're going to have a lot bigger problems than the police," Justin bluffed.

"Fine! Fine. Let go, and we'll talk like civilized human beings," Mr. Ferguson bartered.

"I'm a lot faster than you, remember that," Justin said, releasing the man's wrist.

He rubbed it as he sat down.

Justin loomed over him.

"Are you going to sit or…"

"I'm fine right here." Justin took a few steps closer, preventing the man from getting out.

Mr. Ferguson wore his disdain plainly. "What do you want to know?"

"Who is the killer?" Justin asked.

Mr. Ferguson chuckled. He shook his head. "I can't answer that."

"Can't or won't?" Justin asked, keeping his hands on his hip.

"Can't," Mr. Ferguson said firmly.

"Any suspects?" Justin asked.

"You're not very good at this," Mr. Ferguson said.

Justin set his jaw. He wasn't the stronger fellow, but he was quick and could knock Mr. Ferguson out with a few hits.

Mr. Ferguson said, "You're looking for answers to a murder, great, but that's not my department. I deal with the guests. Check-ins and check-outs, mostly."

"So why won't you give me a list of suspicious suspects?" Justin asked.

"You have my ledgers."

"You must've known something was wrong while you worked there," Justin theorized.

Mr. Ferguson said, "This case is personal to you, isn't it?"

Justin was silent.

"Did you lose a friend? No, that's not it. Something else happened, didn't it? Something you can't explain." A wicked smile grew on Mr. Ferguson's face. "So which one was it? Alesha? Vincent? Trent?"

"Who the hell are you talking about?" Justin asked.

"You know," Mr. Ferguson said seriously. "Trent was the first to appear to me. I was taking a shower and suddenly I wasn't alone. A naked man wearing only a necktie stood behind him. His eyes bulged. His swollen tongue poked out of his purple lips. I'll never forget it."

Justin listened intently.

Mr. Ferguson said, "Alesha was the next to see me. I knew her when she checked in. Gorgeous woman. Not so much now."

"You did this to them," Justin said.

"Me?" Mr. Ferguson asked, "You don't think I'm the first one the police always suspect? I've had my name cleared over and over again. You can talk to my various alibis. Most of them work down at the street corner by the bus stop."

Justin wasn't sure if he believed them. The man's convictions were strong. If he was acting, he was good.

Mr. Ferguson said, "Now would you please sit down, for Pete's sake. I'm tired of talking to your groin."

Not taking his eyes off him, Justin lowered himself to the bench. He kept some space between them. If Mr. Ferguson were to reach for a knife or gun, Justin was confident he could snatch the weapon before the man had a chance to aim.

"Finally," Mr. Ferguson mumbled.

"Why are Alesha and the others still around?" Justin said.

"Club Blue is special," Mr. Ferguson replied.

"Does it have to do with the rituals?" Justin asked.

"Anything is possible. All I know is that it started happening after the fire," Mr. Ferguson explained. "Many guests were plagued with strange visions for years. However, when the arsonist was *apprehended* by the police, the hauntings stopped."

"The police never apprehended anyone," Justin called the man out on his lie.

"Not formally," Mr. Ferguson said. "They instead put him in the back of a squad car, drove him out to the woods, and put a bullet in his head."

"Why? That could've been the story of the century," Justin said.

"Because Club Blue isn't what you think it is. Sure, it was a secret Masonic lodge and, yes, it was a middle ground where the elite and ambitious upstarts would discuss under the table business ventures while indulging in their wildest fantasies. But Marco Blanc had something much bigger going on. Club Blue was a honey pot."

"What's that?"

"Let me describe it like this: if you had a very specific fetish, Mr. Blanc would find avenues to give you what you desired. It could young or old, black or white, disposable. You would pay Mr. Blanc a little extra for his discretion. Little did you know, Mr. Blanc filmed your stay behind hidden walls and mirrors. A few months later, you might get a call from one of Mr. Blanc's employees asking for a favor. Maybe it was to invest in a certain business or to pull out all your stock on a certain day. You get the idea."

Justin nodded along. "If they refused, he'd release the tape."

"As you can imagine, this made people very angry with Mr. Blanc. One particular client, Hugo Green, heard that there was a film of him with a dead man. He got very angry at Mr. Blanc. While staying on the fourth-floor suite, he locked the doors and started a fire. Eight prominent figures died and another ten unnamed women and children went with them. Hugo escaped somehow. Blanc and the police agreed the fire was an accident. See, the police chief had a film about him too. What he didn't know was that the true reason for the fire was so Hugo could destroy the films."

"Did he?" Justin asked.

"He did, but Blanc kept it a secret. After all, he was vulnerable now. He used his resources and contacts to find Hugo, but he'd fled to Canada. In 1978, Hugo thought everyone had forgotten about his stunt and wanted to return to the U.S of A. He was killed two days after entering the country."

Justin said, "Geez."

"Suddenly, the haunting stopped," Mr. Ferguson said. "Marco and his heir were both dead and I was in charge now. I never tried to restart the honey pot, but I did preserve the elegance of the fine hotel."

"When did you start working there?"

"In the early '70s. I was a bellhop, but my discretion and loyalty helped me to earn my position," Mr. Ferguson said. "Life was good, but then the hauntings began again."

"Someone else was killed."

"Yes," Mr. Ferguson said. "Over the thirty years that followed, more and more specters appeared. They'd speak to me, and I soon got used to it."

Justin interrupted him, "You said Trent was the first one you saw."

"Of the latest batch, yes," Mr. Ferguson replied, "I was annoyed. The burn victims were gone. The other specters roamed the halls. I knew there was a killer about, but I had no power to stop him. I stopped promoting the hotel, hoping it would save lives."

"Why not shut it down?" Justin asked.

"I still needed to make a living. Besides, there are certain powerful people that warned me what would happen to me if I left my post," Mr. Ferguson explained.

"Well, more than fourteen people have gone missing since the fire. Why are we only seeing three?" Justin asked.

Mr. Ferguson replied. "That's because the killer of the first fourteen is dead now."

"How?"

"I don't know, but one day, they all vanished," Mr. Ferguson replied. "Fifteen years later, specters started to appear again."

"Obviously the killer is using the hidden passages. Why didn't you block them?" Justin asked.

"Those passages are the killer's domain. The only reason why I'm still alive is because I refused to investigate them."

"Not even one time?" Justin asked, not believing him.

"Never," Mr. Ferguson said seriously.

Justin stroked his chin. "I guess this leads me back to my first question. Who is the killer?"

Mr. Ferguson replied, "All I can say is that he is a reoccurring guest."

Justin was annoyed. "Obviously."

Mr. Ferguson reached into his jacket.

Justin went tense, ready to attack if he saw a gun.

Mr. Ferguson withdrew his wallet and pulled out a small photograph. "This is from twelve years ago."

Justin held the picture. It showed two rows of ten men. The first ten were seated and the other ten stood behind them. "Who are they?"

"Loyal guests," Mr. Ferguson replied. "I offered them all a free week's stay for their frequent reoccurrence at Club Blue. If you're looking for your killer, he has to be one of them."

Justin studied the photo. A grey-haired man in the back row stood behind a teenage boy. The adult man had the same eyes, square jaw, and nose as...

Justin's jaw fell open. "Who is this one?"

"That's Pierce," Mr. Ferguson said. "He died of a heart attack two years after the photo was taken."

"What's his last name?" Justin asked.

"Ryder," Mr. Ferguson said.

Justin said, "Was he ever a suspect?"

"All these men were."

Justin pulled out his phone and snapped a picture of the photo. The wind screamed. The temperature quickly dropped. The storm was coming a lot faster than he'd expected. "One last question."

"What?" Mr. Ferguson asked.

"Were you the one staying in the unburnt fourth-floor suite?" Justin asked.

Mr. Ferguson's silence spoke volumes.

Justin said, "I want your number."

"Why should I give that to you?"

"Because if you don't, I'll call the police," Justin said.

"How long are you going to use the same leverage to get your way?"

"Until it stops working. Phone number now."

The concierge begrudgingly recited it.

Justin called him. Once he heard the ring in Ferguson's pocket, he hung up. "Keep that on. If someone else goes missing, you're the first one I'm calling." Justin sped-walked away from the bench.

"You'll be wasting your time!" the concierge yelled.

"We'll see about that!" Justin shouted back.

He sprinted to the SUV and locked the doors behind him.

Fat raindrops pelted the windshield. Justin used the overhead light to review the ledgers. It took a while, but he was able to match four of the missing person's visitations with Pierce's time at the hotel. Pierce might've been dead, but his son wasn't.

"It must run in the family," he mumbled as he called his mom.

The phone rang a few times before going to voicemail. He tried again. Same result. Frustrated, he left a message. "Mom, it's Justin. I need you to call me right away. You're in danger."

He sent her a few texts, demanding that she call before trying Asher's phone. He didn't pick up either.

Justin punched the steering wheel.

35

THE KITCHEN

he fork speared the last chunk of fresh grouper. Anna bit it, savoring the lemon-zest taste. Her eyes almost rolled in pleasure.

"Good, huh?" Cameron asked.

"Uh-hmm," Anna chewed. She hovered her hand over her mouth. *Good is an understatement.* Anna said, "I need to hire your chef."

Cameron replied, "He's a local legend. He used to work here."

"No kidding," Anna replied. She glanced over, seeing the tall and wide chef lingering by the kitchen door. He wore his white garb and traditional hat. "When my finances are in the black again, he'll be the first person I hire."

Cameron said, "He might be worth the investment now. Imagine having a cook-to-order chef as one of the hotel's perks."

"That would be fancy," Anna said.

"Fancy attracts the wealthy," Cameron said. "You can't have more freeloaders like me taking up useful space."

Anna said, "I didn't realize you thought so lowly of yourself."

"I was hoping the fancy clothes and food would help you ignore my many flaws," Cameron said with a wry smile.

"Well, it's working." Anna sipped her wine. She set down her glass and rested her knee on her interlocked fingers. The alcohol was a lot stronger than she realized, but she wasn't at the point where she was seeing double. Yet. "What's next for you?"

Cameron dabbed the corner of his cheek. "What do you mean?"

"You can't stay in Club Blue forever," Anna replied. "Surely the agency will call you to some other small town."

"About that." There was a seriousness in Cameron's tone. "I'm not on active duty."

"Oh? What happened?" Anna asked.

Cameron said, "A few months ago, I lost my temper and hurt someone I shouldn't have. I thought he was guilty. I was so sure of it, too. When it turned out I was wrong, they put me on leave."

"This whole time then…"

"Yeah, I've been unemployed. I'm sorry I've not been honest with you. I thought I could earn my way back on payroll after cracking the Club Blue case," Cameron confessed. "There goes our relationship, huh?"

"Are you kidding me? No. It's just a job," Anna said. "In full transparency, your career terrified me."

Cameron smiled lopsidedly. "Why's that?"

"I don't know. It felt like I always had to look over my shoulder while you were around," Anna admitted. "I know it's stupid, but I've always felt awkward around authority figures."

Cameron took a drink of wine. "1962. Strong stuff."

Anna agreed. "Let's go back to talking about your future."

Cameron replied, "There's a lot of uncertainty. If I don't get this job back, I don't know where I'd go. Perhaps I could be your bartender. You really need one, by the way. It's not fair for the rest of us that we have to wait until your evening shift to get drinks."

"I'll take your resume into consideration," Anna teased.

"Oh, that's cruel," Cameron said.

"Tough," Anna replied.

The chef checked his watch. He approached the table and leaned down to whisper to Cameron. The agent pulled a few twenties out of his pocket and slipped them into the chef's hand. The chef thanked Anna and Cameron and left for the night.

Anna yawned, covering her mouth.

Cameron asked, "You like it here?"

"That's a loaded question."

"Seems pretty *yes or no* to me."

Anna said, "I like the idea of it, but in light of current events, I have doubts."

"Like Lance," Cameron remarked.

"He's one of many issues. Thank you for saving me, by the way," Anna said. "You were a godsend."

"I don't know about all that," Cameron said, trying to stay humble. "I just couldn't stand by while a beautiful woman was being attacked."

"You're really laying on the sauce thick tonight," Anna remarked.

Cameron said, "I think it's healthy to know your partner's intentions before agreeing to anything."

"And what are your intentions, Agent?" Anna asked.

"To get to know you, first and foremost. Then, maybe we could travel. I've not had many long-term relationships, but it's something I'd like to try with you."

"Why me?" Anna asked. "You're charming enough to have a lot of girls."

"You're a fighter," Cameron said. "Life hits you and you get back up. Most people would've fled months ago. You stayed. From the moment I saw you in York's police station, I knew you had a predator instinct that didn't just overcome challenges, but crushed them completely."

"That's a kind of creepy way of saying it," Anna replied.

Cameron locked eyes with her. "You get it, right? It's like that instinct to thrive. Sometimes, we have to remind ourselves who we are. Overcoming a challenge is one of the best ways to do that."

"I agree," Anna said. "You don't know how fast you can run until you start moving."

"Exactly," Cameron replied.

The lights flickered.

Anna glanced around.

Cameron said, "Storm's here."

"Maybe that's our cue to turn in for the night," Anna said.

"Whatever you want to do."

"I'll put these dishes in the kitchen. Maybe I'll wash them tomorrow," she said.

Cameron grabbed his plate and the glasses. Anna took her plate and the wine bucket. Without bothering to turn on the massive kitchen's lights, she put the dishes in the sink.

"Wine?" Anna asked.

"We'll take it back to my room."

Anna put a hand on her hip and raised one eyebrow.

"What?" Cameron said innocently. "It's really heavy."

"Uh-huh," Anna said slowly. "I got your number, buster."

"You talk like you're from the '80s," Cameron said. He held open the kitchen door.

"It was a good era," Anna replied.

"Debatable," Cameron said.

"Agree to disagree, how about that?" Anna said.

They joked and laughed all the way up to Cameron's room. Anna felt extra tipsy. She could keep her balance, but couldn't stop talking. She was a loud drunk. Her trek ended at Cameron's door.

Cameron turned to her. "Thank you, Anna."

"Thank me? I should be thanking you," Anna said.

"No, I'm serious. I've been on my own for so long I almost forget what it's like to have fun. A couple of hundred bucks and calling in a big favor from my favorite chef is a small price to pay for a night like this," Cameron said.

Anna looked deep into Cameron's eyes. "Sometimes I can't tell if you're a hopeless romantic or learned all your lines from cheesy novels."

"Maybe both." Cameron neared her lips.

Anna shut her eyes and met his kiss halfway. She tasted the wine in his breath. The kiss was brief and simple but left Anna's heart fluttering.

Cameron brushed the back of his index figure down her cheek. "Have I told you you're beautiful yet?"

"A few times," Anna replied. She leaned in for another kiss but pulled away before their lips touched.

A wry smile accentuated her tease.

Grinning ear to ear, Cameron opened the door. "You can place the wine on the counter. I may have a little more tonight."

Anna peered into the tidy suite. *He'd cleaned today.* Anna handed him the ice bucket. "It's late, Agent. I should get to bed."

Cameron hid his disappointment. He quickly gathered his composure. "A kiss goodnight?"

Anna sighed exaggeratedly and kissed him. She held the back of his neck and felt a spark she hadn't felt since she first met James.

When the kiss ended, she wished him goodnight.

He did likewise and watched her walk away for a moment before closing his door.

Feeling like a million bucks, Anna quickened her pace. She thought about turning in for the night but remembered to secure the lobby. It wasn't long after 10 pm, but she was okay not receiving any new guests tonight. She locked the glass front doors, her mindset on the bubble bath that awaited her.

Humming, she put a sign to call her in case of emergency on the counter and headed to the ballroom where she had forgotten her purse. She grabbed it off the chair, pushed her seat in, and stopped. Having dirty dishes in the sink nagged at her.

She decided to give them a quick wash. It wouldn't take long and she wanted to make sure the chef didn't break anything.

Upon entering the large kitchen, she toggled the light switch. The fluorescent tube lights buzzed to life. Some turned on faster than others. The chef's cooking tray and the knives he used were already clean. *Nice guy,* she thought as she washed the gunk off the plates. She scrubbed them hard and set them on a cloth to dry.

After wiping her hands on a nearby rag, she noticed something strange about the meat locker. Slowly putting the rag down on the countertop, she neared the large metal freezer. An unfamiliar lock secured the door's latch.

She wondered if one of the boys switched it out, but why?

Anna tugged on the lock. It was secure.

Compelled by curiosity, she pulled out her lock-picking tool kit from her purse.

SCARRED

A lightning bolt struck the ocean. Torrents of rain blitzed the lighthouse.

Nervous, Asher swallowed a glob of spit. He waited for Raven to reveal her dad was the Club Blue killer.

Raven's gaze fixed on the treacherous waters beyond. "If I tell you what happened, you promise you won't freak out?"

Asher nodded. "Yeah."

"Swear it," Raven pushed.

"Just tell me," Asher pressured her.

"Not until you swear."

"Fine, I swear. Cross my heart. Hope to die," Asher replied hastily.

Raven collected her words. She said, "My father brought me to the hotel a long time ago."

Asher's heart raced. "And?"

"He was trying to write his book back then, too. He'd researched a lot about Club Blue but wanted firsthand knowledge. He hoped it would be the thing that would launch his career. He bought an old typewriter to complete the book as a marketing tactic," Raven said. "Meanwhile, I was bored out of my mind. Dad didn't do anything but work and sleep. One night, a hidden door in the bedroom opened. I remember sitting up in the bed. The lights were out. Someone was watching."

"Was it your dad?" Asher asked.

"He was sleeping in the bed next to mine. A figure entered inside. He shined a flashlight into my face. I screamed. He was quicker," Raven said.

Asher's palms sweated. "What are you trying to say?"

Raven grabbed the bottom of her shirt and started to lift it.

Asher turned his eyes away. "Whoa. Slow down."

"Look," Raven demanded.

Asher slowly turned back to her

She held the shirt just below her chest. A large gash was cut into the right side of her pale belly. It was inches deep and bloodless.

"Oh my—we need to call an ambulance!" Asher exclaimed.

"The cut is twelve years old, Asher," Raven said plainly.

"But that would mean…" The revelation hit him. He quickly scooted away from her. "No, no, that's fake. This is just one of your creepy stunts. It's not funny."

Without even the slightest reaction, Raven put four fingers into the cut.

Asher scrambled to her feet.

Raven drew out her bloody fingers and held them at eye level. Her expression was pained.

"You're one of them!" Asher pointed and shouted.

"My father and I both are," Raven said.

Asher put both hands on his head. His eyes were so wide, he thought they'd pop out of his head. "I can't believe this is happening."

He felt his chest tighten and his breathing strained.

"You promised me you wouldn't freak out," Raven replied, staying calm.

"I thought you would tell me your dad is a serial killer or something! Not this!" Asher pulled out his inhaler. His legs felt like jelly. He leaned against the window to keep his balance.

"How is this worse?" Raven asked, her eyes watering.

"It just is!" Asher shouted. He pulled out his inhaler and took a hit. It only calmed him down a little.

Raven stood up. "Asher, I'm still me." She neared him. "Nothing has changed."

Horrified, Asher ran for the stairs. He tumbled down the final three steps, pushing himself to his feet and running into the deadly tempest.

37

MEAT LOCKER

*A*nna picked the unfamiliar lock. She didn't hear her phone buzzing in her purse. Successfully removing the lock, she put it aside and pulled open the large freezer door.

Light from the kitchen spilled into the meat locker. Two rows of rusty meat hooks dangled from the ceiling. Something was snagged on the last hook. Something bloody and meaty.

Knives of various kinds rested by a functional sink lining one wall.

Anna's heart fluttered. She entered one step at a time, walking between the rows of hooks. She stopped in front of the eight-inch strip of bloody meat. One side was maroon and the other was pale. Anna reached out a hand to touch it but stopped herself. *This can't be real*, she thought. She looked into the sink. Plastic sheeting lined the inside. Dried blood and flesh rested at the bottom. The skin was a day old but distinctly human. Anna knew not what part of the body it originated from. She didn't want to know.

Pale as death, she backed away from the sink.

She took deep breaths. She pulled her phone out of her purse as she ran for the door. She kicked off the heels that were slowing her down. She dashed into the kitchen and made a hard right, slamming into someone's broad chest. Her phone was knocked from her hand and skidded across the floor.

"Anna?" Cameron looked down at her.

Anna pointed back to the locker. "There's…"

She noticed he'd changed his clothes. He now wore a long-sleeve shirt, cheap jeans, and shoes wrapped in grocery-store bags. He held a small key in his gloved right hand.

"You find something?" he asked innocently.

Anna suddenly became light-headed. Her pulse quickened and her body trembled. She opened her mouth to speak but found no words.

Cameron glanced past her shoulder and at the open freezer door.

Without any more hesitation, Anna swiftly slipped by him. She hit her shoulder against his as she ran for the phone.

Cameron grabbed the back of her dress and yanked her back. Her scream echoed off the kitchen's walls.

Cameron hushed her. "It's just a big misunderstanding."

Anna rammed her elbow into his groin.

Cameron grunted and doubled over.

Anna dashed away, the back of her dress tearing as she raced for the bar. She threw her body at the door, busting it open. Soft music played over the speakers as she smashed into a table. Pain thumped through her side, but she kept going. She saw the glass bar door.

Like being hit by a bus, Cameron tackled her to the ground.

Screaming, she struggled to escape his weight but was no match.

"Don't fight," Cameron said calmly. "You're not going to win."

Her arms and legs flailed as he put her into a chokehold. His muscles pressed into her throat. Her screams were silenced. Her face glowed blood red. A vein bulged in her forehead. Darkness closed into the corners of her vision.

Cameron continued hushing her. "It's okay. Everything is going to be okay. That's it. Go to sleep."

Anna lost her fighting spirit. Her body went limp.

Cameron kept her pinned for a moment longer. He looked at the side of her tear-stained face. She was out cold. He cursed under his breath. "Why couldn't you just stay in bed?"

He let her go and sat up. Adrenaline pumped through his being. With the power of life and death in his hands, he felt like a god. He thought maybe things could change for the better between Anna and himself. She was a killer too after all.

"Mom!" someone shouted from the lobby.

Cameron cursed.

Justin dripped across the glossy lobby floor as he ran by the counter. He kept his phone close to his ear, listening to his mother's voicemail again. She'd locked the front door early this evening and wasn't in her office. Justin beelined for the elevator.

He jogged by the bar's glass door, noticed something in his peripheral view.

"Mom!" he shouted, seeing her face down the bar floor. He rushed into the room, dialing the first 9 in 911.

The moment his foot stepped into the bar, a wine bottle swung out of his blind spot and slammed into his nose.

Justin was knocked off his feet and landed on his back. His head rested to the side. Blood streamed from his broken nose.

Cameron kept the wine bottle in a striking position. Blood smeared the side.

He kicked Justin's side. "Get up."

The teenager didn't move.

"C'mon. Don't play with me." Cameron kicked him again.

Either out cold or dead, Cameron assessed. He set the bottle aside and checked Justin's pulse. There was a faint heartbeat.

"It would've been easier if you died," Cameron mumbled.

He grabbed the boy's ankles.

Seventeen... he thought coldly. *I've killed younger.*

38

DARK WATERS

Sheets of rain flooded Asher as he ran from the lighthouse. Raven ran after him. His feet clacked on the dock. He slipped on the wood and hit his chin. He scrambled to his feet and reached the dock. Lightning flashed, revealing the boat for a mini second.

"Asher, please!" Raven shouted.

"Stay away from me!" Asher yelled.

Asher picked the lock and pulled on the rusty chain. The corroded metal cut into his palms. He gasped in pain. Water and blood rolled down the metal links. He held the chain like a leash, keeping the boat from drifting away. Inches of water sloshed around the inside.

Raven took two steps on the dock before stopping. "You'll drown if you go there."

Asher lowered himself to a seated position. The freezing downpour soaked him to the bone. He put one foot in the boat. The waves rocked the bow.

Raven carefully approached him. "Why don't you let me help you?"

"You're one of them," Asher shouted. "You lied to me this whole time!"

"I didn't lie... I just didn't tell you the whole truth."

"Same thing," Asher said, at his wits' end.

He pushed off the dock and landed in the boat. Inches of water soaked through his shoes and socks. He grabbed the paddle and rowed.

Rain and darkness kept him from seeing the shore. The sidewalk lamps dozens of feet from the cliffs were his only source of light. He twisted back. Raven stood at the end of the dock. She was unfazed by the rain falling over her.

Asher kept his head low. The wood plank made for a horrible paddle. The waves rolled under him. The wind slapped his face. He spat out water. He got twenty yards before a large wave rolled over his boat.

Before he could scream, he was under the icy water. The riptide spun him around. His only means of escape was to swim upward. His head breached the water. He kicked hard. The current had carried him dozens of yards away from the lighthouse.

He struggled to keep hold of his glasses. He coughed. The icy water numbed his fingers and toes.

Something grabbed his ankle.

He shrieked just as Raven popped her head up out of the water. "Hold onto me!"

Asher wrapped his arms around her waist, and she swam quickly. Asher felt the ridged wound below her shirt. He gagged but didn't let go. His teeth chattered.

They neared the rocky coast. The current sucked them toward the jagged rocks. "Let go!" Raven shouted.

Asher obeyed.

She grabbed his hips. Lightning flashed in the sky. The jagged rocks were only twenty feet away. When they were less than ten feet away, Raven launched Asher. He shot out of the water. His arms flailed as he flew through the car and across the muddy grass. Pain shot through his elbow. He rolled to his back. The rain pelted his face. He guarded his eyes with a hand.

Like a creature from the deep, Raven crawled up the small cliff and towards Asher.

He froze in fear.

"If we don't get you inside, you'll end up like me." Raven helped him to his feet.

Trembling and in agony, Asher leaned against her. She helped keep his balance. They rushed through the woods. Club Blue stood ominously in the storm. Only a handful of windows shone golden light. The rest of the hotel was dark as night.

They headed to the front entrance. Anna's Kia Sorento was parked outside of the door. The doors were closed but the vehicle was running. Asher and Raven neared it. There was no one inside. Asher got a bad feeling. He pulled on the lobby door. Locked.

He cupped his hands and peered through the glass. The counter was vacant.

"Do you have a key?" Raven asked.

Asher felt in his pockets and removed the master key. "Can't you walk through walls?"

Raven said, "Something like that would break your fragile mind."

Asher's jaw fell open.

Raven smirked.

They stepped into the lobby. The warm, dry air was the closest thing Asher ever felt to heaven. The rain added an extra twenty pounds of weight to his clothes. Hugging himself to stay warm, Asher said. "I've got to find my mom. Tell her that the car is running."

He hurried to the elevator.

"After saving your life, you're just gonna run off then?" Raven asked bitterly.

"Raven, I can't handle this right now." Asher rapidly pressed the button.

Raven balled her fists. "I knew you'd react like this. Ugh, part of me wishes I let you drown."

Asher turned back to her, a horrified expression on his face.

Raven said, "We could've been together that way."

The elevator dinged.

Raven continued. "After all the years being here, you're the only one that actually talked to me."

"I'm sorry, I have to..." Asher's voice trailed as he slipped into the elevator. "My mom needs me."

The dead girl watched him as the elevator doors closed.

Asher's teeth chattered. Water puddled around his drenched shoes.

"Hurry up," he said anxiously.

The elevator dinged.

He took one step before noticing a crimson droplet on the floor. He glanced into the second-floor hallway, seeing another one a few feet ahead.

A cloud of dread fell over him. He stepped out and followed the bloody droplets. The trail became less frequent the farther he went and eventually ended outside an unoccupied suite. Asher glanced around the hallway. He ran back to his suite and grabbed his phone. Justin had called a few times. Asher redialed him. His phone went straight to voicemail. Asher thought about calling the cops, but he knew his mom couldn't handle another scandal. He grabbed a towel from the restroom and dried off. His clothes were still soaked, but at least they weren't as heavy.

He returned to the suite where the bloody droplets stopped and unlocked the door. Remembering back to the time where he spied on the guests, he knew there was a tunnel entrance to this room, but he just had to figure out what corner. He tried the wall behind the tall lamp standing in the corner of the room.

Trembling from the cold, he brushed his hand up and down the wall until he found the hidden switch. It was near the ceiling where no one could accidentally trigger it. It opened with a click. Asher slipped inside. He followed the corridor, using the flashlight on his phone as his guide. He continued through the inner walls. He saw the naked fat man standing at an elbow in the hallway. Asher swallowed his fear and went that way. Maybe the fat man was the one who had left the bloodstains? Asher hoped so. The fat man walked down the branching corridor. Asher followed him. He peeked through paintings that overlooked the ballroom balcony. He continued until reaching a dead end. The fat man phased through the dead end. *There must be a hidden door there, too. Much like the one with the old film camera.*

A thin light shined through a little peephole. Asher turned off his flashlight. He stood at eye level with the peephole and peered inside.

The room was well lit and tidy. It was twelve feet wide and fourteen feet long. Shelves lined the left and right wall. They were full of different trinkets. The back wall had a variety of tools, surgical and otherwise. At the middle were two dental chairs where Anna and Justin were strapped.

Asher nearly wet himself.

Their mouths were gagged with plastic balls. Their hands and ankles were bound by leather straps. Justin's nose was swollen and bent to the side. Dried blood stained his lips and chin. Anna's make-up was smeared and her hair tangled, but she had no visible wounds. They were both awake.

Agent Cameron eyed the tools on the back wall,

pondering which instrument he should use. "I cut off a man's face once right where you are sitting, Anna."

Anna whimpered through her gag. She squirmed, but her binds were unrelenting.

Cameron looked over his shoulder. "Guess who was in your chair, Justin?"

Justin roared in rage. His fists were balled so tightly his knuckles turned white. He tried mightily to break the binds.

Cameron smirked. "Father Stephen. Do you know what's funny? He even tried praying for me in the end. Me? As if I'm the one who needed help." Cameron laughed and shook his head. "I have to respect the man. He died with integrity." Cameron pointed to the box cutter. "I used this one to open his throat. It was a hell of a clean-up. Thank goodness for that meat locker. It took me a little while before I could properly dispose of him. I wasn't done, as you are well aware."

Cameron grabbed the Taser off the wall. Content with his choice, he walked between the chair and faced his victims. "You have questions. I'm not going to bore you with answers. Long story short, Dad and I had a particular taste that only this place satisfied. The FBI was just a means to remove the scent. Understand? Good. We have a long night ahead of us, and then I have to leave town. No doubt the police will look for you. It's *obvious* you left because the police knew you killed your husband."

Anna begged through her gag.

Cameron stood next to her, a sympathetic smile on his face. He brushed her hair aside. "I really cared about you. I just wish this part of my life could've stayed hidden."

Justin screamed through his gag.

Cameron quickly twisted back and shot him with the Taser.

Justin gurgled. Every muscle in his body contracted. He

looked like he was about to split apart under pressure. Cameron kept the trigger pulled.

Asher dialed 911.

"911. What's your emergency?"

Asher whispered. "He has my mother and brother."

"Who and where are you?"

"Cameron Ryder. We're at Club Blue. Hurry."

Cameron suddenly turned to Asher.

He backed away from the peephole. *He saw me!*

The tasing stopped and Justin's noises with it. Replacing the Taser's needles, Cameron approached the hidden door.

Asher ran down the corridor.

Alerted by his footsteps, Cameron ran after him. "Hey! Come here!"

Water squished in Asher's shoes. He scraped his shoulder against the wall as he ran. He jumped through the hidden door and scurried through the suite.

Andrew Warren stepped into the hallway. He saw Asher. "What's wrong, boy?"

"Run!" Asher shouted.

Cameron bolted out of the door.

"What's going on?" Warren shouted.

Cameron flicked out a knife and slammed into the old man, knocking him over like a bowling pin. With his belly split open, Warren sprawled out on the floor. Blood leaked out the side of his lip. His mouth opened and closed like a fish out of water.

Cameron kept moving forward, a bloody knife in one hand and the Taser in the other.

Asher ran down the ballroom stairs.

Cameron reached the balcony and fired his Taser.

It zipped by and hit the pillar near Asher.

Cameron cursed. He let go of the Taser and ran down the steps.

Unable to breathe, Asher crumbled to the checkered floor. He squeezed his chest and sucked in gasps of air.

Winded, Cameron slowed his sprint as he neared the boy.

Asher fished his inhaler out of his pocket.

Cameron stepped on Asher's wrist, pinning his inhaler hand to the floor.

Asher gulped air, but none seemed to fill his lungs. He was drowning.

Cameron watched him, a pitying expression on his face. "I liked you, kid, but you just had to keep snooping around."

Asher's face turned purple. He felt splinters in his throat. His heart rate skyrocketed.

The blood trickled down the knife and onto Asher's shirt.

Suddenly, they were surrounded.

Raven, David, Rosy, Christophe, Stephen, the faceless man, the naked obese man, the couple from months ago, and Andrew Warren each stood on a black or white tile.

"You!" Cameron exclaimed, unable to comprehend what he was witnessing.

In his final breath, Asher reached out his free hand and grabbed the knife.

Cameron was in too much shock to realize what Asher had done until the weapon was no longer in his grasp. He glanced down just as the blade stabbed into his inner thigh.

Cameron yelled and stumbled backward, falling between David and Raven.

Unable to breathe, Asher's world turned black. He listened to Cameron's last words. "No. It can't be. Not like this. Not like this…"

39

CLOSURE

Snow fell over Sebring and topped its buildings with white. Club Blue stood alone in woods of leafless trees. The rising sun cast its crimson rays across the calm ocean and clear sky above.

Inside Anna's suite, Justin sat on the rocking chair and watched Anna grab one of the few presents from below the evergreen tree. She smiled widely. "This one from you?"

"Just open it," Justin said.

Anna ripped apart the wrapping paper and pulled out the little cardboard box. She opened the top flap and drew out the snow globe. Inside was a miniature version of Club Blue. Equally excited and horrified, she said, "You're serious? How did you find this?"

"eBay," Justin replied.

Anna shook it and set it on the lampstand. "I love it," she said.

A half-smile crept up Justin's face. His nose was healed but slightly crooked. They all had scars from that night, but some were on the inside.

"My turn," Asher said. He blew on his hot chocolate and sat cross-legged by the Christmas tree.

Anna handed him a gift.

He tore it open, revealing the latest Call of Duty video game. "Thanks, Mom," he said kindly and gave her a hug.

"Don't get too excited," Anna said sarcastically.

"I like it. I do," Asher said, a tad bit of insincerity in his tone. He looked at the game. There was sadness in his eyes. He was thinking about someone.

"All right, Justin," Anna said.

He got off his chair and grabbed the present. It was long and rectangular. He tore off the paper, revealing the MacBook Pro. His eyes widened. "This is expensive, Mom."

Anna said, "You're going to need a new computer if you're going to be homeschooled."

"Yeah, but this cost upwards of three grand. Take it back and get something cheaper."

"Relax," Anna said calmly. "It's a tax write-off. The first of many when we re-invent this place."

"Or we could accidentally start a fire and collect the insurance," Justin suggested.

It was a touchy subject for Anna. She focused their attention on opening gifts. They were mostly candy and gift cards.

Anna handed Justin an envelope. It was from Sasha Grimes. He didn't recognize the name. Perplexed, he ran his finger down the crease and pulled out the letter. It read, *Thank you, Justin. You were there when I needed you most. I'm sorry I left without saying goodbye. I just wanted you to know that I'm safe and with my daughter. I hope you can visit us sometime. My address is listed below. Merry Christmas, Justin. Xoxo – Sasha Grimes "Cherry."*

Justin's eyes watered. Joy welled up inside him knowing she was alive.

"You good, bro?" Asher asked.

"Yeah," Justin sniffled. "Stop being so gay and let's play some of Call of Duty."

Asher smiled ear to ear. "I don't even play anymore and I'll still destroy you."

"Try me," Justin replied.

They quickly hooked up the Xbox to the TV. None of them were annoyed that they'd all moved into the same suite. Sure, it was cramped, and sharing a single suite led to some embarrassing encounters, but they felt like a family again. One Anna was proud of.

The hotel was still in the red, there were a million little problems that always needed fixing, and the future had never been more uncertain. Yet somehow, Anna was at peace. Being strapped in that chair and almost killed put her life into perspective. Sink or swim, rich or poor, she'd have her family, and that was all that mattered.

Her boys talked smack to each other as their game loaded.

A small smile appeared on Anna's face.

The paranormal encounters stopped the night Cameron died. Whenever Anna felt a chill or heard a strange noise, she'd think for a brief second it was one of them contacting her from the other side.

Asher went to the restroom after the first round. He put his hands on the sink and glanced in the mirror. From the other side, Raven looked at him. She smiled. He smiled back.

When the paramedics arrived that stormy night, they found Cameron on the ballroom floor, but not Asher. Raven had taken Asher's body far away and left him in a place where no one would find him. Despite this, Asher somehow showed up to answer all the police's questions and even led them to his mother and brother. After the police had cleared out Cameron's corpse and the spirits of the dead passed on,

Asher stayed with Raven as permanent residents of Club Blue. Since then, his mother had questioned his sudden recovery from asthma. Asher chalked it up to a miracle.

The End.

CPSIA information can be obtained
at www.ICGtesting.com
Printed in the USA
LVHW041316151019
634130LV00004B/145/P